Dream & Drake 3

A Cartel Love Story

By

Princess Diamond

Twitter & Instagram: author princess
Facebook: authoress princess diamond
Pinterest: princess diamond

Dream & Drake 3: A Cartel Love Story
Copyright © 2016 Princess Diamond

Text COLEHART to 22828 to sign up for the mailing list & for updates on New Releases. Also, Check out Cole Hart Releases at www.colehartsignature.com

Acknowledgements

I give all praises to God who anointed me with this wonderful gift of writing. Through Christ I can do all things.

To my father in heaven, you passed away too soon. You never seen any of my work, but I write in your memory. Love always.

To my family and friends, I couldn't have done this without your endless days of listening to me talk about my stories, offering ideas, and giving me advice. You all are my rock. Thanks for everything.

To all the authors that have helped me. From giving me advice to supporting my work to the positive interactions. You are my inspiration. Much love.

To my readers, without your support, there is no me. I appreciate you all.

To my readers, without your support, there is no me. I appreciate you all from the bottom of my heart. You are invaluable.

XOXOX
Princess Diamond

Princess Diamond's Books

Element of Surprise

Element of Surprise 2: Lust Unleashed

Put My Name On It

Vacation Series

Hott Girlz Series

Dream & Drake Series

Chapter 1

Dream

"Hi, Dream. I'm Dr. Kelly. How are you?"

"I'm not sure, doctor," I answered truthfully. "I think I'm okay, but I still feel a little weird. Is there something wrong with me?"

The doctor gave me the warmest smile. "No, Dream. Despite the trauma that you've sustained. You've recovered almost one-hundred percent."

"What about my memory? Will I get that back too?"

"You see, your brain is a tricky organ. Sometimes, in traumatic cases such as yours, the brain needs a little more time than the rest of your body to heal. We're still running tests, but I have faith that you will get all your memories back. I'm just not sure when."

I nodded as a fresh stream of tears came. I didn't understand why I couldn't remember that Drake guy. For some odd reason, him being mad at me had me feeling so emotional.

"Don't cry," the sweet nurse holding my hand said. "You have to save all of your strength for the baby."

"What baby?" I pondered.

The doctor and the nurse looked at me strange.

"The baby that you're carrying," the doctor answered.

I'm pregnant? "How far along am I?" I wondered.

Princess Diamond

The doctor wheeled the portable machine over to me and squirted gel on my stomach. I remained still while he moved the wand around.

"You appear to be about sixteen weeks."

I jumped, knocking the wand out of his hand onto the floor. "How can I be that far along?"

The nurse held my hand again, trying to calm me down. All that rubbing that she did the first time wasn't working this time. I wanted to know what the hell was going on.

"Well," the doctor said. "I'm not sure. You appear to have gotten pregnant the day of your accident, but then again..." his voice trailed off.

"What is it doctor?" I asked frantically. The shocked expression on his face scared me.

"Unless you got pregnant after the fact?" he asked and said at the same time.

The nurse and I just looked at him crazy.

"Right. That makes no sense at all." He chuckled in disbelief. "You've been in a coma for quite some time, so there is no way you could have gotten pregnant after your accident. That would be impossible. So, I'm assuming you're sixteen weeks, and you conceived before you went into a coma."

I was not sure why, but for some reason, those words bothered me. There is no way that you could have gotten pregnant after your accident? That's what he said, but I had the strangest feeling that maybe that wasn't true.

"I'm not feeling so well," I said, quickly lying down.

"We'll let you get some rest," the doctor said.

"No," I voiced. "I want to talk to the nurse in private."

The doctor nodded his head. "I'll be back later. Press the call button if you need anything."

"I will." I waited for him to leave before I spoke again.

"What is it?" the nurse asked with a look of concern.

"What's your name?" I asked her.

"Nurse Agnes."

"Okay well, Nurse Agnes, what do you know about Drake?"

"Drake?" she questioned, as if she heard me wrong.

"Yes, Drake. The man who claims I know him, but I have no memories of him at all. What can you tell me about him?"

Agnes took a seat on my bed. "I don't know him personally. However, I can say that that man has been up here every day to see you here in the hospital."

"So, you've interacted with him."

Nurse Agnes gave me a warm gaze. "Yes, of course. He has been polite to me and the rest of the staff, asking if there is anything more he could do to help you. He even helped us take care of you. Many days, he's spent the entire time here in the hospital with you, reading to you, showing you pictures, and talking to you. He even prayed for you."

Nurse Agnes had me thinking. Maybe I jumped to conclusions about Drake. Maybe I didn't give him the benefit of the doubt. "What do you think? Do you think I overreacted?"

She stared at me closely before answering. "Let me start off by saying that I've been a nurse for twenty years. I've taken care of many patients in a coma. I-"

"What does that have to do with me, Nurse Agnes?"

"Well, baby, sometimes when people are sick and away from the world in an unconscious state, they don't have a clear sense of reality. You just woke up, honey. Maybe you didn't give Drake a fair chance. I truly don't believe that man was trying to hurt you."

For some reason, I believed Nurse Agnes. She didn't seem like she had any reason to lie to me. It was weird, but I sensed her presence while I was in a coma. I remember hearing her voice. She was around me a lot. Also, I trusted her judgement. If she said that I should rethink my accusations, then that's exactly what I planned on doing. Even though I felt great, I knew that I wasn't one-hundred percent.

"What do you think I should do?"

"I think you should talk to him. Give him a fair chance."

"Okay, I'll do that." I noticed how much she emphasized on Drake. I wondered why she never mentioned Spencer. "What about my boyfriend? Did you see him here?"

Princess Diamond

Nurse Agnes looked at me, confused. "As far as I know, Drake is your boyfriend."

"So, you never saw Spencer here visiting me?"

"I'm sorry, honey, I don't know who that is."

That's crazy. How was it a man that I didn't even remember managed to visit me every day, and the man who I remember didn't even show up? He was the one I last had sex with, at least that's what I remembered. He's the father of my child, and he abandoned me? Spencer was going to have some explaining to do. There was going to be hell to pay if he hadn't been up here to see me. I wouldn't be able to forgive him if he left me hanging in the hospital, like he did time and time again when my car broke down.

I was just about to ask Nurse Agnes another question when my parents walked in.

"Oh, baby," my mother exclaimed, rushing towards me. She hugged me, squeezing the life out of me. It hurt, but I didn't say a word because I was glad to see her too.

My mother pulled back with tears in her eyes. "I thought we had lost you." She hugged me again, kissing my cheek. "I prayed and prayed for this moment. God finally answered my prayers." My mother and I cried as we hugged. We were definitely having a moment.

When she let me go, my father stepped forward, kissing me on the forehead. "Baby girl, you scared the hell out of us. I didn't know..." He stopped speaking abruptly. I could tell that he was holding back tears. My daddy was a macho man, so he would never admit to his emotions.

"Daddy, I'm fine," I said, wiping my tears.

My father cleared his throat a few times. "You just scared us, baby girl."

"It's like I was never in an accident." I thought for a moment. "Well, except for a small case of amnesia."

"Amnesia?" my mother inquired. "Does that mean you don't remember all of your birthdays and stuff?"

"No, mama. I remember all that."

She sighed in relief. "So, what is it that you don't remember?"

"Drake," I said with mixed feelings. I still didn't know if there was a reason why I didn't remember. My daddy's next statement didn't help matters.

"I'm glad you forgot that punk. He's no good for you. Ever since you met him, you haven't been yourself. I blame him for your accident." Daddy punched his fist into his hand in anger. "I almost lost you because of your affiliations with that lying, cheating dog."

I was really conflicted now. Nurse Agnes seemed to paint a different picture of Drake than my father did. Daddy didn't seem to like him at all. I wondered why. "What did Drake do, daddy?"

He grimaced. "For starters, the raggedy punk is married. You're already being two-timed."

"Married?" I asked in shock. "I was dealing with a married man?" That statement bothered me. I would never talk to a married man willingly. I took marriage very seriously.

"Apparently," my father groaned. "That man had you brainwashed. You even ruined your relationship with Spencer for him."

I gasped, putting my hand over my mouth. "You mean, Spencer dumped me?"

Maybe waking up was a bad idea. I seemed to have made a huge mess of my life. I had no idea my parents were going to come to the hospital and drop this bomb on me. There was no way I could tell them about the baby now. I needed to talk to Spencer first and see where his head was at.

"No, you broke up with Spencer because you wanted to be with that Drake guy."

I couldn't believe my outrageous behavior. "Well, I'm going to get to the bottom of this. One thing I know for sure, I'm not going to run from my past. I intend on talking to Spencer and Drake."

The pissed off look my father gave me let me know that he disapproved of me talking to Drake, period.

"Listen, daddy, I know you're concerned about me but, evidently, I made some mistakes. The only way for me to get to the bottom of my amnesia is to face my fears. If that meant confronting Spencer and Drake, then that's what I plan to do."

"Donald, let me talk to her alone," my mother said to my father. My parents had their share of issues, but they were happily married. Even though, they lived in two separate homes. They claimed that it made their marriage spicier. I didn't see how, but to each its own.

My father gave my mother a grimace, but he left just like she asked him too. She got up and closed my room door, so we could have some privacy.

"What are your true feelings about all this?" my mother questioned. "I can see the emotions written all over your face."

I felt hot tears on my cheeks again. "Mama, I don't know. A part of me knows that I have history with Spencer, but I would be lying if I said that Drake isn't constantly on my mind. Even though I don't remember him, I can't help the fact that I want to know him on a deeper level."

My mother grabbed some tissue, dabbing at my tears. "Your father is going to always be super protective of you. That's how he's always been, and he's going to continue to be. That's why I didn't tell him all the things that you and I talked about pertaining to your love life."

"Did I tell you what happened between me and Spencer, and me and Drake?"

"Yes, you did. I don't want to replace your memories by going into detail. I feel that you will regain your memories in due time. However, what I will say is, you cared deeply for Drake. You may not remember him now, but at least hear the man out. If things work out between you two, fine. If not, that's fine too. At least you would have tried. That way, you won't have any regrets."

"What about him being married though, mama?"

"Chile, your father was married when I met him. He was separated and about to get a divorce."

"Thanks, mama," I exclaimed, hugging her once again. "Where's Bey?"

"Your sister is doing that dumb shit again. She's mad at the world. Ain't no telling where she's at. I'm sure she'll turn up soon."

I made a mental note to find out what's going on with Bey. I didn't know if she was acting out like she normally did or if something was really wrong. There wasn't nothing I could do while I was in here. However, when I got out, I'd find out the truth.

Chapter 2

Drake

I stormed into my hospital room with an attitude that would tear this building down if someone tried to stop me. Fresh stopped reading the newspaper and Quay looked up from his phone. Neither one of them said anything, as I marched over to where my clothes were.

"What happened?" Fresh asked.

Quay stopped texting. "Aww, fuck. Something must've happened with Dream."

"Don't mention her name to me ever again," I snapped.

"Damn, what's her room number?" Quay exclaimed. "I'ma straighten this shit out. I don't know who did what to who, but I can't live with you and your attitudes. The shit is too much."

"What happened?" Fresh asked again.

"Dream is awake," I huffed. "And she doesn't remember me," I spat before they could start asking a million questions.

"Whaaaat?" they both asked.

"Don't ask me a bunch of fuckin' questions!" I snapped again. "I'm not in the damn mood. Now, is this all the clothes I have?" I asked in disgust. I saw some flip flops and jogging pants. I held the ugly shit up for them to see. "What the fuck, man?"

"Um, yeah," Fresh answered vaguely. "We had to dress you as fast as we could. Quay grabbed the first thing he saw. We were more worried about your health."

I ice-grilled both these niccas. Quay had the nerve to shrug. "All them fuckin' clothes in my damn closet and this is all you two knuckleheads could find?"

Quay looked up from his phone, but he didn't say a word. He eyeballed me as I walked around the room, dressing.

"I'm ready to go," I voiced. Yeah, I looked crazy. I had on a hospital gown, jogging pants, and flip flops. I looked like a fuckin' crackhead. It didn't matter. I was out this bitch whether they came or not.

"You don't need to leave," Fresh said. "You're not well."

"I'm not trying to hear none of that shit. I'm walking the fuck out of here with or without you two. Y'all can keep my room warm if you want too."

Fresh looked as if he was going to dispute what I just said. Then, he sighed and tossed the newspaper aside. "Your ass is going to be right back in here."

"I think not," I replied.

"His head hard as fuck," Quay said to Fresh, while putting away his phone. "He won't be satisfied until he's forced to be in this bitch."

"Get off my back," I snarled, walking out the room once again.

"You can't leave," one of the nurses at the nurse's station said as I strolled by.

"Watch me," I told her. She must've realized how serious I was because she didn't bother getting in my way.

"Where the car at?" I asked Fresh when we got to the front entrance of the hospital.

"I'll go get it," Fresh said, pulling out his keys. "Watch him," he told Quay as he walked off to get the car.

"You're going to have a setback because your head is hard as shit."

I glared the fuck outta him. "Who died and made you King Quay?"

9

"Nicca, I'm just telling your stubborn ass. And my dick got me crowned as King Quay, if your ass must know."

"Fuck you and your dick, nicca. I hope that bitch falls off, all that nasty pussy you keep falling in."

"Such a hater," Quay grumbled.

When Fresh pulled up, we all got in. I didn't want nobody to see me in these rags. Fresh pulled off into traffic and I could have sworn there was a car that pulled off right behind us. I looked out the back window a couple of times, but I didn't see the car anymore.

"What's wrong?" Quay asked while immediately grabbing his gun, turning all the way around.

"I don't know. I thought someone was following us," I stated, feeling paranoid. "I guess not. Anyway, I'm starving. Let's hit up Three Chefs."

Quay was still looking all around with his gun exposed.

"Did you hear me, crazy ass?"

Quay stopped looking out the back window. "What color was the car?"

"I thought it was a car. It was a truck. A Suburban or something."

"Aight, well keep your eyes open while I go in here and get this food. I'ma leave a gun under the seat for you." Quay got out of the car and walked toward the restaurant.

Fresh's phone vibrated. I assumed he got a text because he started typing immediately. Meanwhile, I was still looking around. I had a bad feeling that I just couldn't shake. Something told me that shit wasn't right.

"I need to run in this pharmacy right quick and grab something for Precious. Did you hear me?" Fresh asked.

I snapped my neck in his direction. "Huh?"

"What's wrong?" Fresh asked, picking up on my nervousness.

"Oh, nothing." I didn't tell him I felt something was wrong because I was starting to regret leaving the hospital. On top of sensing that something was about to happen, I was starting to feel very weak. My pride wouldn't allow me to ask Fresh to take me back to the hospital. Quay was right. I should have never left.

"Aight," Fresh exclaimed, staring at me funny. "I'm going to be in and out. When I get back, if you need something, let me know."

I nodded my head. When Fresh got out the car, I hopped out too and sat in the front. Without hesitation, I reached for the gun that Quay had under the seat. I promise, I couldn't even grab the gun when shots rang out, hitting Fresh's car, spraying it up. I crouched down. The bullets seemed to be coming from the opposite side. I wasn't too worried when I realized that Fresh's car was bullet proof. Man, I was glad his ass was on point.

A brother would have been shot the fuck up. When I lifted my head up, I saw that same black truck driving towards me, full speed ahead. I jumped in the driver's seat and threw the car in drive. I cut the wheel as far as it would go and stepped on the pedal. As soon as I pulled out of the parking spot, the truck rammed into me. The car flipped over and skid down the street. I heard more gun fire erupt. There was no doubt in my mind that my cousins were hitting that truck up. I must've been right because I heard tires screech and then the sound became more and more distant.

There was banging on the window. I couldn't see anything because I was trapped upside down. Thank goodness I was strapped in or I would have been ejected. However, I felt like I was being smothered by the air bag and choked by the seatbelt. The combination saved my life, but it felt like I was about to die because I couldn't breathe.

"Drake!" Quay yelled. "Drake! You aight?"

I went to speak and my throat felt tight. Sweat began to pour down my face and I felt extremely sick. Light headed with chest pains. I was afraid at any moment I was going to pass out again and not be able to wake up this time.

"I'ma break the window, Drake!" Quay yelled.

"You can't," Fresh countered. "He might get cut by the glass, and we don't know how badly he's hurt."

Princess Diamond

I saw Quay bend down and look inside the car. "Drake! We gonna get you out. Hold on, cuz."

Sirens sounded in the distance. I could only assume they were coming to my rescue.

Quay was still on the ground looking inside the car. "Fuck, man, the gawddamn car is leaking gas." He stood back up and all I saw was his expensive kicks. "Hurry the fuck up and get my damn cousin out of there."

More sirens were in the distance. An ambulance, I assumed.

All of a sudden, the car shook. Then, there was a loud buzz-saw noise. I guess they were using the hydraulic tool to open the side of the car. Moments later, the light shined into the side of the car. After that, I saw several firemen. The air bag was popped, the seatbelt was cut, and oxygen was placed over my face. I got that oxygen just in time because the car was very hot and I didn't know how much longer I could hold on. I was lifted in the air and placed on a stretcher. My vision was blurry, but I saw the paramedics rushing toward me. Everything went black after that.

Chapter 3

Drake

"Where am I?" I asked, feeling very groggy.

"You're in the hospital," Quay said, approaching my bed.

I went to speak and felt a sharp pain in my chest. "Fuck!" I groaned.

"I'm going to get the nurse," Quay said, rushing out of the room.

When he came back, a nurse and a doctor followed.

"What seems to be the problem?" the doctor asked.

I went to speak and couldn't, so I just pointed to my chest.

"Oh, you're going to experience some soreness. You were pretty banged up from the car accident. Scrapes and bruises all over your face, chest, arms, and legs."

That's when I noticed that one of my legs was in a cast, and my arm was in a cast too.

"Let me give you something for the pain," the nurse said, using the syringe to put pain medication into my IV.

"What's wrong with me? Why does my chest hurt so bad?"

The doctor replied, "You suffered a lot of bruising to your chest. It probably hurts more than the injury actually is. The steering wheel was pressed against your body. As for your leg and arm, you fractured them both. It'll take about eight weeks."

"Did you say eight weeks? I don't have eight weeks. I need to get back to work," I responded.

"What type of work do you do?" the doctor asked me.

Quay cleared his throat loudly.

I gawked at him, letting him know that I got this. "I own several laundromats that won't run themselves."

"I'm sorry," the doctor stated. "You're going to be out of commission for about eight weeks. If you don't take it easy, it might be longer, maybe ten weeks."

I sighed. "Whatever, doc, when do I get to leave?"

Quay spoke up. "You're not leaving again, Drake."

"Shut up, man," I snapped at Quay. "I'm not asking your ass. I'm asking the doctor." I stared directly at the doctor, waiting for an answer.

"You're cousin is right, Drake. You're gonna be here for a few days. Your blood pressure is through the roof. I can't allow you to leave until your numbers are stable."

"Damn," I said, getting angry again, which hurt my chest again. My pain meds must not have kicked in yet.

"I'll be back later to check on you," the doctor said while leaving, followed by the nurse.

I pleaded, "I can't stay in here, Quay."

I threw the covers back and swung my feet over the bed and cringed, once again, in pain.

Quay stared at me as if I had lost any good sense that I might have had. "Nicca, you have to. You almost died out there. Shit ain't safe. Niccas trying to take you out like Breeze."

"Okay, so what's up with that?" I asked as I got back into the bed and rested comfortable against the pillow. Maybe the doctor was right. I was exhausted just from sitting up and lying back down.

"Oh, I'm all over that. I got the license plate and a picture of the driver. I'm running his face through recognition as we speak. We about to get these niccas."

"That's why I need to get out of here. I want in on the action."

"Nah, Drake. Your ass is sick. You're here for a reason. You should have never left."

"C'mon, Quay. This is me. I always bounce back."

Dream & Drake 3: A Cartel Love Story

Quay stopped leaning on the window and walked closer to my bed. "You must've really bumped your head. Do you not realize that you almost lost your fuckin' life? Muthafuckas not only shot the gawddamn car up, but they tried to run your ass over too. You could have muthafuckin' died. Do you get that? We could have lost you?"

I went to speak, but Quay stopped me. "I'm calling rank. You're keeping your ass up in this bitch."

"You can't pull rank on me; I'ma boss. Nobody is over me."

"I can't, but Papi can."

"You didn't?" I couldn't believe Quay told my father.

"I did, Drake. It's for your own good. You're staying in the hospital until the doctor releases you. Then, you're going to take eight weeks off to heal. This street shit will be here when you get back."

I was so angry with Quay; I didn't know what to do. "Fuck you, man."

"I don't care about your nasty attitude. Be mad at me all you want, at least you'll be alive to see another day. As of right now, you can't even shoot nobody. Your trigger hand is fucked up."

"My arm is in a cast, not my hand."

Quay walked over to the bed and asked me to text on his phone. I snatched his phone with my good hand and tried to text with my hurt arm. It was nearly impossible. The cast was all the way down to my wrist, which prevented me from using my hand the way I wanted to.

"That's my damn point. This time, you lived. The next time these niccas catch you slipping, your ass will be history, and I can't have that on my watch. I got your back, even when you don't want me to."

"Whatever," I mumbled, turning over with my ass in his face. He could take the gesture however he wanted to. I was sick of all this shit.

"I'm positive Yolo is behind this. I don't care what y'all say. He knocked Breeze off. You're down for the count."

15

"Nicca, I'm not down for the count," I interrupted. "I'm just out of it temporarily. I'll be back on my feet in no time. Believe that shit."

"Whatever the fuck. You in this bitch right now, laid up with casts. Like I was saying, this nicca is picking us off one by one. I'm sure he's trying to get me and Mega next. Fuck that. I'ma catch his ass slipping. I know what we did wrong last time. We put a nicca on his ass instead of a woman. I'm setting that shit up now. He's back in. If he thinks we're all cool with him, especially me, he'll fuck up. I'll be right there when he does."

I yawned. "Do what the fuck you want."

Quay started texting, while I called myself being mad at him and ended up falling asleep. The pain medicine kicked in and I was out like a light.

Chapter 4

Dream

Every time I closed my eyes, I thought about Drake. I mean, for someone who couldn't remember him, he sure was always in my thoughts. That puzzled me too. The more I talked to people who knew me, the more I realized that Drake was a lot more relevant in my life than what I thought. When I first woke up, I thought he was some random nicca. From what my mama said, I loved him. I trusted my mother's opinion. If she said I was in love with this man, then that's exactly what it was. One way or another, I was going to get to the bottom of our relationship.

"Can, I get you anything, baby?" Nurse Agnes asked as she was about to leave my room.

"Is Drake still here in the hospital?" I inquired.

"Let me check and see. I think he left, but I'm not sure. I'll be right back."

Nurse Agnes walked out of my room to the nurse's station. I silently prayed that he was still here. I didn't want him to be sick or nothing but, at the same time, I really wanted to see his handsome face and talk to him.

She came back inside with a look that I couldn't read. "Looks like he did leave, but was just readmitted about an hour ago."

I gasped. "Is he okay?" I wondered. I was sure something bad must've happened for him to be admitted back to the hospital.

"He was in a car accident," Nurse Agnes told me. "From the look of his chart, he was banged up pretty badly, but nothing life-threatening from what I could tell."

Tears welled up in my eyes. "I feel so bad. You think that the way I treated him might have triggered his accident?"

"No, no, sweetie." Nurse Agnes comforted me, hugging me against her bosom. "From what I heard, it was a freak accident. It has nothing to do with you."

After hearing that devastating news, I just had to see him. "Okay, but I need to talk to him. If he's back here, in the hospital, it's meant for us to speak."

"I'm sure he won't be up for talking today. Let me see if I can get him down here to see you tomorrow."

"Will he still be here tomorrow?"

Nurse Agnes patted my hand. "Oh, honey, I'm positive."

The next day, I patiently waited for Nurse Agnes to enter my room. I ate breakfast. I watched tv. I even played games on my new phone. Finally, she appeared in the doorway and said that she was about to go get Drake and bring him to me. I was happy as a kid in a candy store. I still didn't know why I got so excited every time I thought about seeing him again.

All the excitement drained from my face when I saw the nasty look on Drake's face. He looked at me as if he hated me. I quickly shook that thought away. Maybe he was upset because of the accident. There were bruises all over his face. Scars that I didn't see yesterday. Not to mention, the casts on his arm and leg. I'm sure he was in pain. I continued to smile at him, thinking that maybe my happy attitude would rub off on him.

Chapter 5

Drake

I held my gun effortlessly in one hand, as I shot at the dude strapped to a large bullseye. I was fucking him up too. He already had two shots in each limb. His screams didn't bother me. He shouldn't have come for me and I wouldn't have to kill his ass. After shooting him in the groin and two more times in the stomach, I decided to take him out of his misery. A single shot to the head. My best aim yet.

"Drake?" I heard someone say. "Are you okay?"

I opened my eyes and realized that I was dreaming. I thought I had just killed the dude who tried to end my life. I quickly frowned when I found out I was still in the damn hospital.

"Yeah, I'm good, why?"

"Oh, I was just wondering because you mumbling something about dying. I hope you don't plan on leaving us anytime soon."

Nurse Agnes smiled at me and I found myself smiling back. She had always been nice to me when I came to see Dream. So, if she was my nurse, I wouldn't give her the same attitude that I gave other nurses.

"How about we go for a little stroll? Would you like that?" she asked, holding tight to the wheelchair.

"I'd rather walk."

"I know you would, but you need to stay off that leg. The doctor doesn't even want you on crutches yet. So, you'll have to settle for a wheelchair for now."

I felt like snapping on her, but I didn't. I let her help me out of the bed, hopped on one leg over to the wheelchair, and flopped down. I felt like a cripple for real as she pushed me down the hall to the elevator. Quite a few people stared at me and I glared at them, hard, until they turned their heads. I even mouthed fuck you to a few of them. I was in a sour mood to say the least. I never asked where we were going. It didn't dawn on me until I was being wheeled into Dream's room.

"Why am I here?" I asked Nurse Agnes.

"Dream has some things she wants to say to you."

"Well, I'm not talking to Dream, so you can wheel me right back to my room."

"Just hear her out for me," she pleaded.

"Tell her she got two minutes," I replied to Nurse Agnes. At this point, I didn't even want to hear Dream's voice.

"That's all I ask," Nurse Agnes.

"Drake," Dream said when Nurse Agnes left, as if she really knew who I was. I guess she caught the nasty look on my face and decided to defend herself. "You act like I can't say your name?"

"You can't. You aren't allowed to say my name because you don't know me," I fired back.

Dream rolled her eyes and huffed. "Why are you making this so difficult?

"Difficult?" I countered. "You try spending all of your moments with someone and they don't remember that you exist."

"That's kinda why I wanted you to come and see me."

I cut my eyes. "I don't know why. I don't have nothing to say to you."

Immediately, I felt like a girl but, at this moment, I didn't care. I was in my damn feelings. I loved this woman and she

20

didn't know who the fuck I was. I was afraid that, at this rate, she might not ever know my ass.

"I'm sorry, Drake."

I stared at the ceiling, ignoring her.

Dream sighed, as if I was getting on her nerves. "I said, I'm sorry. I'm trying my best to remember you. From what I have been told, we were once an item. It seems like, at one point, we might have been very close. That's why I wanted to talk to you. If that's true, I don't want those memories lost forever."

My head stayed tilted towards the ceiling. I heard every word she said but wasn't about to answer.

"Damn, Drake, I'm trying," Dream pleaded. "This is ridiculous."

I felt like she should beg me after the way she embarrassed me yesterday. I looked like a damn fool up here every day being concerned about her ass, when she had the nerve to wake up with another nicca on her mind.

"You got a lot of nerve being mad," I exclaimed, breaking my silence. I tried to stay quiet. I just couldn't. Dream always pushed my buttons, even when she wasn't trying to. "What's up with you? One minute, you want me out of your life, the next minute, you want to talk. Fuck outta here. I ain't one of these weak niccas."

I wasn't supposed to stand up, but I had to. I was pissed off. I made my way over to Dream's bed, crippled looking and all. This time, she didn't seem to be scared.

Just like before, I leaned into her. "You think I'm a joke?"

She smirked at me. She never did that before. I studied her while she stared at me.

"Of course I don't." Her mouth might have said that, but the fake smile she wore told me otherwise.

Who the fuck was this chick, and what happened to my baby, Dream? I would be lying if I said that her newfound attitude didn't turn me on. I felt my dick getting hard as she eyed me with major attitude.

"I think you're a lying ass trick," I spat. Never in a million years did I think I would have to address Dream in this manner.

This whole situation had me in turmoil. I immediately regretted talking to Dream like that. No matter how mad she made me, I realized it wasn't her fault. I was just hella frustrated that she didn't remember me.

"Listen, I know you're mad, but I refuse to be disrespected. I might not remember you, Drake, or whatever your name is, but let's get something straight, I will beat your ass. I don't care how much of a past we shared. I'm nothing like the old me. I heard the stories. That weak ass Dream is dead. I was trying to be nice, but all this intimidation that you're trying to do, the shit won't work."

And just like that, she flipped on me. Now, the repercussions of the accident were really starting to show. She was crazy as fuck. Maybe it's good that she didn't remember me.

"I don't even know if I want to know your ass again. I think you hit your head a little too hard. I had enough of this shit. This conversation is over."

I pressed the call button and Nurse Agnes answered, "Yes."

Dream cut me off. "I accidently hit the button," she lied.

"Is everything alright between you two?" Nurse Agnes inquired.

I was about to answer when Dream grabbed my hand. The physical contact threw me off. I was so disgusted with her that I didn't even want her to touch me.

"We're fine," she replied with an intense stare.

"Okay, sweetie," Nurse Agnes said, hanging up.

Chapter 6

Dream

This is how I heard our conversation…

Drake was in a sour mood from the moment he was wheeled into my room; looked like he had been sucking on lemons all day.

"Why am I here?" Drake barked.

My heart dropped. I thought maybe he would be just as happy to see me as I was to see him. That's the impression he gave me yesterday.

Nurse Agnes put the stoppers down on his wheelchair. "Dream has some things she wants to say to you," she politely told Drake.

Drake looked from her to me. "Well, I'm not talking to Dream, so you can wheel me right back to my room."

"Just hear her out for me," I pleaded.

"Tell her she got two minutes," he replied to Nurse Agnes.

"That's all I ask," Nurse Agnes.

"Drake," I said when Nurse Agnes left.

Drake looked at me funny, like I shouldn't be saying his name or something.

"You act like I can't say your name."

"You can't. You aren't allowed to say my name because you don't know me," he fired back.

This nicca was crazy. I rolled my eyes and huffed. "Why are you making this so difficult?

"Difficult?" he countered. "You try spending all of your moments with someone and they don't remember that you exist."

"That's kinda why I wanted you to come and see me," I said with a softer tone.

I cut my eyes. "I don't know why. I don't have nothing to say to you."

Immediately, I was hurt. This man had me all in my feelings. I was trying my best to talk to him and he was steadily pushing me away. He acted like I didn't remember him on purpose.

"I'm sorry, Drake."

He stared at the ceiling, ignoring me.

I sighed because this whole situation was getting on my nerves. "I said, I'm sorry. I'm trying my best to remember you. From what I have been told, we were once an item. It seems like at one point we might have been very close. That's why I wanted to talk to you. If that's true, I don't want those memories lost forever."

His head stayed tilted towards the ceiling. I was positive that he heard every word I said, but he didn't even bother to answer me.

"Damn, Drake, I'm trying," I pleaded. "This is ridiculous."

"You got a lot of nerve being mad," he exclaimed, breaking his silence. "What's up with you? One minute, you want me out of your life, the next minute, you want to talk. Fuck outta here. I ain't one of the weak niccas."

He gave me an angry stare. I guess I pissed him off once again. He stood, making his way over to my bed. From the way that he walked, I could tell that he shouldn't have been on his bad leg. For some reason, I wasn't scared like the last time when he approached me. Several things had changed. I wasn't confused anymore. After talking to the people close to me, I knew that Drake wasn't trying to hurt me like I originally thought. That's why I had to make things right between us.

He leaned into me and I stared into his cold eyes without flinching. "You think I'm a joke?"

I smirked at him. I didn't mean to. He was just so damn handsome.

"Of course, I don't," I answered with a sweet smile. I hoped that he didn't mistake my smile as sarcastic.

"I think you're a lying ass trick," he spat. Why was he talking to me like this? For a man who was supposed to have once cared about me, he surely didn't act like it. The disappointment must've been all over my face because his expression softened a little.

"Listen, I know you're mad, but I refuse to be disrespected. I might not remember you, Drake, or whatever your name is, but let's get something straight, I will beat your ass. I don't care how much of a past we shared. I'm nothing like the old me. I heard the stories. That weak ass Dream is dead. I was trying to be nice, but all this intimidation that you're trying to do, the shit won't work.

"I don't even know if I want to know your ass again. I think you hit your head a little too hard. I had enough of this shit. This conversation is over."

Drake pressed the call button and Nurse Agnes answered. "Yes."

He was about to speak, but I cut him off. "I accidently hit the button," I lied.

"Is everything alright between you two?" Nurse Agnes inquired.

I grabbed Drake's hand, catching him off guard. He paused and I spoke up before him again.

"We're fine," I replied with an intense stare. I wanted Drake to know that I meant business. I wasn't backing down just because he wanted me to.

"Okay, sweetie," Nurse Agnes said, hanging up.

"Let go of me," Drake barked. The veins in his neck popped out as he spoke.

Drake pinched my arm and I let go of him.

"I was hoping we could be friends."

"Friends?" he snapped. You expect things to be platonic after you already gave the pussy up?"

I was speechless. He made a valid point. I only said friends because I didn't know what else to say. Until I got my memory back, I couldn't be anything more.

"Ain't no damn way you and I can be friends after we done fucked all over the damn city." He chuckled in disbelief. "You on that bullshit. I'm out."

"Whatever Drake. If we're connected to each other as much as I was told we are, I'm not going nowhere, and you'll be back."

"That's a damn lie. I refuse to come back to your room."

"Shows how much you know; I'm not talking about here in the hospital. I'm talking about in general. That's why I suggested for us to be friends until we figured this thing out."

"Ain't shit for me to figure out. I know what I want. It's your ass that conveniently forgot."

"That's not fair."

"Life's not fair, shit."

Drake finally made it back to his wheelchair. I could tell he was exhausted when he flopped down and let out a long sigh. I would have helped him, but I was tired of his attitude. I'd let him cool off before I tried to approach him again. Our conversation wasn't what I hoped for. I thought he would fill me in on some of the missing details that nobody else seemed to know.

"Bye, Drake," I said in defeat as he wheeled towards the door.

Drake didn't even bother to respond. He just glared at me before he rolled out of my room.

He probably thought I was playing games because I didn't remember him, but I wished I had. Waking up out of the coma, I was slightly confused and trying to get my bearings. Now that I was starting to adjust, I could tell that Drake wasn't trying to hurt me, and my actions really affected him. We had some type of relationship before my accident. I still didn't know what happened. At this point, no one knew what really happened to me but Drake because he was there.

Dream & Drake 3: A Cartel Love Story

I asked my mother about him to see what she had to say because I wanted to know him better. She said we seemed happy. She couldn't shed much light on our relationship though. Obviously, I kept some things from her. I guess I'd continue to pester Drake until my memory did come back. I planned on chasing him until he cooperated.

I pressed the call button.

Another nurse answered, "Yes."

"Is Nurse Agnes available?"

"She stepped away. May I help you?"

"No, thank you. I'll just talk to her when she comes back."

"Okay. I'll leave her a message."

I thanked her and leaned back in the bed, more conflicted than ever. Drake was still heavily on my mind. All of a sudden, I got an odd feeling. I couldn't say it was pain because I didn't hurt anywhere. It was more like a knowing type of feeling that made me stop and think. I sat back on the bed and closed my eyes. I saw bits and pieces of my relationship with Drake flash in my mind.

I was still slightly confused about a lot, but it was enough to let me know that what we had was real. I knew in my heart of hearts that I loved him. That powerful feeling that I just got took over my body and forced me to concentrate. Lying in bed, I realized that what I felt was love all over me.

Normally, I would just sit here and wait for things to happen. Well, today wasn't that day. Drake was going to talk to me whether he liked it or not. I got out of my bed, grabbed my robe, put on my slippers, and made my way to the nurse's station.

"Excuse me, can you give me the room number to Drake, um, um…" I had no idea why I was at a loss of words. I knew his last name a minute ago. Now, I couldn't think of it. It was on the tip of my tongue too. Since I awoke from my coma, I did that forgetting thing a lot.

"Are you talking about the guy that just left your room?" the nurse asked. I assumed it was the nurse that I just talked to. She sounded like the same nurse if she wasn't.

"Yes. That's him."

"He's on your visitor's list. I'll tell you in just a moment." She searched through a few papers, and then she began typing on the computer. "His last name is Diaz-Santana. Here's his room number." After writing it down on a piece of paper, she handed it to me. "Good luck, girl."

"Is it that obvious?" I asked her.

She laughed. "Yes, it is. He wheeled out of your room with the meanest mug I'd ever seen. You pissed that man off something terrible."

That's exactly why I was going after him. "Well, thank you, I need all the luck I can get."

"No, you don't. Just be honest and true. Lay it all out on the table and allow him to accept you for you. Tell that man exactly how you feel, instead of playing games like we women do, saying and doing everything to piss our men off even more."

"You really think that'll work?" I asked. I planned on making some shit up if I had to, in order to win him back.

"Yes. You young girls don't know nothing. I know his type. Be real with him and he'll be real with you."

I hugged her. "That's exactly what I plan on doing."

Chapter 7

Drake

It took me forever to get back to my room. Who knew that wheeling myself would be worse than any workout I ever endured. Dumb fucking idea. Next time, I would let one of these nurses push me around. Using all of the strength that I had, I lifted myself from the chair and squirmed back into the bed. Resting my head on the pillow, I laid there trying to catch my breath, when there was a commotion at my door. I looked out in the hallway and saw Dream being held back by the two officers that stood guard at my door. Since there was an attempt on my life, extra security secretly followed me. I ain't gonna lie. My first thought was to leave her no memory having ass out there, but I couldn't. Despite how much I was hurt, I still cared for her. They were about to escort her away when I stopped them.

"Let her in!" I shouted.

Both of the officers stopped tussling with Dream. She was going off for someone straight out of a coma.

"She's good," I reiterated. They still hadn't let her go.

Dream closed the door and walked in, smiling as if she was back in good with me. It was time for me to bust her bubble.

"What do you want Dream? I can't do this back and forth thing with you anymore. I'm tired. I have a million other things to think about. I don't have time to play mind games with you." I sighed. "I'm exhausted. I'm constantly being judged. I can't do anything right in people's eyes. I'm put on a pedestal. I'm not allowed to make mistakes. I'm running in circles and I barely have a life. I live, eat, and breathe The Cartel, and still Drake isn't good enough. The last thing I need is you on my case too. I can't take it. So, if you came in here to say anything that might set me off, turn your ass around and walk your ass back out of my room."

Dream stood there listening to me vent. I really expected her to butt in. She didn't. She just stared at me with a listening ear. I was all talked out by the time she did speak.

"I'm not going anywhere, and since when do you care about other people's opinion of you? Let them talk. The Drake that I know is fearless. He's rich, handsome, and powerful. The world is his. Fuck what they say."

She smiled and, instantly, my anger subsided. I smiled back.

"Did you say the Drake that you know? Does that mean you remember me?" I asked with a goofy wide grin.

She giggled and sat on the edge of my bed. "Well, I don't remember everything but, after you left, I saw bits and pieces of our relationship. Kinda like snap shots."

"So, that means I still need to prove myself to you?"

"You don't have to prove anything to me, ever. The things that I remember are proof of your love for me. I just want to apologize for forgetting you. I can see why you were mad."

"So, we're good?" I wondered.

I had this strange feeling that the other shoe was about to drop. I had no idea why. It just seemed like Dream's speech was leading up to something. My thoughts were confirmed when she started bawling.

"C'mere," I said, reaching for her with my left arm. She was sitting on that side of the bed, so it wasn't much of a reach for me. "What's up? Whatever it is, you might as well get it out. Now is the time, since we're getting shit off of our chests."

Dream laid on my chest, continuing to cry. "You're going to be mad at me."

She had me curious now. "What did you do?"

I expected her to answer right away, but she didn't. She remained quiet, silently crying in my arms. I kissed her forehead and rubbed her back. Her head was starting to hurt my chest a little, but that didn't stop me from consoling her though. I was more afraid of what she was about to say than the pain I felt. I could take the pain. Depending on what she said, it might hurt more than having my chest compressed.

"I'm so selfish," she said, lifting her head from my chest as if she just heard my thoughts. "You were in an accident and I'm lying on you."

"I'm good," I lied. I didn't want to tell her I was in pain.

"No, you're not," she stated. "I can tell."

I was about to speak and she stopped me.

"No more lies, Drake."

Dang, she was trying to make a brother look weak. "Maybe a little bit. So, what was the secret that you had to tell me?" I braced myself for the bad news as she stared at me with teary green eyes.

"Promise me you won't get mad."

How could I say no to her? "I promise."

"I cheated on you with Spencer," she blurted out.

I felt my temper go from zero to ten thousand. "What the fuck do you mean, you cheated on me? When? With who?" I wanted to kick her ass.

She sniffled. "Now, you said that you wouldn't get mad. You even promised me."

Why did I make that damn promise? "Okay, Dream," I said through gritted teeth. "What... else?"

"I'm pregnant and I don't think it's yours."

I closed my eyes and held the bridge of my nose. She was asking for something impossible.

"Drake? Talk to me?" she whined.

"Give me a minute," I said, still in thought.

Pregnant? How could this be? How could she be pregnant by that nicca? Damn.

"So, there's no possibility that the baby could be mine?"

Dream stopped sobbing. "I never thought of that, but I don't think so. I mean, I wish it was. I... I... don't think so. To my knowledge, no."

Man, was I hurt. "So, what are you really telling me, Dream? You fucked around on me. You pregnant by the next nicca. How could there possibly be a future between us?"

"I don't know, but I was hoping that you would have me and the baby. I know I'm asking for a lot, but I don't want to be with Spencer. I want to be with you."

I closed my eyes and sighed. I think I was more hurt by her actions now than when I carried her in here bruised and bloody after the accident. Then, I thought she was going to die. Now, I felt like she was killing me. Silently, I prayed.

God, why? When I asked you to bring Dream back to me, I had no idea it would be like this, with child. Another man's child. I hate that man and you know this. Yes, hate is a strong word, but I can't lie. It's how I feel.

"Drake?" Dream asked, interrupting my talk with God.

I put my finger up, signaling her to shut up. She must've gotten the hint because she was quiet after that, allowing me to be with my thoughts again.

Lord, please direct me on what I should do in this situation. You know me. If this nicca gets out of line one time, I won't be held responsible for what I might do. I'm trying to change, but it's hard. Should I accept Dream or not?

I had no idea how I was going to be a father to the next man's child but, if this was what I was supposed to do, then that's exactly what I was going to do. I might be an alcoholic in the process. I sighed. That's when images of Channa being pregnant flashed before me. I saw Arizona and Arabia too.

Then I heard, He that is without sin among you, let him first cast a stone. I knew that scripture well. John 8:7. My Meme said it all the time. Until this point, it didn't have a true meaning in my life. I had to accept Dream. I wasn't innocent either.

"I have a confession too," I finally said, opening my eyes.

"What?" she asked, wiping away more tears with the back of her hands. "Wait a minute. If your confession involves you leaving me, I don't want to hear it."

"Nah, nothing like that. You said you got some memories of me. Did you remember that I was married? Technically, I'm separated, but you know what I mean."

"I didn't remember that, but my parents filled me in on it. My mama loves you. My daddy hates you."

I wanted to tell her that I hated her father too. "Sounds about right. Enough about your parents, what do you think?"

"I don't listen to my parents or anyone else. I'm grown. I pay my own bills and I live in my own home. That's the reason why I went to college and landed a great job, so I could be my own woman."

I couldn't help but smile as she spoke. She was definitely a new and improved Dream, with the ability to hold her own now.

"Channa's pregnant!" I blurted out. "I have two babies on the way."

"Twins?" Dream asked.

I nodded yes.

She glared at me. "Okay, what else?"

I looked at her like she was crazy, but I continued to talk. "And I cheated on you while you were in the hospital with two women, an ex-girlfriend and her sister."

Once again, Dream stared at me for a moment before she said, "Okay, what else?"

"That's it," I admitted. Hell, she already knew what I did for a living. "I have nothing else to hide."

"Do you want to be with them?" Dream questioned.

"No, none of them. All three of them are history. The only thing I want to do is take care of my kids. I'm divorcing Channa as soon as I can recover from this bullshit."

Dream grinned. "Well, it's settled then. We're together, right?"

"It's that easy?" I asked her. "I mean, you can forgive me for all that in an instant. I needed to pray to get over what you said."

"Of course I can. All I wanted to do was get back to you. I woke up confused and disoriented, but now that I know that you have my heart, I can't see myself with no other man. While I was asleep, I prayed too. I asked for a second chance. I got one and nothing will stop me from living it. Not a baby by another man. Not a baby by another woman. Not an ex-wife or an old girlfriend. Now, I'm asking you once and for all, do you want me, all of me, baby included?"

It pained me to say it, but I felt the same way. I couldn't see myself without Dream. My answer was simple. "Yes."

In the back of my mind, I felt like that baby was mine. Dream's mind was all jumbled up. How the hell would she know if that baby was mine or the next nicca's? She didn't. Easily, she could have swapped my memories with Spencer's. I was not buying it. Until it's proven that the baby was Spencer's, I was claiming that the baby was mine.

Chapter 8

Dream

"So, now that we've agreed to be together, what are we going to do about Spencer and Channa?"

I looked into Drake's handsome face as he thought. "I was thinking, you go home with Spencer and I'll go home with Channa."

"That's absurd. Not after we've went through hell to get back together. Are you trying to break us up again?"

"Hear me out," he commanded. "I won't be well for another eight weeks. So, the last thing I need is for a nicca to act a fool and I can't handle his ass. I want to be there when you drop this nicca. For now, go home and play your part with him, but don't sleep with him. When the time is right, you'll leave him."

I thought about what he said for a second. "Okay, you might have a point."

"Exactly. You feel me now?"

"Yes, but what about you? What are you going to do?"

"I'm going to do the same."

I gave him a knowing look. "You better not sleep with her."

"I'm not. The last time I had sex with Channa was before we met. Honestly, I don't think the babies she's carrying are mine. The fuckin' dates don't add up."

"Get a paternity test," I suggested.

"Oh, I plan on it but, for now, I need to keep Channa around so that when the hearing comes up for our divorce, she'll show up. If I don't pacify her until then, she can drag this shit out for years. As of right now, we have a decent relationship because she's pregnant. If she finds out that I'm back with you and not her, she will skip town or worse; she might come after you. I can't afford for her to do either."

I laid back in his embrace. "She can come after me if she wants to. I'm going to have something waiting for that bitch," I said with venom dripping from my voice.

Drake looked taken aback when I said that.

"I'm not that old Dream. If that bitch comes after me, I'm going to end her life. So, you better do what you have to do to keep that hoe in line."

Drake looked me over with lust in his eyes. "You sound sexy as fuck right now."

"So, you don't care if I beat the shit out of her?"

"Not at all," he replied. "Just do it after the babies are born. That's all that I ask."

"You got my word." I snuggled closer to him. "I don't want to be away from you."

He ran his hand over his beard with disgust. "I hate it too, but we gotta do what we gotta do. After that, our exes will be out the picture, and we can live happily ever after."

"I seriously doubt that, but I'm willing to try. My gut tells me it's about to get real bumpy."

"Don't be afraid."

"I'm not," I confessed. "I'm getting me a gun when I'm discharged. Anybody that threatens me is about to get shot."

Drake laughed at me and I couldn't help but to laugh with him.

"My lil gangsta boo," he said, still laughing. "Real talk, if you need me, I'm only a phone call away. If I can't get to you, I'll send someone in my place to assist you."

I frowned. "Yeah, I know. I just wish we could leave the hospital together."

"It's only eight weeks. You can do this."

I exhaled. "I have no choice."

"Show me how much you want to be with me," Drake said, rubbing my ass through my gown. I didn't have on the cheap hospital gown anymore. I wanted to be cute for him, so I had on a feminine pink cotton gown with the matching robe and slippers.

"You so nasty." I pecked his lips. "What makes you think that I can do something like that?"

He smirked. "I saw the way you were beating the officers up. You need some dick in your life."

I giggled and then smirked too. I was more than ready to sex Drake. Truth be told, I'd been wanting to feel him inside of me since I saw him naked. His body was flawless.

"I got something for you. Something that I've been waiting to do."

I dived under the sheet head first. I could tell that Drake didn't know what the hell I was doing at first. Quickly, he got with the program when he felt my warm hands on his joint.

"Ah, your hands are so soft," Drake murmured.

"My mouth is even softer," I said, admiring his neatly trimmed private area.

I slowly stroked his penis. My sweaty hand went from the base to the tip in a half-twist motion. I couldn't see Drake's face, but I could tell he was feeling my strokes from the way his dick twitched.

I'd never done this before, so I allowed my instincts to lead the way. I did what came natural. I thought about how much I wanted to please Drake and, just like that, giving head was a piece of cake. I decided to give his balls some attention as I kept stroking his member. After gargling on them for a few minutes, I was finally ready to give him head. His dick was stiff as a board when I finally put my mouth on it. My tongue tickled the tip before I sucked on it like a succulent piece of fruit. Bobbing my head up and down, I took his thick phallus into my mouth, swallowing him whole.

"Shiiiiiit," Drake said, thrusting into my mouth. "Sssss. This is exactly what I needed."

"I know, papi. Let me take away all the stress," I exclaimed before putting his dick back in my mouth. "I'm going to make up for lost time."

"Is that right?" Drake asked, touching my face.

"Hell yeah," I answered before slurping on his dick again.

"Damn, your mouth so juicy."

"My pussy is juicy too."

"Let me see what it feels like," Drake said, motioning for me to get up.

I rose to my knees, pulled off my gown, and straddled his hips.

"Wait," Drake said, stopping me. His eyes darted to my small pudgy stomach. "I'm not about to hurt the baby, am I?"

"No," I said, sliding down on his pole. "Ohmigod, it feels so damn good."

My hands were palming his stomach as I rose up and down on his dick. Instantly, I was cumming. My eyes rolled into the back of my head. My body tingled all over as my body quivered.

Drake grinned. "Damn, you cumming already?"

The orgasm felt so good that I couldn't even answer him. I continued to rock my hips in a circle, savoring the feeling that went through out my whole body.

"Ah, you got some good dick," I moaned, ignoring his question. "Ohmigod! I'm about to cum again"

I felt a stream of juices leave my body. The shit was so intense that I couldn't do nothing but continue to rock. I hadn't even been sitting on his dick for five minutes, and he managed to make me cum twice. I leaned forward, grinding against Drake as he kissed me. A sweet savory kiss that felt like a million dollars. Allowing the feeling to take over me, I arched my back and worked my vaginal muscles in a way that felt good to us both.

"You trying to make a nicca nut?"

"Yeeeessss," I mumbled against Drake's lips. This sexual experience was ultimately incredible. It's like every nerve in my body had been unlocked, and Drake's dick just turned the key.

"You're the best," I moaned. I meant that shit.

"Stop lying," Drake said with a smirk. "You just missed getting dick on a regular."

I rode the fuck out of his dick. "I... promise... it's... good."

"Damn, Dream, I'm about to nut."

Drake held my hips, vigorously hitting my spot again and again.

"Oh, Drake, me toooooo," I wailed as my clit fluttered, and then my whole body quivered.

Within moments, I felt his seed spill up inside of me. I collapsed on top of him, forgetting all about his chest pain.

"I promise, that shit was the best I ever had."

"Don't be pumping a nicca head up, ma."

"No, Drake, I swear. My pussy still twitching."

Drake chuckled. "I feel that shit too."

When I rose off his dick, it was coated with thick white cum.

"You enjoyed yourself, huh?" Drake pointed to the cum leaking down my thigh.

I blushed.

"You want some more baby?"

I nodded. I didn't know what was wrong with me. I was so damn horny that it was driving me crazy. "I don't know what's wrong with me, but I'm so damn hot."

"You're pregnant," Drake announced. "You got some good pussy. I bet it taste good too. Come ride my face."

I got in the bed, ready to sit on Drake's face when the door opened. It was Nurse Agnes.

Drake pulled the sheet over both of us, covering our naked bodies. I was sure I looked like a deer in the headlights as she stared at us.

"I knew that you two would make up," she said while grinning at us.

Drake smirked.

"Dream, Mercy is here to see you," Nurse Agnes stated.

"Oh, okay. I'll be there in a minute." That was all I could muster. There was no denying what we were in here doing, so I didn't even try to cover it up.

"Make sure I get an invite to the wedding." Nurse Agnes smiled, laughed, and then she left. "I'll wait for you outside."

As soon as she left, Drake kissed me. "I'm not done with you yet. You got me hooked on that pussy. Come back and see me after Mercy leaves."

I winked at him. "You just make sure you're ready to put that work in."

Drake flexed his dick under the sheet. "My shit stay ready."

"You so nasty."

He snickered. "But you like it though."

"I don't like it, I love it."

We kissed for a minute.

"Tell Mercy I said, what up doe?"

I grinned at him. "I will."

I put my gown, robe, and slippers back on. I kissed Drake once more before I was forced to sit in the wheel chair. Nurse Agnes insisted that it was too far for me to walk, so I was wheeled back to my room.

"There you are," Mercy said, hugging me as soon as I was wheeled into my room. "Girl, your ass almost gave me a heart attack when I walked in and your bed was empty."

Nurse Agnes helped me into the bed and then she left.

"No, I'm fine," I said with a wide grin. I couldn't help but smile as I thought about being intimate with Drake a few minutes ago.

Mercy stared at me. "I know that look. You got some dick."

I hushed her. "Sssssssshhhh. Don't tell the whole damn hospital."

Mercy took a seat on my bed. "Your ass is nasty. I was worried about you and you come straight out of a coma fucking."

We both cracked up laughing.

"It wasn't that simple," I confessed. "I didn't remember Drake at first. I called him Spencer and everything."

Mercy gasped. "Bitch, you lying. I know Drake went crazy on your ass. You lucky to be alive."

I giggled. "He did. I thought I lost him."

Mercy waved her hand at me. "You ain't never going to lose that man. He looooves you," she stressed. "I spent a lot of time with him while you were unconscious and all he talked about was you."

"Yeah, well, he admitted to fucking two women while I was out."

"Fuck them hoes. Bitches always gonna be on Drake's dick. What you have to do is play your part and show them why you're wifey. If you do it just right, he won't have eyes for no other woman but you."

Mercy was right. I felt that deep inside. "My instincts were leading me do to just that. That's why I didn't trip when he opened up and told me."

"The nicca told you," Mercy said, getting all hyped. "Girl, you got him wrapped all around your damn finger. He loves your ass for real. Don't fuck it up, though. What you about to do about that rotten ass nicca Spencer?" She rolled her eyes at the ceiling.

I ran the plan down to Mercy that Drake and I had discussed. "So, what you think?" I asked her.

"I don't know. Spencer ain't about to let you go that easy, and I met that piece of trash wife of Drake's. She's a real piece of work. I almost had to beat that bitch black and blue."

I cracked up. "Why you crazy? I could see you fighting her too."

Mercy cracked her knuckles. "You know how the fuck I get down. I will murder that bitch. That's why I keep pink passion on me," she said while patting her handbag, referring to her pink gun. "You need to get you one too. Shit ain't safe out here."

"I been thinking that too. I want a purple one."

"It's whatever," Mercy said. "I can teach you how to shoot and everything, cause my aim is tight."

"I already know it is. You stay poppin' niccas."

She twisted her lips. "All day."

We both laughed again.

In the middle of us laughing, Mercy grabbed me and held me tight. "I thought I lost your ass forever," she sobbed. "You better not ever scare me like that again. You know I will shoot up Chicago if your ass dies."

I laughed through my tears. "I know you will too."

"Hell yeah. You're my ride or die," she said seriously.

I wiped her tears. "Well, stop crying because you got a baby shower to plan."

"Get the fuck outta here!" Mercy shouted. "I can't believe it. I'm about to be an auntie. I'm mad at you, tho. I should have been the first to know." She paused and smiled. "Oh, wait, that's why you had to make up with Drake."

"Well, not really," I said, avoiding her stare.

The smile wiped right off of Mercy's face. "I know that look." She gasped. "I'ma cut you if this is Spencer's baby."

I stayed quiet, looking down.

Mercy jumped up off the bed dramatically. "You gotta be kidding me."

I knew Mercy was going to be all in her feelings when I told her I was pregnant by Spencer. I just couldn't keep the news from her.

"Imagine how I feel."

"What Drake say?"

"He was mad at first, but we worked it out."

Mercy did a body roll, trying to imitate me riding Drake. "Oh, I'm sure you work, work, work, work, work, work." She made a sex face and giggled. "Now, I see why you were missing when I got here."

I threw my pillow at her. "Shut up, crazy girl."

"I guess I have to accept the baby because it's yours, but I'm not planning shit for that nicca. I hate Spencer's weird ass."

"So, you're not going to plan my baby shower, for real?"

Mercy rolled her eyes and folded her arms across her chest, posing with an attitude. "Let me think about it."

"C'mon, Mercy. For real."

"For real, I don't like his ass, but I'll do it for you. He ain't invited tho. Punk ass nicca."

"That's cool. He ain't gotta come."

"So, how you plan on saving your goodies for Drake? Cause you know Spencer is a horn-dog. I wouldn't be surprised if he wasn't sneaking in here at night, humping on you."

She laughed, but I didn't. Something about her words resonated with me.

"I'm not giving him shit. I already know what I'm going to do, get a doctor's note. It's gonna say I can't have sex for eight weeks."

Mercy busted out laughing. "Spencer about to be half-crazy for real, now."

"Aye, you know what I wanted to ask you. Where's Bey?"

"I ain't seen her. I thought she was on her tirades again."

"Nobody has seen her since my accident. That's a long time. I think something might have happened to her."

"Don't jump to conclusions. Let's get you well first. Then, we can worry about her. You're not one-hundred percent and you're pregnant. When the doctor says that you're well enough to start searching, then I'll be right by your side."

"Well, let me go," Mercy said, standing to her feet. "My lunch break been over. I'm working from home today, dealing with one of your problem accounts."

I laughed. "I'll bet you really miss me now."

"Damn right. Your clients are nuts. I can't wait for you to get back and take over."

"I'll be back before you know it."

"You better because I can't stand none of those bitches at that job. I ain't got nobody to eat lunch with."

I cracked up. "All you're worried about is food."

Mercy smiled. "Don't act like you don't know how I do. Now, give me a hug." Mercy hugged and kissed me.

"Let me go see how Drake's doing before I leave. I'm sure his ass is sleep after getting a dose of that hot coma pussy."

I cackled loudly. "You know you wrong for that."

"So, you didn't put it on him?"

I blushed. "Maybe."

"This nicca probably snoring with drool. I'ma text you if that's what I see."

Mercy did another body roll before she waved goodbye and left out of my room.

I laid down, preparing to turn in for the night. I didn't look forward to facing Spencer tomorrow. I remembered everything about him. It's funny how I removed Drake from my mind, yet I kept all my memories of Spencer. He was an asshole. I hated that I slipped up and got pregnant by him. I used to want to be with him, but my feelings had changed.

God, if there is a chance that my baby could be Drake's, please, please, please let it be. I don't want any ties to Spencer. I didn't want Spencer in my life for the next eighteen years. Drake and I had been through a lot in a short period of time. *I just want to have his baby and make our lives complete.*

I got a text before I drifted off.

Mercy: *Girl, I just went to visit Drake and he's in here snoring with drool on the side of his face. You got that snap back cooch. Put his ass to bed.*

I laughed hard as hell. Mercy was definitely a character.

Chapter 9

Spencer

I pushed Destiny off of me and rolled out of bed.

"Where you going?" she had the nerve to ask me.

"To work," I spat. "Where do I always go during the week?"

"Don't get smart," she said while rolling over, going back to sleep.

She should be tired. Her ass stayed up all night. I was glad she was staying in bed. Normally, she got up and followed me around the damn house while I got my shit together for work. This girl didn't have no kind of life. No friends or nothing. What the fuck was on my mind when I fucked around with her. Shit, I gotta make better choices in the future.

My phone vibrated and I jumped. I whipped my neck over at the bed as I cut my phone on silent. When Destiny didn't move, I checked my text message. It was from Lois, the night nurse who watched after Dream.

Lois: *Dream is awake. She's been up for three days now.*

Me: *And you're just now telling me. Why the fuck do I pay your ass if you're not going to come through?*

Lois: *I was on vacation. I just got back to work and found out. Besides, you wouldn't have been able to see her anyway. Her visitor's list was restricted until today.*

Princess Diamond

This bitch was on some country fried bullshit. It's cool because her day was coming. She was going to look for that payment and the shit was going to bounce. Her ass was about to miss me and my money in a major way. I didn't need her ass no more now that Dream was awake.

Me: *Aight cool.*

Lois: *Something else you should know... she's pregnant.*

"HELL YEAAAAAH!" I shouted. My plan worked. I knew it would.

"What's wrong, baby?" Destiny asked in a groggy voice.

"Oh, nothing baby. Go back to sleep."

"Quiet it down then."

"I will, baby."

Me: *Thanks for letting me know*

Lois: *Oh and she has a slight case of amnesia too.*

Me: *What does that mean? She doesn't remember me?*

Lois: *From what I can tell, she remembers you. She just doesn't remember everything, but the doctor said she should get all of her memories back soon.*

I didn't give two fucks, as long as she remembered me.

Lois: *Did you deposit my money yet? Rent is due.*

I wasn't a damn cash cow for her ass.

Me: *You'll have it later on.*

Lois: *Text me when you send it.*

I didn't even text her back. I left her ass hanging.

I jumped around, doing my happy dance. I was super excited. There was no way that Dream could deny me now. That other nicca was history. She was carrying my damn seed. I wish he would step to me on some fuck nicca shit. He was going to see how I got down. I was going to shoot his punk ass. Although I never met him, I heard he was bad news. A thug type who was deep in the streets. I had no idea what Dream saw in him. To my knowledge, she never had a thing for bad boys.

I crept back into the bedroom and grabbed my things without bothering Destiny. I was not sure if Destiny knew she was awake or not. If she knew, she didn't mention it to me. I couldn't imagine the family not telling her. She probably didn't mention it because she's afraid that I was going to leave her ass, and she should be.

As soon as she went to school, I was going to come back and clean out all my shit and go home. I could have gone home a long time ago, but things just didn't feel right there without Dream. In fact, I tried to stay there quite a few times and it felt weird. Almost like Dream's spirit was there with me. It was creepy as fuck to say the least, so I just remained at Destiny's house. Now, I had a reason to return.

After I dressed, I decided to call in today. I needed to see Dream this morning. I couldn't wait to talk to her about the baby. Once I left the hospital, I was going to come home to our house and clean it from top to bottom so that it would be sterile by the time she came home. I hoped she didn't plan on going to her mother's house. I wanted her home with me, so I could nurse her and my baby back to health.

"Heeey," I said to Dream when I entered her hospital room. Immediately, I was greeted by a million flowers and cards.

"Hi," Dream said dryly. If I didn't know any better, I would think that she didn't want to see me.

Wow, she was gorgeous. Her once short haircut was long flowing curls.

"I'm not cutting my hair, if that's what you're thinking," she stated matter of factly.

"No, no, baby. I wouldn't ask you to do that," I said, taking a seat next to her on the bed.

I sat the roses down next to all the other gifts and then pulled the card out to give to her. I had it specially made to announce that I knew about the pregnancy. Dream took the card from me with an attitude and opened it. Her eyes glanced over the card and then she closed it, handing it back to me. She didn't even read it.

"This card won't make up for the way that you've treated me."

"I guess I deserve that. I've been a rotten boyfriend. After losing you in more ways than one, I came to my senses."

47

She rolled her eyes at me and sucked in air. I knew this wasn't going to be an easy process, so I came prepared to beg and plead.

"Listen, while you've been asleep, I've been getting my shit together. I got a promotion and a couple bonuses. I've put the money up just for you. I'ma buy that car that you wanted."

"Whatever, Spencer."

Damn, she wasn't budging.

"I know you're mad at me. I deserve all of the attitude that you're giving me right now. I was supposed to have your back and I didn't. So, whatever I need to do, I'll do."

Dream just stared at me, unfazed that I was pouring my heart out to her.

"I know you're pregnant," I said, breaking our silence.

"How? Because hardly anyone else knows."

I thought of a quick lie while she stared me down. Surely, I couldn't tell her that I paid off one of the nurses looking after her to get the information.

"Nobody would tell me how you were, so I kinda looked at your chart at the nurse's station. I hope you're not mad. I was just concerned. I'm happy about the baby."

Dream kept the same snide look that she previously had.

"Are you not happy about the baby?" I asked. I was concerned now because I was doing all the talking, while she kept giving me crazy looks.

"I just woke up out of a coma. What makes you think I would be excited to be pregnant? Since you looked at my chart, you would know that I have amnesia. That could affect my child."

"You mean, our child," I corrected her. I knew that she was feeling some type of way, but I was super excited. I couldn't stop smiling.

I went to reach for her stomach and she popped my hand. "I can't feel my son?"

"Spencer, you ain't been here all of five minutes and all you've done is get on my damn nerves." She cut her eyes at me. "And how do you know it's a boy?"

Dream & Drake 3: A Cartel Love Story

As mean as she was treating me, I smiled every time I thought about my child. "Because I just know. Please, let me touch him."

Dream sighed loudly. "Okay. I guess."

I went to raise her gown and she popped my hand again.

"Ow! What was that for?"

"You can touch my stomach through my gown."

"Okay," I whimpered. "I didn't know."

Dream finally laid still and I touched her belly through her gown. I was amazed at how big her stomach was. "How far along are you?"

"Sixteen weeks."

"Wow," I exclaimed. I was amazed that I actually got her pregnant. My hands gently roamed all over her stomach. "You're so big."

"Actually, I have gotten bigger since yesterday. When I first woke up, I had no stomach. The next day, I had a small pouch. Now, I'm actually showing. I guess my body was waiting for me to wake up before I blossomed. I look about four months now."

"I love it," I said, rubbing my face against her belly. I kissed all over her stomach. "I can't wait to see him."

Dream sighed. "Are you going to leave him hanging like you left me?"

"I'm sorry, hell. You are never going to let me live that down."

"Whatever. I'm tired," she said, faking a yawn.

I didn't want to stress her and the baby, so I let it be. "Okay, I caught the hint. I'll let you rest, but I'm taking you home from the hospital, and you and the baby are staying with me."

She acted like she wanted to say no. "Yes, that'll be fine. Now, let me get my rest, please."

I tried to kiss her on the lips, but she turned her head, and I ended up kissing her on the cheek. I didn't object. One more thing I let slide. She was coming home with me. I had plenty of time to be up underneath her. More importantly, being inside of her. I smiled to myself as I left her room. She had that good-good, and I couldn't wait to slide up in it once again.

My phone vibrated and I nearly flipped the fuck out when I saw that I had twenty missed calls from Destiny's paranoid ass. Wasn't nothing that fucking serious. This girl was beyond delusional. Shit was so bad with her that I seriously considered faking my own death, just so I could get away. If she wasn't so damn crazy, I would change my number and move on with my life. But, see how her brain was set up, she might come after a nicca. I was not trying to die over no fatal attraction bullshit.

I couldn't lie and say that I didn't know how she was. I knew. I just thought that maybe I could pass the time with her until Dream came back to me. Obviously, I was thinking with the wrong head because now I was in a real life Lifetime movie. The more I tried to pull away, the clingier this bitch got.

Chapter 10

Channa

Arizona and Arabia were overrated. Now that I was pregnant, I didn't need those twin bitches around anymore. They could go back under the rock they crawled from under. That's exactly what I intended on telling them. I no longer needed them because I was pregnant with not one baby but two. The fertility drugs and In-Vitro fertilization worked perfectly.

The only reason why I kept them around was just in case I miscarried. After talking attentively with my doctor, she assured me that I would carry these babies full-term. Of course, she was well aware of my history of miscarriages. I found out that I was missing a vital enzyme that would help with the implantation of the fetus. I understood what she was saying basically but, when she started talking all those medical terms, I tuned her out. As long as I got my prescription of whatever it was that would help me carry my babies for nine months, I didn't give a fuck.

I was four months and working the hell out of my pregnancy glow. Drake had been cooperative too, even though he'd been giving me the side eye. He didn't think the babies were his. Of course, he had no idea of my little trick. That's why I needed Arizona and her side kick to get the fuck out of dodge. I could handle shit from here.

Princess Diamond

I waited in the cut while those twin hoes strolled into the hotel, carrying bags full of designer shit. I was sure it came from the money that I gave their trifling asses. They were giggling and talking about how nice of a time they had at the mall. Stupid bitch shit. They were so sickening. I prayed that my daughters wouldn't be pathetic like them.

As soon as Arizona opened the hotel room door, I rushed out of my room across the hall, shoving them both inside of their room with two guns pointed at them.

"Well, well, well, bitches. Is this my money you're spending?"

"Do you mean our money?" Arizona had the nerve to say.

"No, bitch, I mean my money. I gave it to you."

"No, we earned it," Arabia cosigned.

I pointed both my guns at her. "Bitch, shut your fuckin' mouth. You were never a part of the deal. I suggest you keep your opinion to yourself before I put a bullet down your throat."

I expected Arabia to pop off like Arizona did, but she was smart. She shut the fuck up. I was glad because my finger was itching. I had thoughts of shooting her, especially since Drake seemed to like her more. I didn't know why. She was a weak bitch if you asked me. This was why I needed to be in Drake's life. He had a soft spot for dumb bitches.

"Listen, twin bitches, and listen good. I'm only going to say this once. Get your fuckin' shit and get the fuck out of Chicago."

I threw a knot at Arizona's feet. "That's six grand. Take that fuckin' money and relocate."

Arizona looked as if she was about to speak and I took one gun off Arabia and put it back on Arizona. "Bitch, I will blow your ass away."

"No!" Arabia shouted. "We'll take the money and leave."

Arabia might have agreed to what I was saying, but Arizona hadn't said a word.

"And what about you, bitch?" I asked Arizona's funky ass. "Are you going to take the money and leave like I told your ass to do, or are you going to be carried out of this bitch in a body bag? What you gone do, bitch?"

"I should hit you in the stomach," Arizona said, jumping at me.

I fired off a single shot and the bullet just missed her head. "Fuck with me if you want to bitch."

"It's two of us and one of you," Arizona spat. "We can take your pregnant ass."

"You wish you could take my pregnant ass, bitch." I laughed in her face. "Let me tell you something. If you make me lose my babies, I'm killing your whole bloodline. That means this cheap looking hoe to the left of you that shares the same face as you, your mama, your pappy, and other siblings you might have, grandparents, uncles, aunts..." my voice trailed off. "Do you need me to keep going?"

"Let's just leave," Arabia advised her sister.

"You should listen to this weak bitch. She's going to save your life."

"Fuck you, Channa," Arizona said, spitting at me.

She's lucky the shit missed.

"You're just threatened because Drake likes us more than you."

"Bravo bitch. He does, that's why I want you scheming, double-teaming ass hoes gone. I don't do competition. There is only one wife, which is me, and not you two raggedy bitches. So, I'm telling you one last time. You have until the end of the night before I send my people after you."

"Okay," Arizona finally conceded. She knew that I meant business. I wouldn't hesitate to kill her or her sister.

"It was nice doing business, ladies. Now, fuck off and get lost." I confidently turned my back. I wished like hell one of them would run up on me; I was going to shoot them both dead. I wanted to do that anyway. The only reason why I didn't was I felt like I owed them this much. They did help me get the babies that I thought I would never have. Thanks to them, Drake and I were working on our relationship. Well, he didn't actually say that, but he'd been nice to me because of the babies. I'd been eating that shit up too.

"You won't get away with this Channa," Arizona spat.

"Bitch, I already got away with it. You can't do shit to me."

I looked over my shoulder at them. They both wore devilish smirks. I was sure they had something up their sleeves. I wasn't sure what and, right now, I didn't give a fuck what it was. As long as they left town, I was cool.

"Time is ticking, twin hoes. You better be gone before midnight or that's your ass." I pointed from Arizona to Arabia. "You were born together and you can die together. Or..." I stood before them, as if I was deep in thought. "Maybe, I'll kill you, Arizona, and let a pack of ruthless niccas have your sister. The would love to fuck her pretty ass."

That comment wiped the smirks right off of their faces.

"You don't have to be acting all crazy, Channa," Arizona said. "We're leaving."

"Bye, bitches." I waved my fingers over my shoulder before I walked back across the hall and flopped down on the bed. I only intended to rest my feet. I was sleep before I knew it.

Chapter 11

Arizona

"I hate her ass," Arabia said to me.

"I do too, sissy."

"Do you really think that she'll kill us if we don't leave the city?"

I sighed. "Not only do I think she will kill us, I think she will enjoy it. She's crazy, for real."

Arabia sucked her teeth. "Why should we have to leave? We haven't messed with Drake in weeks. She asked us to dodge his calls and we did as she said. So, why is she forcing us to leave? We did as she asked. Ugh. I swear, I hate her ass. She never means shit that she says."

"Because bitches like her think that they rule the world until they fall."

I walked over to the closet, pulling out my suitcase. I knew this day would come because Channa was an unpredictable, greedy bitch. The only reason why I agreed to her bullshit plan was because I wanted to get something out of the deal— Drake. She knew he was feeling us more than her. That's why she was threatening us. She was so greedy for his love that she didn't realize that I had a trick up my sleeve. I knew that Drake would desire me when I accepted her offer. I made sure when I included my sister. Drake asked me for a threesome quite a few times while we were together. I always said no but, after being away from him, I was ready to fulfill his fantasy. I was right about him loving me and my sister because here Channa was threatening to kill me and my sister, if we didn't leave the city. That's how afraid of us she was.

"I can't believe we're allowing her to run us away," Arabia said with an attitude. She grabbed her suitcase, tossing it across the bed as if it was Channa.

"We're leaving, but it won't be quietly."

"What do you have in mind?" Arabia inquired.

"I'll think of something. If the bitch wants to play dirty, so could we. Besides, I heard that Dream is awake from her coma. I'm sure that bitch doesn't know that or she would be more worried about her than us."

"Obviously, she's as stupid as she looks. What makes her think that Drake won't find out what she did?"

"See, that's just the thing; she thinks she's invincible. That's cool. We're going to leave but not before we hit her ass up."

I was trying to figure out how we were going to rob her when my cell rang. It was none other than Drake.

"Come see me," he cooed with his sexy ass.

I didn't know if I was signing my death certificate with Channa by seeing him, but I decided to go see Drake anyway.

"Okay, where are you?" I asked.

"I'm at Christ."

"OMG! Are you okay?"

"I'm cool, ma. Just get here."

I hung up the phone.

"We gotta go," I told my sister.

"Why? Who was that?"

"Drake. He's in the hospital."

Arabia threw the shirt she was holding on the bed. "What about Channa?"

"Fuck that rotten bitch. If she wants us to leave, the least we can do is go see Drake and tell him bye."

"You think that's what he wants to talk to us about?"

Dream & Drake 3: A Cartel Love Story

"Sissy, I'm not sure," I told Arabia. "However, I think we owe Drake the truth."

As Arabia and I drove to Christ, I was scared, but my fear turned to concern when I realized that Drake was actually hurt. He was in casts, had cuts on his face, and appeared to be in pain.

"What happened to you?" I asked, rushing to his bedside. Arabia stood on the other side of Drake's bed.

"Oh, ain't no thang," Drake said with ease. "Listen ladies," he continued, "being in here, I had a chance to think. And some things just don't add up. I'm not as stupid as you two think. Before I jump to conclusions, is there something that you want to tell me?" His eyes were glued to mine and I felt the sweat gather under my arms.

"Think wisely before you answer," he said. "I'm giving you two a chance to tell the truth."

I knew Drake well. If he called us here to ask us questions, then he was on to us. Arabia stared at me and I gave her the same knowing look. We both looked at the two burly officers that were waiting by the door. They looked like more than just security. They looked as if they were about to set some shit off.

"So, neither one of you have anything to say?" Drake probed. He had the nastiest look on his face. "Both of your mouths stayed open when we were in the bed. Now, you can't say shit."

Arabia was already afraid. Her fear was evident. I was built for the streets, but she wasn't. She didn't know how Drake rolled, but I did. I didn't know everything because I didn't see much. All I knew was he worked for The Cartel, and they were very powerful. I feared that me and my sister were about to be killed because we helped Channa out. I really should have thought about helping Channa's no good ass before I did it. The truth was, I just wanted to see Drake again. I missed him. Call me stupid, but I took the only opportunity I could in order to be back in Drake's life. I loved that man.

"I'm sorry, Drake," I whimpered, holding back tears.

I was emotional and Arabia immediately became emotional too.

"What are you sorry for?" Drake asked with a mug look on his face.

I shrugged my shoulders.

"Are you sorry for setting me up?"

I gasped. "I-I just wanted to see you again. That's all."

"So, you admit to setting me up?"

I had no intention of coming clean, but my back was against the wall. The last thing I planned on doing was telling what me and Arabia did. However, I would if that meant throwing Channa under the bus to save our asses.

"Channa made us do it," I lied. "She threatened to kill us both if we didn't help her."

"Help her do what?" Drake pondered.

"Help us get your sperm. She was desperate to have your baby, so she asked us to capture your sperm."

Drake shook his head, as if he just had an epiphany. "And that would be why the dates don't add up with her pregnancy. She's four months and I know I didn't fuck her four months ago."

"She lost that baby," I said, singing like a bird. "She was pregnant the last time you two had sex, but she lost it when she found out about you and Dream. It stressed her out. That's why she came back to Chicago. Her plan was to break you two up by getting pregnant again."

Drake faced Arabia. "So, what part did you play?"

"I tagged along to seduce you," she said, crying her eyes out. "Believe me, I wouldn't have done it, but I owe my ex-boyfriend money. He threatened to kill me if I didn't pay him back."

"Is he paid off?" Drake asked her.

"Yes."

"Text me his name anyway." Drake looked from Arabia to me. "Is there anything else I should know?"

"No," I said, blinking back tears. I was so afraid that Drake was going to harm us.

Arabia put her hands up to her face, sobbing even harder. "No," she mumbled.

"I understand if you have to kill us," I lied. I didn't understand shit. I was hoping that he had sympathy on us, even though we were disloyal. I knew that bitches died over shit like this. I'd never seen Drake do anyone harm, but I knew he was very capable. Muthafuckas didn't fear him for nothing.

"Stop crying," Drake told Arabia. "I already knew that bullshit, ma."

A single tear fell and I quickly wiped it away, trying to save face. "You knew?"

"I didn't know at first," he said. "I just found out today. Don't get me wrong; I'm still disgusted with both of you for being a part of Channa's conniving plan. However, I don't have any ill feelings towards either of you."

"How did you find out?" I wondered.

"Channa records everything. She had one of your conversations on tape," he said to me.

I sighed and Arabia looked as if she was about to cry again.

Drake wore a serious expression. "Listen, there is a street beef brewing that could turn deadly at any moment."

"Is that what happened to you?" I asked, looking at the cast on his arm and his leg.

Drake was beat up pretty bad. I was not sure what happened to him. I had a feeling that it had to do with this street beef that he was talking about.

"Yeah, but you know can't shit stop me. I'm not worried about it. When I get well, niccas about to be sorry. Until then, you two need to leave. I can protect y'all from the niccas in the streets, but I can't protect you from Channa. If she threatened you, then she means every word. One thing about her, she's ruthless. Obviously, she thinks that you two are a threat."

"She definitely does because she threatened us at gun point. She said she was afraid that we were getting too close to you."

Drake winked at us both. "She's right. I find you two very sexy, but my heart belongs to Dream."

It hurt me to hear him say that, but I'd heard Channa say it a million times, so I already knew.

Princess Diamond

"Don't look so sad," he said, looking from me to my sister. "I still care about y'all. Even though we can't be together, I'ma make sure you're straight. Here's what I want you two to do. Wait until Channa leaves the hotel. She's coming to pick me up from the hospital today because I'm getting released once the doctor brings the discharge papers. I'll have someone come and get you and put you two into hiding so that she won't find you. Because she's gonna be pissed off when she realizes that you two robbed her. Trust me, she will be after you."

Drake kissed us both on the cheek and we left.

We did just like Drake said. We went back to the hotel, packed our shit, and waited for Channa to leave. Within an hour, she was rushing out of her hotel, and we were using the key card that the man at the front desk gave us, thanks to Drake.

It took us a moment to find her safe. We tore her room up trying to find that money. She had it hidden well. It was in a box that looked like a suitcase. I pulled out my phone and put in the code that was text to me from an unknown number. Sure enough, the safe popped opened and there it was, stacks of money.

"How much you think it is?" Arabia asked with her eyes lit up like a Christmas tree.

"I don't know, but let's take this shit and go. I don't want to be here when Channa comes back."

We moved like an assembly line, working together to put the neat stacks of money into the extra suitcase. Once we had every dollar, I reached for the bleach and fucked her room up. This bitch was crazy if she thought she was going to run me out of town and I didn't get her ass back. She's lucky I didn't hit her in the back of the head with a pipe.

"You leaving that bitch a letter?" Arabia asked me.

"Yep. Sure is."

After handwriting a nasty ass note, Arabia and I left out of the room, closed out our tab, and got into the car that was waiting for us, courtesy of Drake.

"I wish I could see that bitch's face when she comes back," Arabia said with a smirk.

"Me too. She about to be sick as fuck when she realize what just went down. We took all her damn money. Stupid bitch."

.

Chapter 12

Channa

A few hours later, I woke up to my cellphone ringing. I reached inside my purse and retrieved it. I didn't recognize the number, but I answered anyway.

"Hello," I said with an attitude. "Who this?"

"Hello, may I please speak to Channa Diaz-Santana?"

I loved hearing my last name. "Who's calling?"

"Nurse Felicia at Christ Hospital."

I sucked in air. "This her. What you want?"

Nurse Felicia took a deep breath. I guess I was getting on her nerves. The feeling was mutual. "I was calling you because your husband is here in the hospital. He is about to be released today and you were down as a contact person. He can't drive and someone needs to pick him up."

"Ohmigod!" I gasped. "Is he okay?" I was worried now.

"Are you coming or not? The doctor has released him today and he asked that you come and pick him up."

"I'll be there," I said, feeling emotional. These damn babies were making me soft. "Tell my husband I'm on my-"

Her rude ass hung up before I could say another word. I stared at the phone with an attitude before I tossed it in my purse. I needed to get to my husband asap. He needed me.

"Drake, I'm coming, baby."

Dream & Drake 3: A Cartel Love Story

I jumped behind the wheel, driving like a bat out of hell. Everyone needed to watch out. Pedestrians. Kids. Old People. I was on a mission and I didn't mind hitting a muthafucka.

"Get the fuck out of my way." I swerved around a dude riding a bike. "You lucky I didn't hit your ass!" I screamed out the window before laying on my horn.

The guy on the bike ran into the curb and nearly crashed into another car.

"Stupid bitch!" the female driver hollered.

"Fuck you, ugly frog-face cunt!" I hollered back.

She turned off and I thought about following after her ass and shooting her, but Drake needed me. She better be glad or she would have been surrounded by dirt. I drove to the hospital at full speed. I heard what the nurse said, and I just hoped that Drake wasn't hurt too bad.

I came into Christ like a whirlwind. People cleared my path. I guess the nasty look I had on my face said that I meant business. Not only would I cuss their ass out, I would hold a nasty ass grudge until I got payback. Basically, they'd wish that they never fucked with me.

"Excuse me, I'm here to pick up my husband."

"What's his name?" the woman at the admissions desk asked.

"Drake Diaz-Santana."

The lady began pecking on the keys, as if this was her first day. "Can you hurry up?" I asked, impatiently tapping my fingers on the desk.

"I'm trying," the woman said. "This is my first week."

"Listen, boo boo, I don't really care. If you can't do the job, they shouldn't have hired you. Burger King is hiring. I'll bring you back an app."

The woman sighed, but she kept it professional. "Let me write down the room number for you."

As soon as she finished writing down the number on a piece of paper, I snatched it out of her hand.

"You need another job because you suck at this one."

Princess Diamond

I walked away while she looked stupefied. Hell, someone had to tell her ass. If I see her on my way out, I'ma tell her to get a job on the pole. She's pretty enough. They had Drake all the way on the other side of the damn hospital. My feet were killing me by the time I made it there. Of course, I had on high ass heels and a mini dress, trying to be cute for my husband. A bitch should have put on some flats and jeans.

The doctor was in the room when I walked in. He was just the person that I wanted to see. I needed an update on Drake's condition because he looked pretty banged up.

"Is my husband going to be alright?"

"Yes. He'll be just fine after eight weeks."

"Eight weeks?" I nearly choked. Not because of what I heard, but because I was already plotting. That gave me just enough time to win his heart again.

"He has restrictions too," the doctor chimed in. "You'll get that with his discharge papers."

"Okay," I said, not fully understanding what the doctor was talking about.

The doctor walked out and I rushed over to Drake.

"Baby, are you alright?"

Drake nodded.

I hugged him and tried to kiss his lips, but he dodged me.

"I need to get dressed. Can you call me a nurse?"

"I can help you dress," I offered. I would do anything just to see him naked.

"Nah, we ain't rocking like that."

Not yet, I thought. "Drake, you ain't got nothing I ain't seen."

"Yeah, but you haven't seen it in a long time, tho."

I rolled my eyes. "We're married, shit, with a babies on the way. I got your dick etched in my mind. I'll never forget it."

"I see calling you was a mistake. As usual, you're on that selfish bullshit."

Drake shocked me when he pressed the call button, and a nurse stepped into the room.

"Is there anything I can help you with?"

Dream & Drake 3: A Cartel Love Story

"Yes," Drake exclaimed. "Can you help me put on my clothes?"

"Sure," she said.

I saw the funny look she gave me, but I decided to be quiet. I didn't want Drake mad at me. I sat there while this beautiful nurse giggled in my husband's face and touched his body. She was a little extra, if you asked me. I wanted to fuck her up when she helped him put his underwear on. I probably would have, if I wasn't trying to get back in good graces with him.

Apart of me wanted to leave, but I wouldn't dare leave this hoe alone with my man. I was going to sit right here while she helped him. I wasn't leaving unless we were leaving together. After Drake was dressed, the nurse left and came back with his discharge papers. Some other guy came into the room with a wheelchair. I was tripping because I forgot Drake couldn't walk. The guy handed me Drake's crutches like I was his servant, before wheeling him out the room. Again, he was another one that could have gotten cussed the fuck out. What the fuck I look like?

I trailed behind as Drake was wheeled out. My attitude had gotten bad. I didn't want to show my other side, so I kept my distance. When they stopped at the door, I kept on walking to go get the car. No, I didn't tell them. It's obvious what I was doing. I drove the car around and the guy helped Drake in the passenger's seat and put his crutches in the back.

"I don't know why you called me if you didn't need my help," I said. "You should have called one of your relatives."

"That's cool. I will," Drake replied, taking his phone out of his jacket.

I watched as he texted with his left hand.

"You can drop me off and be on your way."

Well, that's not the response that I was expecting. "I didn't say that I wouldn't help you."

"But you're acting like it. I never call you for shit. When I do, this is how you act, like I owe your ass some shit. You're good. Step the fuck off."

This was not how I imagined our conversation when I drove here. I played out in my mind something totally different.

"I'm sorry," I apologized. "Pregnancy hormones."

"Yeah, right," Drake snarled. "I can't even depend on my wife to help me out. How do you think that makes me feel?"

I had to get my attitude together quick, fast, and in a hurry before I lost him for good.

"Do you need me to come and stay with you?" I offered. I hoped that he said yes because I planned on doing it anyway.

"That would be nice," he said, giving me the answer that I wanted to hear. That made me smile and my attitude was much better. Staying with Drake for the next eight weeks was exactly what I needed. Live-in dick. He had to still have feelings for me, if he wanted me to stay with him. Our marriage wasn't over like I thought it was.

"Are you hungry? Or is your appetite restricted too?'

Drake was still texting. It took him a moment to reply. "I'm hungry, but someone is going to meet me at the crib with my food. I want a home cooked meal. No more fast food."

"Okay," I said, biting my tongue.

I sure in the hell wanted to ask who was bringing him a home cooked meal, but I didn't. It had better be one of his relatives. I swear, if it was another bitch, I was going to lose it. Baby or no baby, I was going to beat that bitch's ass.

We rode in silence as I drove to Drake's house. I had to give myself a pep talk as I drove because Drake was all into his phone, not paying me any attention. It bothered me, but I knew I had eight weeks.

I pulled up and helped Drake to the door. That shit was a task all in itself. He was leaning on my pregnant ass and I could barely hold him up. It was too much on me, so I left him at the door and went back to get his damn crutches. I didn't know how I was going to help him for eight weeks when I was tired already.

"I need to go back to the hotel right quick," I said after I got him settled on the couch. I left him downstairs, so he could get around if he wanted to get something. It was a bathroom on this level too, so he was good. If I took him upstairs, he wouldn't be able to get back down without someone's help.

"You're coming back, right?"

I smiled. "Of course." I hadn't gotten this much attention from Drake in a long time. Unless it had something to do with the baby, he wasn't fucking with me like that.

I handed him the remote and put his crutches by him. "Can I get you anything else?"

"I'm good," he said, staring at the door.

I wanted to ask who the fuck was he waiting for but, once again, I decided to shut my mouth. "I'll be back soon."

"Okay," he said, resting on the couch.

I better not come back and a bitch was up in here. I swear, I was going to fucking go crazy.

I raced to the hotel. I needed to get my things if I was staying with Drake for eight weeks. I didn't need this room if he wanted me there. I could put my things into another bedroom until he wanted me back in the room with him. I was willing to take baby steps.

I nearly had a heart attack when I walked inside of my room. Shit was everywhere. Clearly, the place had been trashed. My first thought was to run over to my safe. I fell to my knees when I saw that my money was gone. Two-hundred fifty thousand. I slid down the wall in agony. That money was all I had. Drake already told me that I couldn't go back to the trap in New York. He definitely wasn't going to put me on with his operation in Chicago. He claimed because I was pregnant. I knew differently. He didn't trust me anymore.

"What am I going to do?" I cried.

I sat on the floor bawling my eyes out for what seemed like an eternity. The only thing that stopped me was the note that caught my eye. It was resting on the bed. I didn't know how I missed it because it was clear as day with my name in bold letters, like it was written in a marker or some type of special pen.

I got up from the floor, picked the note up, and read it. My mouth dropped open when I saw it was from Arizona's punk ass.

Channa. Channa. Channa. Bitch ass Channa. We left town, but not before we took all your money with us. Payback is a bitch, bitch. Fuck you, bitch. I hope Drake leaves your stupid ass. Oh by the way, don't bother looking for us, you won't find out where we are. Next lifetime, bitch!

"No, this lifetime, bitch," I said, balling up the letter. "As soon as I have this baby, I'm fresh off your ass, hoe."

It was hard, but I dusted myself off and gathered the few things that them twin hoes didn't destroy. I left the hotel and went back to Drake's. Surprise number two. A green sports car parked in the driveway. Some expensive shit that looked like it was imported from a foreign country. I swear, I was about to have a miscarriage because I was about to drag this bitch. I rang the doorbell and got ready to go to war.

Imagine the shocked look on my face when Gigi answered the door.

"What the fuck you standing there looking dumb as fuck for? Get your ass in here and tend to my grandson. I don't know why you left him in the first place. It's bad enough I had to bring him some food. What kinda wife are you? Not a very good one, apparently. He wouldn't be relying on me if you did what the fuck you were supposed to do. Don't worry, bitch; I'ma be here the whole eight weeks to make sure your ass is on point."

After the day that I just had, I couldn't do anything but start crying. I hated Gigi and she hated me. She was about to make my life a living hell. If I had any money left, I would leave Drake here with his crazy grandmother and I would have gone back to staying at the hotel.

"Don't cry now, bitch. Bring your ass in here and stop stressing my great-grandbaby out. I'ma kill your ass if something happens to that baby because you doing stupid shit. Fuck with me if you want to."

I stepped inside, afraid. This woman was crazy as they came.

"Get your ass in the kitchen," Gigi demanded. "I gave the maid some time off. Ain't shit wrong with you. I cleaned my house and cooked while I was pregnant with all of my kids. That's the problem with you new bitches. Y'all don't like to do shit."

Dream & Drake 3: A Cartel Love Story

Drake was sitting on the couch, eating the food that she brought. I looked at him and he smirked. I wiped away my tears and sulked on my way to the kitchen. He better be glad I was pregnant. I swear, if I wasn't, I would beat his ass and his crazy fuckin' grandmother's ass too. No, I take that back; she wasn't wrapped too tight. I would leave her alone. She killed people.

Chapter 13

Dream

Last night, I sexed Drake all night long. I couldn't get enough of his dick. Besides, I knew we had to depart today. We went over our plan once again. He was going home with Channa so that he could get a divorce. Meanwhile, I was going home with Spencer so that I could buy us sometime until Drake was well enough to come to my defense, if need be. I didn't want to go home with Spencer, but I had to play things off. Drake was sure of his plan, so I had no choice but to back him up. Call it crazy or whatever, but I trusted him. The more time I spent with him, the more I remembered. I didn't remember everything, but I was hopeful that I would soon.

"You ready, baby?" Spencer asked.

I cringed at his voice. I wanted to be next to Drake so bad but, since I couldn't, I had to remain strong. "Yes, I'm ready."

I was already dressed and waiting on him. He called me an hour ago and told me he was on his way. Minutes before he got here, I exchanged numbers with Nurse Agnes. I had to keep in contact with her. She meant a lot to me. I didn't need a wheelchair, but it was protocol, so I sat my butt down and took the ride.

"I can take it from here," Spencer said, trying to help me out of the wheelchair.

I shooed him away, getting up on my own. "I'm good."

Spencer stared at me funny, but he backed off.

I thanked the guy who wheeled me down and got into the passenger's seat of Spencer's car. Before Spencer could pull off, Nurse Agnes came running out of the hospital.

"You better call me," she said while leaning into the car, giving me a kiss on the cheek.

"You know I will. I'm going to need love advice."

We both giggled at the inside joke. She waved bye once more before Spencer pulled off. She knew about my dilemma with Drake and Spencer. I was thankful that I could confide in someone because my parents were at odds because of me and my decision to rekindle with Drake.

"When is your first prenatal appointment?" Spencer probed.

"In a couple of days."

"I want the exact date and time so that I can leave work to be there."

"Okay," I said. I hadn't even left the hospital good and he was already getting on my nerves. I got a text that made me smile.

Drake: I miss you boo

I squealed and Spencer's eyes darted in my direction. I quieted it down and wiped the grin off my face, texting him back.

Me: I miss you too.

Drake: You miss all this dick

I giggled.

Spencer shot me another look. I ignored him and kept on texting.

Me: You know I miss it.

I sent him the eggplant emoji.

Drake: You really miss this D, huh?

Me: Yep. When am I going to get some more? Don't make me back it up on Spencer lol.

Princess Diamond

Drake: Don't make me beat your ass. You better not give that lame fuck nicca my pussy.

I kept giggling while reading his text. I knew what I said would get a rise out of him. That's why I said it.

"Something is different about you," Spencer said, eye-balling me.

"Please keep your eye on the road. The last thing I need is to be in another accident."

Spencer huffed, but he did as I said. I was being sarcastic, but I didn't want to be in another accident. This time, it just might take me out, for real. As Spencer drove us home, I managed to keep my outburst to a minimum as I texted Drake. I told him I would text him later when we pulled up. Spencer parked in front of our house and then walked around to help me out. I was surprised when he picked me up.

"I miss you," he said, kissing me on the forehead.

I felt uncomfortable in his arms as he carried me to the door. He fidgeted with the keys before opening the door. Carrying me inside, I thought he would sit me on the couch, but he took me upstairs to our bedroom. I got a strange feeling when he laid me down on the bed.

"Damn, you look so sexy."

I gave him a crazy look. "You're tripping. I'm fresh out the hospital; ain't nothing sexy about me."

"Yes, it is."

He tried to rub my stomach and I rolled over in the bed. "What's wrong with you?" He had this crazed look in his eye.

"Nothing, I just miss you."

I stared at his erection and, immediately, I knew what time it was. He was horny.

"Oh, you can't have none of this," I stated with a smirk.

"Why not?" he asked, taking off his shirt, and then his pants.

"Because… doctor's orders."

"You're lying," Spencer spat with his erection straining against his boxers.

Dream & Drake 3: A Cartel Love Story

It was as if I hadn't said a word to him because the next thing I knew, he was in the bed with me, naked. His hands were all over me. He was trying to pin me down when I slapped the shit out of him.

"You must be crazy as fuck."

Spencer rose up, breathing hard.

"So what? You were about to take it?" I probed.

He laughed, but I was very serious. "Baby, of course not."

For some reason when he said that, I didn't believe him. Call it a woman's intuition or whatever, but shit wasn't right with Spencer. He said I was different. Nah, this nicca was different. His whole vibe was off.

Spencer's phone vibrated. He checked it and then began putting his clothes back on. "I need to leave, but I'll be back. What do you want to eat? I'll pick it up while I'm out."

"I'm not hungry. Just pick yourself up something."

"Aight," he said, kissing me on the cheek before I could pull away.

As soon as he left, I FaceTimed Drake with tears in my eyes. "I don't want to go through with this plan."

"Why? What happened?"

I was about to tell Drake what Spencer did, but the phone cut off. Moments later, I got a text stating that Drake was on his way over. Ohmigod! What have I done? I hope Spencer stays gone a little bit longer.

Just to be sure, I texted Spencer and told him that I wanted food from this one spot out West. Spencer didn't give me a hassle. He told me that it would take him awhile, but he'd make sure I get my favorite order. I sighed in relief. I was sure that would by me enough time to get rid of Drake.

Chapter 14

Spencer

I got an irate text from Destiny that she was on her way over to my house if I didn't come to hers. Somehow, she found out that Dream was released today and I brought her home. I intended to tell her, just not tonight. Dream was looking sexier than ever and I wanted a piece of her. I didn't mean to be so aggressive, but I was used to taking pussy from her all these months.

Being forceful with her had become a habit that I developed. I saw the fear in her eyes and I didn't want her to be afraid of me. She was the mother of my child and I planned on marrying her. After she dropped this baby, I intended on putting another bun in her oven. I didn't think I was ready to be a father or a husband until she almost died. Now, I was all for that family life. I wanted four kids. She was having all my babies back to back, stair steps.

SMACK!

Destiny smacked me across the face as soon as I opened the door. "Why the fuck do you keep trying me?"

"What you mean?" I asked, trying to buy myself some time. I knew what she was referring to.

"Your black ass didn't tell me that you were taking Dream home. I talked to you a few hours ago."

"It wasn't even like that," I lied. "She asked me to come and get her because no one else could come."

SMACK!

"You better back up before I hit your-"

Before I could get my sentence out, she smacked me again.

"See, this is why I don't tell your ass nothing. You always putting your hands on me."

"Because your ass ain't shit, and you're a fuckin' liar. You know good and damn well that you intended on picking Dream up. What you didn't intend on is me finding that shit out."

"I'm done with your ass," I said, racing towards the bedroom to get my stuff.

"Oh, so now little Miss Goodie Two Shoes wakes up and your ass is brand knew. You don't know how to bring your ass home."

Yes, I was using Destiny until I could get Dream back. Now that Dream was awake and she wanted to be with me, Destiny had to go.

"I didn't want to tell your ass like this, but you left me no choice. We're done," I said boldly.

I marched off with my chest poked out on my way to our bedroom. I pulled out a duffle bag and started throwing my shit in it. I worried about telling her and how she would take it. Her initial reaction wasn't as frightful as I thought. I should have left her a long time ago.

Destiny stood in the doorway with tears streaming down her face, messing up her make up. A part of me felt bad for messing with her in the first place. I knew that she was into me. As much as I tried, I just couldn't get into her. She might have looked like Dream but, in my eyes, she would never be Dream. Never. Dream had my heart.

"So, you've been using me," she finally said after many minutes of silence.

"Destiny, you knew it was coming to this. We were just hooking up, having fun. Don't make this more than what it is."

She cried even harder, as I walked around the room still packing. "So, you're leaving me for good?" she sobbed.

"Destiny, straight up, don't do this. You knew I was leaving when Dream woke up. Besides, she's pregnant with my baby. I have to be there for her.

I noticed the hurt look on Destiny's face. "She's pregnant?"

"Yeah," I said, putting the last of my stuff into the bag. "I'll be back for the rest." I put the bag over my shoulder and tried to pass her. "Could you move?"

I squeezed pass Destiny because she wouldn't move out the way. I walked towards the steps and she followed behind me.

"Nicca, I'll kill your ass before I let you leave," she spat.

I felt Destiny come up behind me. I was just about to turn around to address what she said when she pushed me. Never in a million years did I take her threats seriously. I mean, she was a little off her rocker, but I had no idea she really meant she would kill me. I lost my balance, missed the first step, and tumbled down the rest. You talking about scared? I saw my life flash before my eyes. I just knew as I rolled over each stair that I was a goner.

When I hit the bottom, I was prepared to check out, but that gigantic duffle bag hit the floor before me, so it broke my fall. A brother was happy as fuck that he was still alive. I closed my eyes and thanked the Lord because this shit could have been real ugly.

"Spencer, are you okay?" Destiny had the nerve to say, trying to help me up.

"Get off me!" I barked, jerking my arm out of her reach. I was determined to leave more than ever. Standing to my feet, I quickly realized that leaving would be impossible. A pain shot through my left foot when I stepped on it. Immediately, I hopped on my right foot and lost my balance, landing back on the floor. My ankle was hurting badly. I didn't know if it was sprain or broke. Either way, I felt like I should have died because the pain was unbearable.

"Call an ambulance!" I screamed while holding my ankle.

"I'll take you," she said in a panic. I guess the severity of what she had done just kicked in.

"No the fuck you won't. Your stupid ass has done enough."

Destiny called an ambulance and they were knocking on the door in no time. I was rushed to the hospital and sat in the emergency room. There were two people rushed in with gunshot wounds, a baby who fell off a swing, a lady who sliced her finger off while she was cooking, and a man who had a knife sticking out his chest. All of their injuries were more important than mine, so I knew that I wouldn't get assisted until the wee hours of the morning.

I looked over at Destiny, who looked guilty as hell. I wanted to punch her dumb ass in the face. I felt my hand twitch and I knew that I was moments from attacking her. I got up and hopped across the room to another empty chair. I didn't even want to sit next to her ass anymore.

I'm sorry, she mouthed.

I flipped her the bird and put my headphones on, tuning her and everyone else out.

Chapter 15

Dream

Someone was laying on my doorbell. I fell asleep while waiting on Drake to come over, so I assumed it was him. When I opened the door, he was standing there with a gun. I felt bad because he wasn't supposed to be on his feet.

"Where's this nicca at?" he asked, barging into my house along with three other big niccas.

I knew that these dudes meant business. All three of them had a gun in each hand. They followed Drake throughout the entire house, looking for Spencer.

Finally, he asked me, "Where this nicca at?"

"He left."

Drake gave me a simple look and told what I assumed were his muscle or maybe his bodyguards to wait outside. They left and went outside to a truck that was parked in front of my house.

"C'mere," Drake said, pulling me into his embrace. "Are you okay?"

"Yes," I mumbled against his chest.

"Pack your shit. You're not staying with this nicca for eight weeks."

"No, Drake, I'm staying. I overreacted. I'm fine. We're going to carry out the plan. The way you said it should be."

"Not if that means that you'll be in danger. I refuse to put you and the baby in harm's way. Fuck that. Now, get your shit."

"Leaving will make things worse," I disagreed.

"How so?" he asked me with a sexy frown.

"Because he's going to lose it."

"I don't give a fuck what he loses. I changed my mind. I'm waiting right here for this nicca to come back. When he does, I'm going to confront his ass."

"Drake, please don't."

He got even more irate when I begged him not to. "Why the fuck are you begging for this nicca? What, you still got feelings for his ass?"

"No, of course, not. I was just-"

"You were just what?" Drake barked. "Choose your words wisely, Dream."

"Forget it," I said, feeling drained. Between Spencer and Drake, I was mentally exhausted. "I can't do this right now." I walked away from Drake and he followed me.

"You can't do what?" he huffed. "Us? Is that what you're talking about?"

"No, not at all," I answered truthfully. I had no idea where he got that idea from.

"Just say the shit, Dream. Spit it out."

"There is nothing to spit out, Drake. You're jumping to conclusions, and I'm tired."

"Shit, you don't think I'm tired. I can barely walk and I rushed over here to save your ass, and here you are defending this wack ass nicca."

"I'm not defending him," I exclaimed. "I'm just trying to keep the peace."

"Fuck it," Drake said, slowly walking towards the door.

Obviously, he was all in his feelings. Normally, I wouldn't chase no man, but he wasn't just any man. He was the man I wanted to spend the rest of my life with. I jogged up behind him when he reached the door. I put my arms around his waist.

"Let me go," he said, still playing hard. He knew he liked every bit of my body being close to his. I felt the front of his pants rise.

"I'm not letting you go, Drake. I love you."

"You don't love me," he said angrily.

"You know I do."

"Whatever the fuck," he said, reaching for the door knob.

I didn't know what else to do, so I said the only thing I knew that would get his attention. "Make love to me."

"Stop playing, Dream."

"I'm not playing. Make love to me, Drake."

He took his hand off the door and turned around to face me. "What about your little boyfriend? Aren't you afraid that he'll come back and see you with another man?"

"What about him? Let him see you stroking my pussy when he strolls in."

Drake grinned. "You're trying to make me kill that nicca, for real, ma."

"So be it." I didn't want to see Spencer die, but I didn't want Drake to leave me either. If I had to choose, it would always be Drake, no matter what.

"Get out those clothes, so I can stroke that pussy then."

I smiled and slowly walked back into the living room, undressing. The way he stared at me made me desire him even more. He was looking at me as if he'd never seen me naked before.

"C'mere, ma," Drake ordered, struggling to sit down on the couch.

I practically ran to him. I got on my knees and unfastened his pants. I wanted to taste him again. I knew this was what he liked and, now, I liked it too. As soon as I freed his erection, I wrapped my warm mouth around it. I went to work on the tip sucking for dear life.

"Aaaaaaah. Ssssssss," Drake hissed. His moans only motivated me even more. "Get off your knees," he directed. "Climb up on the couch and put that ass in the air while you suck on this dick."

I did exactly what he said, hopping on the couch. Arching my back, I spread my legs so that Drake could play with my pussy while I sucked on his dick. I rocked back on his fingers as he slipped two inside of me.

"Your dick tastes so good," I said, loving the taste of his phallus in my mouth. I tongue kissed his dick and then sucked it nice and slow.

"Why are you teasing me?" he moaned.

"Because I can do that to my dick."

Just then, I felt his thumb slip into my asshole, sending shivers down my spine. I sucked even harder as he used his fingers to pleasure me.

"You better suck this dick, Dream."

"I'm sucking my dick," I exclaimed in between slurps. "This dick belongs to me, and if you ever give it to another bitch, I'm going to shoot your ass."

Drake laughed and then smacked my ass. "I see sucking this big dick gave you some balls."

I knew he was trying to be funny, so I intended to do the same. "Oh, if I want balls, I know where to find them." I stopped bobbing my head on his dick and began licking his balls like a wild cat. My hand jerked on his dick and my tongue made love to his balls.

"That shit's not fair," Drake moaned. "You tryna turn a brotha out."

"I'm tryna make a brotha understand what this mouth do."

After sucking on his balls a few more times, I gave my attention back to his dick, sucking it faster and faster.

"Slow down, Dream. You're about to make me cum."

"Cum then. Spill that shit down my throat."

Drake began pumping into my mouth and I knew it was a matter of seconds before he came. I was about to cum too. His fingers worked my pussy like a dick.

"Fuuuuuuuck!" Drake cried out, releasing his seed in my mouth. At the same time, I creamed all over his fingers. I sucked his dick hard again and assumed the position on his lap. I couldn't wait to slide down on his dick.

"Ahhh shit," I hissed as his dick filled me up.

My vagina twitched. I knew it wouldn't take long for me to cum. I jumped up and down, but that didn't last long. I was hopping on it before I knew it.

Drake surprised me by flipping me onto my side. He was behind me, beating my pussy up real good. I was hollering, screaming, and cussing at the top of my lungs while calling his name.

"Remember this dick when you think about that fuck nicca," Drake said, referring to Spencer.

"I will. I will. I swear, I will."

He rammed into me harder, making my clit pulsate. "Stop playing with me, Dream."

"Oh, gawd, I won't play... play... play no more. I swear."

"You don't love me," he whispered in my ear.

I don't know why, but this felt like déjà vu. "Yes! Yes! Yes! I do, Drake."

"You just love my dick. The way I make you cum."

"No. No. No. No. No. I don't," I stuttered.

Drake pulled his dick all the way out and slammed it into me with so much force that I felt the hairs stand up all over my body. Tingles emerged in my toes, ass, clit, and vagina. The feeling was so euphoric.

"Tell me how much you love this dick."

"I love it. I love it. I love it. I..." His dick was so fucking good that my words didn't even make any sense. "Pkenogbungbowhbdbgbgiujbgkmrlienfohhyroenpghqptigbnogi."

Drake chuckled while sucking on my large breasts. My breasts had gotten a lot bigger too. I went from a B cup to a D cup in a matter of days.

"Big ass fuckin' titties," he exclaimed while taking my breasts into his mouth, alternating on sucking them.

"I'm about to cum, Drake," I cried. Tears were literally coming down my cheeks as my orgasm came near.

"I'm about to cum too, all in this we pussy."

I gyrated so hard that I nearly fell off the couch as Drake shot his sperm inside of me. We were humping against each other while breathing hard, enjoying the feeling. I fell back, resting against Drake's hard body.

His hand rubbed my stomach. "How's my son doing?" he chuckled.

"He's good," I laughed.

Drake smacked my ass again. "I'm ready for some more of this pregnant pussy."

I lifted my leg up with one hand and Drake was sliding his hardness back inside of me before I knew it. He stopped stroking me, reaching for his gun. He moved it within his reach.

"Just in case that fuck nicca walks in."

Chapter 16

Destiny

I was so damn pissed with myself that I could have slapped my own face. It was my fault why Spencer and I just spent the last eight hours in the emergency room. I was not sorry that I pushed his ass down the stairs. What I was sorry about was that I didn't really harm him the way I thought I did. I mean, I didn't want his stupid ass dead. However, I did want him hurt. He hurt me, so it was only fair that I hurt him back.

That's what he gets for lying to me. He knew when he left my house this morning that he was going to skip work and go pick up Dream. I asked him where he was going and his ass said to work. He should have known that I was going to show up at his job. I was beyond pissed when I found out he never showed up. Immediately, I knew he was at the hospital. Dream's parents told me when she woke up. You think I told him, hell no. I didn't want my man chasing after the next bitch.

I didn't have anything against Dream, but we were going to have a problem if she thought she was going to take Spencer away from me. He was mine. Just like if he thought he was going to leave me for her, he had another thing coming. I would kill his ass before I let him walk away. I knew I couldn't stop him from seeing her, but he had better give me just as much attention as he gave her. I wanted just as much gifts, sex, and everything else that he gave her.

"Is his ankle broken?" I asked the doctor. We were called back to see the doctor over an hour ago. To say that I was running out of patience was an understatement.

"It's not broken," the doctor replied. He lightly touched Spencer's ankle, and he shrieked in pain. It was swollen four times the size it was when we first got here.

"Well, is it sprained?" I asked, aggravated as fuck. Why wasn't this man saying shit? Ain't this his damn job, shit?

"It's more like sprained," the doctor finally answered.

There was no way that was a sprain. "Did I hear you correctly?" I asked, looking at Spencer's elephantiasis ankle. "Are you sure you're a real doctor?"

The white guy chuckled. "Yes. It just looks worse than it is. He'll be back to normal in about six weeks."

"Six weeks?" Spencer groaned. He was pissed, but I was happy as hell. That meant it would be easier for me to keep my eye on him.

The doctor turned to Spencer and handed him a script. "Here's a prescription for the pain, and I want you to stay off that ankle as much as possible. Keep it elevated for eight to twelve hours a day for the first two weeks. Call me to set up a follow up appointment."

"Can I get a doctor's note for work?" Spencer asked.

"Sure. I'll be right back."

"I thought you broke it," I said, trying to make light of his injury. I smiled and Spencer shot me a death look.

I could tell he was pissed because he didn't say shit to me. He shot me another nasty look and I gave him the same funky ass look. If anyone should be in a foul mood, it should be me. Dream was blowing his shit up. Since I was holding all his stuff, I had access to his phone too. When he dozed off from the pain medication, I checked his phone. Just as I thought, a million texts from Dream. I couldn't see them all because his phone was locked. He changed his password. I tried to guess it.

Princess Diamond

After getting locked out for the fourth time, I had to wait thirty minutes for another retry. I was too through. From what I gathered, Dream was asking him when he was coming home and how much longer was he going to be gone. I promise, if I could get into his phone, I was going to check this hoe something serious. That's okay; I had something for that ass. I was going to confront her. It was about time she knew about me and Spencer.

"Why you keep looking at me crazy?" Spencer barked.

"Because I can," I barked back. "Don't make me break your other ankle."

Spencer's eyes got big. He was about to say something smart when the doctor walked back in. "Here's the doctor's excuse that you requested. My phone number is on there too, just in case."

Spencer jumped down off the hospital bed on his good foot. "Thanks, doc. We done?"

"We are. You take care of yourself."

Spencer shot me a shitty look. "I have a feeling that's going to be impossible."

"Well, you really need to try if you want your ankle to heal properly. Take care."

Spencer was wheeled out and I pulled the car around. He looked like he didn't want to get in with me. I was sure he was skeptical after I pushed him down the stairs.

"Buckle up," I said nicely.

Spencer waved me off. "After my ankle heals, I'm leaving your ass."

"Oh, no, you won't," I said, driving off fast as hell. "I'll kill both of us."

I stepped on the gas and Spencer tried to grab the wheel, but I smacked his hand away.

"You should know by now; if I can't have you, no bitch will."

I started driving in a crazy zig zag motion, scaring the fuck out of Spencer. Immediately, he put on his seatbelt. The horrific look on his face as I did all kinds of stunts driving home was priceless. By the time I pulled up, Spencer was already opening the door, hopping out with his crutches.

I got out of the car and hurried before him, opening the door. "Make yourself comfortable because you will be propped up here for the next six weeks."

"That's a lie," Spencer said, jumping over to the couch. "I wish I would say in this bitch with your crazy ass."

I pulled out a knife from my purse and pointed it at his swollen ankle. "Just so you know, I will stab the fuck out of your ankle in your sleep if you try to leave." Just to drive the point home, I fake stabbed at his ankle.

"I fuckin' hate you," Spencer spat.

"No, you don't. You're just in pain. I'm going to get your prescription. Don't go anywhere." I waved the knife at him again and laughed. After threatening him, I was sure that his ass would be sitting right in the same spot that I left him in.

It was now morning, so I decided to get breakfast while I waited for his prescription. After eating, I was on my way home when I decided to stop by Dream's house. It was about time that she knew that Spencer and I were together. I parked in front of her house and I should have felt bad that I didn't visit her once she woke up or that I hardly visited her while she was in a coma, but I didn't. Apart of me wished she was out just a little bit longer so that, by the time she woke up, Spencer and I would have been married.

I didn't even bother to ring the doorbell. I started banging like I was crazy. I knew she just got out of the hospital, but I was feeling confrontational.

"Destiny?" Dream questioned when she came to the door. "What the hell is wrong with you banging on the door like you're crazy?"

I was amped up now. Finally, I was face to face, about to say what I wanted to say to her for months. "Spencer and I are an item now."

Dream looked at me like I just farted. "Is that what you came by here for? Girl, I don't want his ass. I'm glad he's with you. Is that where he is now?"

"Yes," I exclaimed, balling up my fist. I was ready to sock her if she came out her face wrong.

"Good. Tell his mannish ass to stay the fuck over there. He's not welcome back over here. I'll take care of my baby without him."

Imagine my face when I looked down and saw Dream's round stomach. I was sure I turned white as a ghost.

"That ain't his baby," I managed to say.

"How the fuck would you know? Were you in bed with us? Get your stupid ass off my porch before I knock you off."

I was about to say something slick when she slammed the door in my face. I walked back to the car in defeat. I knew in my heart that Spencer was the father. I wouldn't be surprised if he got Dream pregnant on purpose. Well, in order to compete, I'd be getting pregnant too. We both gonna be having this nicca's baby. Keeping that shit all in the family.

As soon as I got in the car, Spencer's phone rang.

"Who the fuck is this?" I answered.

"Excuse me?" the female voice said.

"Excuse what, bitch? You called me." This hoe was way out of line calling my man's phone. She better back the fuck up.

"I was trying to reach Spencer," she said with an uppity attitude. "Is he available?"

"No, bitch, he's not. I'm available. Whatever you gotta say to my man, you can say to me, bitch."

The lady sighed. "I really need to talk to Spencer, if you don't mind."

"Well, that shit's not going to happen. Either you talk to me or you can get clicked on. It's up to you, bitch."

She sighed again. "Fine. I want my damn money then."

"What money?" I stressed. "I know my man ain't paying you for pussy," I said in disbelief. "I fuck him all day, every day, so I know he's not dropping no paper on your raggedy pussy. Fuck outta here."

She laughed and I had to hold the phone back. This bitch tried it. She was about to make me trace this damn call, find her ass, and beat the shit out of her.

"This ain't about no pussy. Well, at least not my pussy. Tell Spencer to give me my damn two-fifty before I tell Dream about his late night rendezvous in her room."

"Wait, what?" This bitch just threw me. What was she talking about? Late nights with Dream, ain't no way? "Stop speaking in riddles bitch. Plain English."

"Pay close attention, Destiny. What the fuck I said was, Spencer owes me a payment of two-hundred fifty dollars or I'm going to tell Dream about all those late nights that he had in her room. I'm sure she'd like to know that her child's father raped her and that's how she got pregnant."

I gasped. I didn't mean to, but I did. I was low down, but I was totally against rape. Then again, this bitch could be lying. She had to be. Spencer wasn't that pressed to get no pussy. Not when he had me. Why would Spencer have to rape Dream's unconscious ass for?

"Listen, bitch, don't call this phone no more, or I'm going to find out where you live and beat your ass. Leave me and my fuckin' man alone or deal with the consequences, bitch."

CLICK!

Chapter 17

Dream

If I wasn't already pregnant, I was sure I would be by now. Drake and I definitely made up for lost time. We fucked every day and, some days, two or three times. The more I spent time with him, the more I remembered.

His doctor told him to stay off his leg; that didn't stop him from showing me a good time. Since we both had been released from the hospital, he'd taken me out to eat, shopping, and we even went on a mini vacation. Not too far. We went away for the weekend to a bed and breakfast where people waited on us hand and foot. Meanwhile, all we did was screw.

"Are you fuckin' ready?" Mercy yelled to me upstairs. "We about to miss our appointment. You know them Asian bitches will give our shit away if we're a minute late."

She wasn't lying. Ming, the lady that did our nails, she would overbook the second we were late. Mercy and I had been going to her for years. Still, that didn't mean shit. Baby girl was about her bread.

"I can't find shit," I squealed in agony.

I turned five months yesterday and I was bigger than a house. Drake and I just came back from the doctor, checking on the baby. I was having a boy. He's excited because he'd been saying that I was carrying his son. Drake was adamant that the baby was his. I just wished it was. The possibility that my baby could still be Spencer's made me ill. Most of my memories had come back and I still didn't remember cheating on Drake. So, maybe Drake was right. Maybe I was jumping to conclusions about being pregnant by Spencer.

After getting more of my memory, I was trying to figure out when Spencer and I had sex. I was wrecking my brain trying to remember. I remembered everything else about Spencer but that.

And speaking of him, he'd been missing since he left the first night I came home. That was four weeks ago. I ain't seen or heard from the nicca since. I could only assume that he was with Destiny after she popped up over here at my house. Real talk, I really didn't give a fuck where he was. I was just trying to keep the peace until Drake got his casts off in two more weeks. He still would be under doctor's orders, but he would be able to walk freely, able to fuck freely. I couldn't tell you how many times I got excited and hit one of those casts and quickly regretted it. They were in the way of me getting my groove on. I was dying to feel Drake on top of me or hit it from the back.

"I thought you said Drake took you shopping?" Mercy asked, walking into my bedroom. Her impatient attitude quickly changed when she saw my protruding belly. Rushing over to me, she rubbed my stomach like a crystal ball. "You're bigger since I last seen you."

"I know," I said, sitting down. I was tired already and we hadn't even left yet.

"So, Drake didn't take you shopping? Let me find out his ass is cheap," she said with an eye and neck roll.

"No, he took me shopping weeks ago, but I can't fit none of that shit. I've outgrew that shit. My belly is growing at an alarming rate."

Mercy smiled while staring at my stomach. She got on her knees and put her face to my tummy. "Hey baby. You'll be here soon and I'm going to spoil you." She kissed my stomach and sat next to me. "There has to be something you can wear in here. Let me look."

"Good luck trying," I said, keeping my fat ass right on the bed while she looked.

The doctor said, since I left the hospital, I gained twenty pounds. He said considering I was in a coma for so long, it was actually normal. I didn't feel normal. I went from having a flat belly when I woke up to having a small pudge to a huge pregnant stomach. If it wasn't for Drake being by my side, I think I would have been very depressed. He reassured me constantly that I was beautiful and he couldn't wait for me to have his baby. That scared me too. I was so afraid that he was going to leave me if the baby was Spencer's. That nicca was such a dickhead. It was confirmed when I found out he was fucking my cousin. I would have been ready to go to blows if I still wanted his ass. Luckily, I didn't. Otherwise, I would have beat Destiny's ass. I actually wanted to thank her because she took his lame ass off my hands.

Mercy tossed a shirt and pants at me. "Here. I know your big butt can fit that. Drake needs to take you shopping again."

"I'll tell him," I said while struggling to get up, making my way to the bathroom to put the clothes on.

I walked out of the bathroom surprised that the clothes fit. It would take Mercy to dig through my closet to find me something.

"Here's your shoes," she said, handing them to me.

I sat back down on the bed and put them on; surprisingly, they fit. "Thank you."

"You're welcome. Now, bring your ass on so that we can get to Ming before we don't get our shit done."

I giggled. "You right about that."

Ming was just about to give our appointments away when we walked in. I was so glad that she didn't. I didn't think I could wait any longer than what we did. Two hours was long enough.

"You know," I started to say while we were under the nail dryer, "I've been doing everything to get in contact with Bey. Something is wrong because nobody has seen her in months. I know she does some crazy shit, but this is out of character, even for her."

"You think something happened to her?" Mercy asked concerned.

"I'm not sure. If I remember correctly, she told me that she would be studying for her classes for a little while, but she wouldn't have been gone this long. My mother said they fell out before she disappeared. From what everyone said that I talked to, she disappeared the same night that I went into a coma."

"Okay, now that you put it that way, it doesn't make any sense. Plus, you two were good, right?"

"I mean, we had a small issue, but we squashed it. I'm not sure what's going on, but I know in my heart of hearts that something is wrong. I hope she didn't run away again. I left Korvette a message. We've been playing phone tag. She was out of town for a few weeks on vacation and, when she came back, we just couldn't seem to reach each other."

I got a text.

"This is her," I told Mercy.

"You must've talked her up," Mercy exclaimed.

"Hey, cuzzo," I said to Korvette when I answered the call.

"Heeey boo! I'm so glad you're awake. I swear, I was up there all the time to see you."

I smiled. "I know. I remember hearing your voice. I don't remember what you said, so don't ask."

She giggled. "I promise, I was about to ask you what I said."

We shared a laugh.

"Listen, you heard from Bey."

"No," she said, turning serious. "But I have her phone and some weird people have been calling. I think they know where she is."

"What you mean? She owes them money or something?"

"Maybe so," Korvette said. "I'm really not sure. If she did, that would make sense why she disappeared."

I spoke to Korvette for a few more minutes and then cut the conversation short because we were on our way over there. I needed to see her in person. Mercy and I sat at the nail salon for about ten more minutes before we both got up. I was sure her nails were dry. At this point, I didn't care if my nails were dry or not. I needed to see what was up with my sister. I had a bad feeling that she was in trouble. Mercy must've sensed it. She told me to go wait in the car while she took care of our tab and made our next appointment.

Korvette ran up to me, hugging and kissing me. Tears were in her eyes when she pulled away. "I was so scared that you were going to die."

Seeing Korvette tear up made my eyes fill up too.

"Naw bitch," Mercy said. "Don't be crying and shit. We celebrating life."

Korvette giggled and wiped away her tears. She gave Mercy a hug too.

"You right," she said, wiping away her tears. "About to make me mess up my make-up. You know I gotta say on fleek."

Her statement made us all laugh.

Korvette reminded me of Bey so much; it wasn't even funny. Her mannerisms, the way she looked, and even down to her voice. She looked like she gained a little weight. She was still beautiful as ever. Just her face was fuller and her hips had spread some. Her stomach was still flat and her waist was tiny as ever.

"So, what's this you're talking about Bey's phone?" I asked as we followed her inside.

"Let me go get it and I'll show you what I'm talking about."

Korvette showed us Bey's phone. Her last outgoing call was the day that I got into my accident. After that, it was only incoming calls from an unknown number.

"Some strange man keeps calling her phone, asking for her," Korvette told us. "At first, I was thinking that it could be someone that she was dealing with, but she was only messing with Breeze from what I could tell. And I actually had a run in with him and his trifling cousin, Kapri. Ugh!" Korvette rolled her eyes so hard; they almost got stuck in her head.

"I take it you know Kapri well."

She eyed me. "A little too well. I can't stand his ass. I've been telling him for months about these calls. This nicca curbed me. He thought I was tripping off us."

Mercy and I both put our hands over our mouths and gasped.

"You gave him some?" I asked her.

She rolled her eyes again. "Yes. It was a mistake, just like him and I were a mistake."

"Okay, we gonna get back to that," I told her, smiling. I couldn't wait to hear those juicy details. "Can I have her phone? I'm going to give it to Drake."

"Okay," she said, handing Bey's phone over to me.

"I'll get him to trace the calls if he can and see what he can find."

I dialed Drake and he picked up on the first ring.

"Que paso, ma?"

"Bey has been missing since the night of my accident."

I ran down to him everything that Korvette told us and how she told Kapri and he ignored her. Drake said that he would talk to Kapri and he was sending someone to get the phone. He asked me for Korvette's address. I gave it to him and he told us to sit tight. I was trying to be strong while we waited. My emotions got the best of me. I was crying my eyes out before I knew it. It took both of them to console me.

The doorbell rang.

Korvette jumped up. "I'll get it."

Mercy was rubbing my back when Mega walked in. The look on her face made me smile. Priceless.

"Hola, ladies," Mega said, giving me and Korvette a hug.

When he stood before Mercy, he picked her up off her feet, pulling her into a sensual embrace. Mercy was always bad mouthing him, but I could tell that she liked it. She was happy to see him too.

"Hey, baby," he said, grabbing her by her hair. It looked as if he was about to kiss her. She closed her eyes so I knew she thought the same thing. Instead, he planted sensual kisses on her face and down her neck to her cleavage. "I missed you, ma."

Mercy didn't say she missed him, but the wide grin on her face expressed it all. She could lie to herself all she wanted to, but I saw the chemistry between them. She was full of shit if she said she wasn't attracted to this man.

Korvette fanned herself with her hand. "Damn, y'all making me hot."

"Me too," I said, feeling a tingle between my legs. Pregnancy had me hornier than ever.

Mega walked over to the couch, pulling Mercy into his lap. "Let me get Bey's phone?"

I handed it to him and he examined it before going through her call log and contacts. We continued to watch him as he pulled out his phone and started speaking in Spanish. I didn't understand much, but Mercy and I both shrieked when we heard him say muerte. I knew that meant death.

"You think my sister is dead," I bawled.

"No, that's not what I said," Mega told me empathically. "I'm going to keep this phone, if that's okay. If your sister is missing, we'll find her. I will follow back up with you when I have more information."

I nodded my head, still bawling.

"Don't cry. You're going to upset my nephew. Besides, I have a feeling that she's alive and well."

"What makes you say that?" I asked, "If they do have her, that means she's been missing for five months."

"I'll find her," he said, trying to convince me. "I see several calls to her phone. It's not the same number, but it's similar numbers, which tells me it's the same person."

I wiped my runny nose with the tissue that Korvette gave me. "How do you know?"

Mega flashed me a smile. "Let's just say I'm a professional when it comes to these things."

Mega nibbled on Mercy's ear and squeezed her waist. "I gotta go, ma, but just know that I'm around so when you talk that slick shit, I'ma roll up on your ass."

"Whatever," Mercy said, standing to her feet. "Ain't nothing changed. I'm just tired of arguing with your ass."

"So, that means things have changed because I'm getting my way."

"Ugh!" Mercy sighed. "I'm trying to be nice to you."

Mega smirked at Mercy and laughed. "Tell yourself whatever you need to, as long as you know that you belong to me."

Mercy frowned and waved him off. "Bye, Mega. I swear, I can only take so much of you before I get annoyed."

He smacked her on her ass. "I can't get enough of you."

Mercy sucked her teeth while sitting back down on the couch, playing with her phone.

Mega walked over to me and rubbed my belly. "Everything's going to be alright. Stop stressing. Give me some time. I'll find her."

I wiped away more tears and nodded. "Okay."

I said okay, but I wasn't sure if I really meant it.

Chapter 18

Channa

Drake was at the hospital so he could get his casts taken off. I was happy to see them shits go. They were definitely in the way. I tried to seduce Drake on many occasions and, every time, I ended up being hit by one of those fucking casts. I even tried to sleep in the bed with him. That was torture too. Every time I turned over, I was greeted with one of those damn casts. So, I was happier than he was to see them go.

It's a shame that I was in the same house with my husband, and I couldn't even get next to him or spend time alone with him. Thanks to his grandma, Gigi's, cock blocking ass. I didn't care what nobody said, that bitch was the devil. I swear, one day I'ma figure out a way to kill her ass. I was working on it all day, every day.

"I'll be back, baby," I told Drake, kissing him on the cheek.

"Where you going?" he asked with a slight annoyance in his tone.

I wanted to tell him where I was going, but I couldn't. He'd be pissed if he found out. "I'm going to run errands while you're here. I know this appointment is going to take some time. The doctor wants to run tests and stuff."

"What kinda of errands?" Drake inquired with an attitude.

I put a smile on my face. "You know, girl stuff," I lied.

"Can't that shit wait?"

Dream & Drake 3: A Cartel Love Story

It was obvious that Drake knew something was up.

"Baby, do you really want to do shopping and shit after spending hours at the doctor's office?"

Drake thought about it for a minute. "Naw. Hell naw. Go handle that, but make sure you bring your ass right back. I don't want to be sitting here waiting for your ass."

"I wouldn't do that to you, baby," I said, offering up another smile. "I'll be back. I promise."

"You better. Let me find out you're up to some bullshit."

Drake eyed me as I kissed him again on the cheek and waved bye. I sashayed out of the hospital to my car. I knew I only had about two or three hours max, before I had to come back to get him. His doctor had him set up for all these tests after his casts came off, to see if things healed properly. Also, he had to get X-rays, blood work, and physical therapy. He probably didn't need the physical therapy, but the therapist was going to test him anyway. I appreciated that his doctor was so thorough. If he wasn't, I wouldn't have time to go handle some unfinished business.

Driving around the city, it took me a minute to find Crunch. He was a very busy man who didn't stay in one spot too long. I was sure he was always on the go because he was the eyes and ears of this city. He wasn't the only one. He was just the only one I trusted.

"You're a hard man to find," I said, giving Crunch a hug.

"I have to stay busy, shorty. You look like you're about to pop."

"No, not yet. I have a few months to go."

"Wow," he laughed. "Okay, so what brings you by?"

"I'm looking for Arizona and Arabia."

Crunch stared me down. "Does Drake know that you're here?"

"No, he doesn't, and I'd prefer if it stays that way."

Crunch sighed. "Look, I can't help you with that Snow."

"C'mon Crunch. I need to find them."

"Why?"

"I just need to."

"See, it's going to look real suspicious if you pop up where they are. Drake ain't about to come down on my ass for it."

"So, you do know where they are," I fumed.

"Listen, I'm not saying if I know or not. What I'm telling you is, you need to ask Drake."

"He's not going to tell me," I hissed. "You're my last resort."

"I can't, Snow."

I was so angry that I started crying before I knew it. If I wasn't pregnant, I wouldn't have been slinging tears like a softy. Pregnancy had me out here weak as fuck.

"Don't cry," he said, trying to soothe me. "You should be happy they're gone."

"Oh, I would be celebrating their disappearances if they hadn't stolen from me."

"What did they take?" this nosy muthafucka asked.

"Never mind," I told him, drying my eyes. I already said too much. "I know you can't tell me where they are, but maybe you can say if they are still in the city."

Crunch sighed. "Why you want to find them so bad?"

"Because they stole from me."

"Whatever they took must've been valuable," he stated.

"Listen, you gotta tell me where they are. If they are still in the city, I'm going to tear this damn city up until I find them."

"How much money you got? You know I'm not cheap."

Now, it was my turn to sigh. "I'm tapped."

"C'mon, Snow. No dough, no info."

I knew he wanted money. Whenever I needed information, I always paid Crunch. "If I had it, I would break you off. I don't have it."

When he gave me a simple ass look, I knew what time it was. It was time for me to roll out. I turned to leave and Crunch came up behind me.

"I like more than just money, you know."

His erection was poking against my ass. I held my breath as he felt me up. His hand ran over my full breasts and down my wide hips.

"You're so sexy, Snow. I've wanted you for a long time. I won't tell Drake if you won't."

"I... I can't, Crunch."

"How much is this information worth to you?"

That was a good question. How much was this information worth to me? Was I willing to let him fuck me to get it? I reasoned with myself because I'd done worst. I guess Crunch took my silence for weakness because he had my dress lifted up before I knew it. I didn't have on any panties, so he had easy access. I palmed the back of the house since we were outside, and he fumbled with his jeans. His dick was exposed before I knew it and the tip was pointed at my whole.

"Shit, this pussy is good," he said, easing his erection inside of me.

I couldn't lie and say it felt bad because it didn't. No, I didn't want to fuck Crunch, but I'd been so horny lately. Drake wasn't fucking me, and I wasn't getting dick from anywhere else. Feeling Crunch inside of me felt damn good. His dick was shorter than Drake's, yet it was really fat, filling me up.

His hands pushed my dress all the way up around my neck, gripping my breasts. "Damn, this pussy good. Super wet and juicy, just the way I like it."

I palmed the side of the house as I felt an orgasm coming on. I tried not to enjoy myself, but I couldn't help it. Crunch had some good strokes.

He sucked on my ear lobe. "Damn, baby, this pussy got me ready to nut."

I didn't mean to moan. It just escaped before I knew it.

"This dick good, ain't it, baby?" Crunch said, thrusting into me harder. "I'm about to nut all in this pregnant pussy."

I hated to admit it. His filthy talk was turning me on. My clit was twitching and so was my pussy. My orgasm was right there.

"Fuck. Fuck. Fuck. Fuck," Crunch grunted as he came.

Hearing him cum made me cum too. I held onto the aluminum siding, cumming hard. My face was plastered against the house as my body pulsated.

"Damn, I'ma start calling you good pussy."

"No, don't call me that or anything else," I spat, coming down off my orgasmic high. "You said you wouldn't tell Drake, remember?"

"I got you, Snow. This was between us."

I sighed in relief. Just as I was about to ask more about those ratchet twins, my phone rang. It was Drake. I let it go to voicemail and sent a text instead, telling him I was on my way back.

"I gotta go."

"That's cool. You got the same number?"

"Yeah," I said, while fixing my dress and smoothing out my hair.

"I'll hit you up later."

"You better. After getting a sample of this sweet spot between my legs, I better get an address."

"You will, good pussy."

I switched back to my car and took off. Crunch couldn't keep his eyes off me. That gave me a natural high. I always had a way with men. They always gave me what I wanted. I had plans for Crunch. Not only was he going to give me the address, he was going to become my puppet.

Whooop! Whoop!

"Aw, fuck!"

Immediately, I stopped. I didn't even bother to pull over to the curb. My focus was stopping so that I could go live on my damn phone, just in case.

"Hello, ma'am. Can you please step out of the car?"

"Wait, no license and registration?"

"No, this car was involved in a hit and run. You're under arrest."

I wanted to scream at the top of my lungs. I was so worried about getting back that I jumped my stupid ass into the car that I hit Dream in. How fuckin' stupid could I be? Yes, I had the dents fixed, but I forgot to switch out the damn license plate. Fuck!

I got out of the car with my hands raised. "Don't shoot."

Two other officers stood by, while the officer who was talking to me roughly handcuffed me. I wanted to say something so bad, but I kept my mind shut. I couldn't afford for him to throw me on the ground, making me miscarry.

Chapter 19

Drake

That fuckin' Channa, with her no good trifling' ass. I couldn't believe she left my ass at the gawddamn doctor's office. Wait, yes I could. She was the same skank hoe who cheated on me. If the court date wasn't coming up soon, I wouldn't even be dealing with her stupid ass. Now, more than ever, I had to get rid of her. Since she was a no show, I asked Quay to come and get me.

"When are you leaving this bitch?" Quay asked. I called him to meet me here after Channa ditched me.

"Man, it's crazy how shit came down to this."

"Fuck you mean?" Quay questioned. "It was always like this. You just didn't see it. That fuckin' hoe been grimy."

I sighed. "Why you always do that?"

"Do what, nicca? Tell your denial management ass the truth. You like to sugar coat shit. I'm giving it to you straight. Channa was on that fuck shit. Since day one."

"This is the first time I see you in weeks, Quay. I just want you to be here for me. Can you do that? I called you cause I just need you to be my cousin, and be by my side at my doctor's appointment."

I wasn't about to let Quay know, but it was bothering me that he wasn't here to support me. We were tight. The thought of him not caring about my health was fucked up.

"I just want to focus on getting my casts off."

Quay nodded. "Done. My bad. I'm concerned. That's why I'm here. Whatever you need," he said, getting up and hugging me. "I was tripping. You're right. I should have been here more for you, but I'm here now. I mean that shit."

"Thanks," I said. I didn't want to tell him, but sitting in this wheelchair made me feel super helpless. I gave up on the damn crutches a long time ago and bought a motorized scooter. For the past six weeks, I hadn't been able to wash my ass by myself. I had nurses in and out of my house. Gigi was there, driving me half fuckin' crazy. Then, there was Channa's thirsty ass. I wish she wasn't pregnant because I would never lay my eyes on her ass ever again.

I felt Quay's eyes staring at me.

"Nicca, what the fuck are you sitting on? What the fuck is that shit? I fuckin' can't right now."

I couldn't help but bust out laughing. Quay started rolling too.

"Damn, you can't be that bad off. Let me get the doctor now so that you can give the old people back their shit. Get them casts off and be that nicca again. You look handicap than a muthafucka."

I fell out laughing then, for real. "You're an idiot."

"Shit, I'm glad I am here," Quay laughed. "You fuckin' need me, for real, for real. I wouldn't have believed this shit unless I saw it with my own eyes. You ain't getting no pussy riding that shit, I promise."

"Shut the fuck up, stupid ass nicca." I laughed with tears in my eyes.

Quay was stupid as fuck. He had me laughing so hard that I had to roll to the bathroom. As soon as I returned, the nurse called me back. I was pissed at Quay at first, but he came though. He was there right by my side as I got both casts off, went through my tests, and talked to the physical therapist. She had me do a few exercises and told me that she only needed to see me for two weeks. After that, I should be back to normal.

"Are you sure?" I asked her, wiping the sweat from my face with a towel.

She smiled and winked. "I'm sure."

"Damn, you get all the bitches," Quay said, watching the physical therapist walk away.

"Naw, I'm off the market now, man. I just want to be with Dream and raise my shorty."

"I know you do. That's why I called her."

I stared at Quay to see if he was being real or playing. "You serious?"

"Yeah, man, that woman is crazy about you. She should take you home, not me. Handle your shit."

"Good looking out."

"Always, nicca. I got your back, no matter what."

"I know. I've been a real ass lately."

"No, nicca, you been more like a piece of shit lately. Talking crazy, acting crazy, and spazzing the fuck out. If you weren't so young, I'd say you were going through a mid-life crisis or some shit. Menopause acting ass nicca."

I had to laugh because Quay was straight talk no chaser, all day, every day. "Damn, fuck my feelings and what I'm going through."

"Nicca, you're lucky we're family or I'd beat your ass. I still want to beat your ass."

"Don't fight me," I laughed. "A nicca is too weak to get his ass beat right now. You might kill me. I know you don't want to see me die. I'm your favorite cousin."

"Fuck all that."

Quay was really pissed. I could tell my actions hurt him badly. "I'm sorry, man. I'm just not used to leaning on y'all. I fucked up. Don't hold it against me."

Quay cut his eyes at me, as if he didn't want to hear what I had to say.

"I'm being real, Quay. I appreciate you. You've been right by my side helping me. I haven't taken it for granted. Shit just been rough. I'm just really hurt right now. Mentally and physically." I knew that if I didn't open up, I might have lost the special bond that me and my cousin shared.

"I know how your prideful ass is," Quay said, finally smiling. "I was hot with you, but I wasn't going nowhere. We're blood, nicca. Cousins for life."

"Man, don't start with that cousins for life bullshit."

We both laughed because we used to say that after every sentence when we both got in the game back in high school. We thought the saying was tight back then. Hearing that bullshit now made me realize just how ignorant we were.

Quay stopped laughing and stared at me. "You talked to Fresh?"

"Naw," I said in a tone that told him leave it the fuck alone.

"You're wrong, Drake."

Quay shrugged and stood to his feet as soon as Dream walked in. He gave me a fist bump, hugged Dream, and then threw up the peace sign at me on his way out.

"Hey, boo," Dream said, walking up and kissing me on the lips. She smirked. "You're baby mama ain't shit. "You know that, right?"

"Fuck that bitch," I replied. I was so heated 'that bitch' just rolled off my tongue.

Dream gasped. "You said the B word?"

"Yeah, I did," I said, regretting it. "I let Channa take me out of my character. She just had a way of doing shit like that to me."

"I'm not a fan of hers, but she is a woman, you know."

"I didn't ask for much," I vented. "I just asked for her to pick me up and be by my side."

Now, it was Dream's turn to say, "Fuck her. That bitch don't deserve you. She got you all stressed."

Dream helped me up and, surprisingly, I was standing with no problem. Those fucking casts had a nicca self-conscious and shit.

"You good baby?" Dream asked.

"Yeah, I think I am." I stretched a little bit, loving the feeling. I was normal again. Well, almost. In two more weeks, I would be back to the old Drake.

"You look cute," I told Dream. She did. She had on a halter dress. Her belly was much bigger. "How is my son?"

She smiled bright. "Greedy as fuck."

"Let me find out you're not feeding him. It's gonna be me and you."

She laughed. "I'm feeding him. I have no choice."

We walked towards the entrance hand in hand. All of a sudden, I had to pee. I went to a nearby bathroom and pulled her in with me.

"You just gonna pee right in front of me?" Dream asked.

"Yep," I told her, freeing my dick and pissing. The moment I pissed, my dick bricked up. "Give me some pussy."

"What?" Dream asked, stuck on stupid.

"You see my dick is hard."

I didn't wait for her to answer. I pulled up her dress and pulled down her panties.

"Step out of them," I declared.

Dream did as she was told and I wasted no time bending her over the sink, ramming into her. Her pussy was dripping wet, so I know that she wanted to fuck as much as I did.

"Fuuuuck, Drake."

"Damn, ma, you're pussy so juicy."

"Uh! Uh! Uh! Uh! Uh! Uh!" Dream grunted.

"Get this dick, ma."

Dream gripped the sink and threw her ass back. "Ohmigod. Fuck this amazing dick. Shit, it feels good. You got the best dick. I swear, Drake. I swear."

"Cum on it then, ma."

I was hoping Dream came cause I was about to bust off. My nut was seconds from leaving my balls.

"Oh, yeah, Drake. Your dick is working my pussy."

I slid my dick out and then put it back in slowly. I noticed how crazy that made Dream act. Again, I slid my dick out. Dream bucked back against me, trying to ease my dick back up inside of her, but I moved back further until I rested against the wall. Dream backed all the way up until her pussy connected with my dick again. This time, she didn't let me slide out so easily. She bent her knees and arched her back, taking my dick with force. I held her hips as she sucked my dick deep into her pussy.

"Oh shit, this dick. I'ma bout to cum!" she screamed loudly. Then, she bounced on me so hard that I could barely stand up. "I'm cummmming on this big dick," she announced. "Ugh! I'm cummming, Drake. All on your dick."

That was it. I couldn't hold my nut anymore. I thrusted into her with all of my might. My body rested against the wall, but my pelvis was in the air as I pushed my dick all the way inside of her.

"I'm still cumming Drake!" Dream screamed.

"Shit, I'm about to cum too," I replied, shooting loads of cum into her pussy. I pumped and pumped until I released all of my cum.

Dream stood up and fixed her clothes. "I'm not done with you yet. We're going back to your place, and we're going to fuck all over."

"Let's do it then," I agreed.

As Dream drove, I texted Gigi and told her to take the day off. I told her that Channa was missing and I was with Dream. We needed some privacy. Gigi knew about Dream. That's why she treated Channa like shit. We didn't even make it to the bedroom. I stripped her naked in the living room, bending her over the couch dicking her down.

"Damn, I love pregnant pussy," I groaned, loving how Dream's pussy gripped my dick.

We fucked in the living room and kitchen before we showered and retired to the bedroom.

*****

I fucked Dream for three days. The fourth day was court day. I sent Dream home and told her that I would call her after the hearing. I was prepared to find Channa, no matter what. She could stand me up, but she wasn't about to no-show on our court date. I was divorcing her ass if it was the last thing that I did.

Princess Diamond

Just as I was about to leave out the crib to go find her stupid ass, Channa came waltzing in as if she had been laid up in a gutter.

"Damn, you stink," I said, holding my nose.

"Well, hello to your ass too."

She strolled pass me upstairs, as if I was getting on her nerves.

"Hold the fuck up," I stated, right on her heels. "You disappear on me, stand me the fuck up, and you show up with a raggedy ass attitude. That's not how this fuckin' works."

She stripped out of her clothes right in front of me. "Don't start no shit, Drake. I'm not in the fuckin' mood."

"Where the fuck you been?" I asked, turning my head. My dick started to get hard. No matter how much I couldn't stand Channa, our sexual chemistry was always there.

"Don't worry about it," Channa snapped.

She walked into the bathroom and I followed.

"So, you stand me up knowing that I needed you, and I can't even get an answer?"

She closed the shower curtain, and I heard the water running. "Let it go, Drake."

"You're sorry as fuck. This is why I don't fuck with your ass. You're always on bullshit, probably laid up with some nicca fucking while you're carrying my kids. That's if they are even mine."

"They are yours!" she shouted. "I'm positive. I don't know how many times I have to tell your paranoid ass."

"If I'm paranoid, it's because your cheating ass made me that way."

"Get over that shit already. How long are you going to cry about that shit? Fuckin' let the fuckin' shit go."

"Fuck you, man. I swear, you're the worst piece of shit I ever met."

"That's not what you said every time you hit this great pussy," she fired back. "I bet your dick is hard right now."

It was, but I wasn't about to tell her that. Besides, I didn't care how hard my dick got, I wasn't fuckin' her. I'd rather die of blue balls.

"Just get your ass dressed before I strangle the fuck out of your ass."

I walked out of the bathroom livid. She had me so fuckin' pissed off that I went downstairs to the bar and poured me a shot of Cognac. I ain't really fuck with it like that because it made me horny to the max. The last thing I needed to do was listen to my hard dick and accidently fuck Channa.

"Where am I going?" Channa yelled downstairs.

I didn't answer. I was sitting down with my eyes closed, trying to meditate before I snapped.

"Where the fuck am I going, Drake? I know you hear me talking to your ass, shit."

"To the fuckin' lawyer's office!" I shouted back. "As usual, your backwards ass forgot. You out here doing gawd knows what. Damn, I wish your ass wasn't pregnant."

"Well, I am, nicca. Live with it," Channa said, coming downstairs.

She looked absolutely stunning. I often wondered how someone so gorgeous with good pussy could be the devil. She wore an all-tan ensemble. A mini dress with a blazer and matching heels. Her jewelry was gold and her hair was twisted up into a neat top knot.

There was no doubt that she was definitely hot, and that's the problem. Our chemistry was only physical. What I had with Dream was mental and physical. I felt like we were equally yoked. Channa and I just liked to fuck each other. Thinking back on our relationship, we only really got along in the bedroom. That's why I was about to divorce her ass.

She laughed. "Don't give me the googly eyes after you just dogged me out, nicca."

I sighed. "I'm ready. Are you ready?"

"Do I look ready?" She twirled around. "Make no mistake about it, I stay ready."

The Cognac subsided my anger a little. I was calm enough to escort her to my Benz. I even opened the door for her.

"You seem to be in a better mood."

I just nodded and smiled. She was about to pop like a can of biscuits when we got to the lawyer's office. Once she found out why we were there, it was about to be a wrap. I had a doctor on standby, just in case she needed to be admitted to the hospital. I didn't want my kids hurt. Even though I had my doubts because I couldn't remember fucking her to make those babies, I still didn't want them hurt. Knowing Channa, they were probably mine, since she was obsessed with having my baby. I just wanted to make sure.

"Hello, Mr. and Mrs. Diaz-Santana," Ross, my lawyer, said. "Follow me into the conference room, if you will."

Channa looked at me strange, but she followed along. I walked into the room and sat by my lawyer. I urged her to sit by hers. She sat down, clueless as to what was going on.

"Here is the divorce decree," my lawyer said, handing the papers.

"Divorce," Channa objected. "I didn't come here for a divorce. I came here to talk about reversing our separation." Channa looked from me to her lawyer. "I don't want a divorce."

"But your husband does," my lawyer spoke up. "He states you have cheated on him and he's not sure if the children you are carrying are his."

"Drake, c'mon, you know these are your babies."

I looked at Channa and shrugged, as Ross continued.

"My client is willing to pay you alimony for two years as you can see in the decree. He also wants a paternity test before he pays child support and pursues joint custody."

"I... I... wish I would do a paternity test while I'm pregnant. I'm a high risk pregnancy. Drake knows that, due to my medical history."

"Can I have a moment with my client?" Channa's lawyer asked.

"Sure. No problem," Ross countered.

While Channa was talking to her lawyer, Ross pulled me back into his office. "I got something to tell you."

"What's up?"

"Do you know where Channa was for the last three days?"

"No, but I want to know," I stated. I braced myself for the bullshit.

"She was in jail."

My eyes got big as hell. "In jail, for what?"

"For a hit and run. Obviously, the car that she was driving was involved in a car accident regarding a Dream Holloway."

"Wait! Did you say for Dream? As in my Dream?"

Ross nodded. "That's exactly what I said. She's the suspect in your girlfriend's hit and run. At first, they were going to charge you for the incident because the car is registered to you, even though you bought it for your wife. Luckily, I was able to prove that you were driving a separate car on the same night. The street light camera confirmed the same story too. You'd be surprised how much the cameras on the street show."

I sat there with my mouth hung open. I couldn't believe that Dream almost lost her life because Channa was jealous. She hit Dream in cold blood. I saw the accident myself.

"I provided the police with all the necessary information regarding your whereabouts that night, so you're free and clear. However, your wife is in serious trouble. She could face jail time."

I was still in shock. Channa was ruthless, but I never thought she would come after Dream like that. Not after she fucked around on me. She ruined our marriage, and now she wanted to play the victim. "She's not my responsibility after I sign these papers."

"I'm glad you said that because I gave her lawyer a copy of the police report, just so he knew that I knew what she did. We're going to use it as leverage." Ross stood to his feet. "It's time to go back to the conference room."

As soon as we sat down, Ross lit into Channa, telling her that I was aware of the hit and run, and Dream was going to press charges. Channa's eyes bucked as Ross spoke. I could tell that she was scared.

Ross went in for the kill. "Drake is requesting a divorce to-day. You can sign the divorce papers and get alimony and child support, or you can take this to court and we can bring up your hit and run with the evidence to back it up."

Channa and her lawyer quietly discussed what was just said before us. I strained to hear what they were saying, but I couldn't hear shit.

"What do you want?" Channa asked me. Her lawyer tried to calm her down, but she continued. "What more do you want, Drake?" she asked in tears. "You wanted to see me cry, you got it."

"I just want a divorce," I stated truthfully.

"Is being married to me that bad, huh?"

When I didn't answer, Channa got up and snatched the papers from my lawyer. "Here, Drake, you happy. I'm fuckin' signing the divorce papers."

I watched as she scribbled her name.

"Watch your back, muthafucka," she exclaimed in anger. "You have no fuckin' idea what I'm capable of." She stared me down with malice before storming out.

"Do you want an order of protection on her too?" Ross asked.

"No, I'm good. She's just making threats because she's hurt. I'm hurt too. I hope she finds happiness out there somewhere."

"What about the paternity test?" Ross asked.

Her lawyer spoke up in her defense. "I don't think that's possible. With her history of miscarriages, she could lose the pregnancy. I don't advise that."

"I don't either," Ross agreed. "We'll wait until the babies are born.

"I don't want to wait, but I will. I'm just glad she didn't want my house. It's been in my family for years."

Chapter 20

Channa

I got up and walked out because I couldn't sit there and listen to that bullshit one more minute. Yeah, I rode here with Drake, but I'd be damn if I left with that nicca. He was now my enemy. He picked that green ass bitch over me. I was the one who was with him when he wasn't a kingpin, when he was building. I helped this nicca when other bitches fled.

I didn't know why he loved these no street knowing, no common sense having, no drug knowledge hoes. He was going to learn one day just how much he fucked up. I couldn't wait to rub it in his face. I was so angry that I nearly walked into the street and got hit.

"Whoa, ma!" the dude driving the car exclaimed as he slammed on his brakes. "Yo, you tryna die or what?"

I recognized his East Coast accent immediately. This was about to be like taking candy from a baby.

I held my stomach and bent over in fake pain. "Ohmigod!"

He left his car double parked, holding up traffic. "I'm saying, you aight? What you need, ma?"

Out of nowhere, I started crying. I mean, lying on the water works. If I was an actress, I swear, I would get an Emmy.

"I'm just so devastated," I cried.

"Why, yo?"

"Because my husband left me," I cried even harder. "You think you can give me a ride?"

"No doubt."

He walked back to his car in the middle of the street and I followed right behind him. Don't ever underestimate me. Pregnant and all, I keep a trick up my sleeve. Believe that.

"So, you was saying your husband left you?" the dude asked as he drove.

"Yeah. He basically forced me to sign the divorce papers, twisting my arm."

"Yo, that's fucked up."

"Tell me about it. He left me pregnant with his babies for some lame bitch. They got into it and he tried to kill her and blamed it on me. I could be facing jail time, thanks to him."

"Wait!" He sighed and then paused. I guess he was trying to process everything. "You're pregnant with twins?"

"Yes," I sniffled.

"This dude is mad foul."

"He is. That's why I need your help getting him back."

"Whoa! Wait a minute now. I'ma give you a lift and all, but I'm not trying to get involved like that."

"Well, maybe I can change your mind."

I undid my seat belt and slid closer to him, caressing his crotch. We locked eyes and I could tell that he thought I was out of my mind, but he didn't stop me, so I continued. I reached inside of his jogging pants, inside of his boxers, and massaged his growing erection.

I giggled when he swerved a little. "Don't kill us, papi."

"Shit, I'm trying not to."

I lowered my face to his crotch, kissing his thighs and balls. I expected his shit to be sweaty, but it wasn't. He was a cutie, so having a stinky private would have thrown me all the way off.

"Aaaaah fuck," he moaned when my tongue licked his shaft.

I wasted no time pushing the tip of his dick back against my tonsils. He was a decent size, but Drake was bigger, so sucking his dick was a piece of cake.

Slurp. Slurp. Slurp. Slurp.

I got real nasty with it, spitting on his dick and sucking it off.

"Shiiiiit, ma. You sucking the fuck outta my dick."

I didn't answer. I kept my mouth on the prize, bobbing my head like the pro that I was. I knew I had him when he gripped my hair. The shit was so good to him; he had to pull over. Sure enough, about a minute later, he was spilling cum down my throat.

"You wild as fuck."

I just sat back in my seat and smiled. "You think you can help me?" I asked in my most sugary sweet voice.

"Hell yeah. After you sucked my dick like that, shit, you know I got you. What you need, ma?"

I handed him a list and told him to drive me to the hard-ware store. I waited in the car with a smile plastered on my face until he returned. The items were so heavy that he had to push them out with a cart. I made sure he stopped off at the gas station on our way home. After he parked in the driveway, he got out of the car and carried my things into the garage.

"This is a nice house," he said, sitting the stuff down.

"Not for long," I mumbled.

"What did you say?" he said, looking at Drake's luxury cars.

"I said, I might need a place to stay."

He looked at me funny. "Um, I don't know about all that."

"Why?" I asked sugary sweet again.

"Because we don't know each other, ma"

"Well, let's get to know each other. My name is Snow and I like to fuck and suck for breakfast, lunch, and dinner. Also, I take it up the ass too."

His eyes nearly popped out of his head. I watched as he swallowed hard. I kept on talking, while he was thinking about what I said.

"I'm just going to grab a few things from here and put them in storage. Afterwards, I was hoping that you could pound my pussy out." I seductively sucked on my finger for emphasis. "Don't you want some of my sweet, sweet pussy?"

We locked eyes and I knew I had him.

"How long you plan on staying?"

I smiled. "Not long."

He grabbed my phone and put his number in. "Okay, just call me later."

"Thanks luv," I exclaimed before I stuck my tongue into his mouth. I lightly squeezed on his dick and balls, giving him a kiss that he'd never forget. "I can't wait to choke on that dick and gargle those balls."

"You're crazy than a muthafucka, but I like it. Make sure you call me."

I winked at him. "I definitely will."

I waited until he pulled off before I went to work. The things that he carried into the garage, I left there. Before I got started, I backed out one of Drake's cars. I made sure it was one of the newer ones he got before he went into the hospital. One that didn't have a tracking device or a kill switch in it. He fell off with taking care of business since he'd been out of commission over the last few weeks.

Marching upstairs to our bedroom was where I started. I cried while packing all my shit. Before I started to destroy it all, I put my suitcases into the car parked in the driveway. I set the camera up on record and went to town wreaking havoc. I wanted Drake to see everything that I had done. But first, I wanted to give him a little speech.

"Muthafucka, you pissed the wrong bitch off. It's cool tho. If I can't have none of this shit, neither will you. You have to be the dumbest nicca alive if you thought I walked away peacefully. You think I give a fuck that you holding something over my head? Nicca, I don't give no fucks about that. I just didn't want to sit there and look in your face, but I got your ass tho. I'm coming for you, and I'm never going to stop coming for you. I'm going to take out every bitch that you seem remotely close to. Muthafucka, I know you helped Arizona and Arabia escape. I'm sure you had something to do with them hitting my safe up too. If I find out your ass was involved, you're going to have to sleep with one eye open forever. These ain't threats nicca, they are promises. I'm about to fuck all your shit up to prove it."

I cackled hysterically before I sat my phone down to capture everything.

"Let's get it," I said into the camera with a smirk.

I ripped out all of Drake's designer shit. Threw everything from the closet on the bed. All his expensive shoes and suits included. Going back and forth to the closet was wearing me out, but I was determined to do this. A few times, I had to stop and catch my breath, holding my big belly. Finally, the closet was clear. Next, I took a hammer and busted out everything I could see. TV's, stereos, appliances, mirrors, all that shit. I hit every fucking thing that I could see. If it was breakable, I made sure I destroyed it.

By the time I was done going through the house, cutting cords and fucking everything up, I went back to the garage and mixed up a recipe to put into Drake's gas tanks. Yes, I said tanks because I was hitting every fuckin' car he had. Since he liked green bitches, I put a mixture of fertilizer and plant food in his tank. I would love to see his face when he tried to start this shit up and couldn't.

I laughed all the way back inside to the kitchen. That's when I filled up gigantic spray bottles of bleach and started spraying everywhere. I was determined to fuck everything up, squirting bleach like a water gun from the top to the bottom of this bitch. My last and final move, I poured gasoline around the outside of the house and lit a cigarette, just like she did in Waiting To Exhale. I smoked the cigarette for a moment and then tossed it, watching the house go up in flames.

"That'll teach his ass," I said, backing out of the driveway. "If I can't have this house, his muthafuckin' ass can't either. I'll be dammed if him and that bitch live happily ever after while I'm living from pillar to post."

Chapter 21

Drake

For the millionth time, I had a fuckin' headache dealing with Channa's ratchet ass. I really didn't know what I saw in her. I was salty as fuck that I couldn't get the paternity test done while she was pregnant. My lawyer tried, but her pregnancy was high risk. She could lose one baby, if not both. I would feel bad if that happened, even if they weren't mine. That was the only thing saving her slick ass.

"So, what now?" I asked my lawyer, Ross. I was sitting in his office after he finished things up with Channa's lawyer.

"I'm going to run by the courthouse on my way home and file the divorce for you."

"How long will it take?" I asked, feeling so antsy.

"Not long. Depends on how backed up they are. Usually, anywhere from two weeks to thirty days. The worst case scenario is six weeks. She has a small window to contest the deal that we made today."

I sighed. Man, that was the shit I was hoping he didn't say. "How likely is that?"

"Drake, I'ma keep it straight with you. Channa is a loose cannon. Who knows what she might do. Her lawyer will inform her of that clause. It will be up to her to exercise her right or not."

"Fuck!" I said, punching his desk. I stood up and walked over to the window to calm down. "Ross, I swear, I know the meaning of young, dumb, and full of cum. I'm paying for that shit right now. Thinking with my dick is what got me in this predicament. I wish I had listened to my family."

"Drake, you're not the first man to think with your dick. You won't be the last. Women are smart, especially women like Channa. Look at her. She's stunning. A woman like that could fool the world."

"True, but I should have known better. I'm not the average nicca. I'm that nicca. I run shit. I make shit happen. I don't make stupid ass mistakes like this. Even my father warned me. I went against him for her. I'm shocked he hasn't disowned me over this shit."

"You know, I know your father personally. He's one of my closest friends. He loves you Drake, you and all your siblings. What you need to realize is your father is not exempt from secrets. He has things from his past that he regrets too. Trust me when I say he understands why you did what you did and what you're going through now. You should open up and talk to him."

I exhaled loudly. "I know, Ross, but Dream almost lost her life fucking around with me and my bullshit. Crazy ass Channa rammed into her like she was nothing. That shit hurt my heart. She came at Dream because of me. All this shit is my fault."

"Drake, stop being so hard on yourself, man. You didn't know. A pretty face and good pussy will trip a man up every time. You're not exempt. You're just stronger than most. It's a mistake. It happened. The shit's in the past now. Dream is good. She's back better than ever. You're finally getting rid of Channa, and now you can live happily ever after with the woman of your dreams."

"You think that shit gonna be that easy? Ain't no fuckin' way. Dream is going to leave my ass when she finds out she nearly died because of Channa. "

"I wouldn't tell her no time soon," Ross interjected.

"So, you don't think I should tell her at all?"

"No, I didn't say that. What I'm saying is don't tell her while she's pregnant. She just came out of a traumatic experience. Personally, I think you better put your game down for real. I mean eating pussy for breakfast, lunch, dinner, and snacks. If you don't suck toes, you better do that shit now. I would fuck her like my life depended on it because it does. I wouldn't tell her until her pussy responded on your command. She should be practically creaming when you call her name."

I chuckled. "You sound like my father now."

Ross put his hands up in surrender, smiling. "Hey, I'm guilty. That shit works. Also, once this divorce is final, you need to make Dream your wife. After she drops this load, you need to put another bun in the oven immediately. I wouldn't let her see her feet for about five years. Load her up with a bunch of babies. She definitely won't go nowhere."

"But I'm not trying to pump her full of babies and she don't want to be with me."

"Nicca, stop questioning the shit and just do it. Dream loves your prideful ass. You're just making sure she can't do nothing too stupid. Good dick and babies keep bitches on locked."

"Why do you think your mother has so many kids?"

Now, that statement made me really chuckle. My father stopped arguing with my mother a long time ago. Every time she got too out of line, he served her the dick. He told me that personally. He said it was his go-to method. Obviously, it worked. They are still happily married. My mother wouldn't stay if she wasn't happy. She was a strong black woman. She wouldn't think twice about packing her shit and leaving my father with the quickness.

"Why do you think your mother is always smiling? Good dick. A woman like your mother, a woman of her caliber, you can't do nothing else. She's a thoroughbred. A born gangsta. Her street shit is official. She's rich. There's nothing else she needs but multiple orgasms."

"Okay. Okay. I get the picture. The thought of my mother having multiple orgasms makes my head and my stomach hurt."

Ross cracked up. "I gotta give it to you straight, young nicca. You need to hear this shit."

"Yeah, I suppose I do. I just hate that Dream and Channa are both pregnant at the same time. How I managed to fuck up like that is beyond me. Then, on top of all that, there is Arizona and Arabia. I sent them away to save their lives. I had no idea that Channa used them to get to me, but I knew that, at some point, she would try to take them out. I can feel that shit in my bones. Channa don't know that I know what she did to Arizona previously. She beat that girl unconscious." I paused momentarily. "I should have known that Channa would go after Dream, based on what she did to Arizona."

"Cross the bridge when you get to it. It's not here yet, Drake. Let the past be the past, deal with the present, and handle the future later. If you keep thinking about what should have and what could have, you'll be crazy than a muthafucka. Your father trusted you with shit because he knew you could handle it. Has he called you fussing about any of this?"

"No," I admitted. "I had been waiting for him to call me to get in my ass, but he never did. All of his calls have been supportive."

"That's my point. Let me tell you something. I was there when you were born. Your father was the happiest man alive when you came into the world. He told everyone that you were going to be his legacy. You've lived up to his expectations."

"Yeah, I guess so. I'ma go see papi as soon as my doctor clears me. I got other shit to handle too. This fuck nicca Spencer. I know this muthafucka is up to something. I just know it."

"I don't understand why you allowed Dream to go home with that nicca no way."

"I had no choice. I didn't want Channa to know about Dream. I'm glad I did do it that way, especially since she tried to kill her before. My gut was like leave Channa in the dark, so she didn't go after Dream. The only way to do that was to allow Dream to go home. I wasn't worried about that nicca spazzing out, until Dream called me crying her first night home. Now, I'm just trying to get well, so I can handle that muthafucka. He thinks my baby is his baby, so I'm probably going to have to kill this nicca."

Ross snickered in disbelief. "There is no probably to it. You're going to have to get rid of that nicca. Whether that baby is yours-"

I cut him off, "The baby is mine either way."

"Aight, I hear you. I'm just saying this nicca ain't about to let nothing go. If you think Channa's a problem, this nicca about to go crazy. You're going to have to stop his ass before he does."

"I plan on it. I got less than two weeks to go. My casts are off, but my strength isn't there. I can use my arm and my leg, but I'm tired a lot faster than usual. My physical therapist said I should be one-hundred after our two-week session."

"So, where is the nicca now?"

"I don't know, but he needs to stay wherever the fuck he's been at for the last six weeks, if he knows what the fuck is good for him. That nicca definitely on borrowed time."

My phone vibrated, interrupting my conversation with Ross. It was Fresh. I forgot that I texted him. Our relationship hadn't been the best since I accused him of wanting Channa again. I even went so far as to say that she might be pregnant by him. He came to see me in the hospital and I snapped out. I said a bunch of hurtful things. I took jabs at him that I shouldn't have. All this shit was driving me crazy and I was taking a lot of it out on Fresh.

Me: I need to talk to you. Can you meet me for lunch?
Fresh texted me right back. Just tell me where.
Me: Hooters
Fresh: On my way

"I'm out, Ross. That was Fresh. I'm about to make things right."

Ross gave me a one arm hug. "It's about time. You can't have your right hand man upset. He's the first person to have your back. Squash that shit and get back to business."

"I am. It was my fault anyway."

Dream & Drake 3: A Cartel Love Story

On my drive to Hooters, I realized that I pushed the two closest people to me away. Fresh and Quay had been by my side since day one. If they ever needed me, I was always right there, no matter what. Now that I actually needed them, I didn't know how to react. I'd always been the rock. I never had to lean on anyone. I just had to keep it real with Fresh. I owed him that much.

Fresh was there when I got there. He was seated babysitting a drink when I walked up. Normally, we were ecstatic to see each other. I didn't think I ever felt knots in my stomach over a strained relationship before. Sitting here with Fresh and we were barely speaking, that hurt my fuckin' heart.

"What did you want to talk about?" Fresh asked with a slight attitude. "Everything's running smoothly, if that's what you want to know. Everyone's in place. Nothing's out of order. Even with this beef with who the fuck knows who, shit is still intact and moving like it should."

"That's not what I called you here for, but I appreciate that. I never had any doubts. You're one of the best. I trust your decisions."

Fresh sighed and cut his eyes at me before he went back to babysitting his drink.

"How you been, man?"

Fresh sighed again. "How do you think I've been? Precious had the baby, another girl. Her name is Pinky. She's six weeks."

I closed my eyes and shook my head. I was fucking up left and right. "Damn, I missed her birth."

Fresh shrugged and looked away. I knew that shit pissed him off, but he was such a hard ass. Fresh would never say it.

"I didn't mean to," I mumbled. This shit was harder than what I thought. "I'm a dickhead, Fresh. I never should have said what I said to you."

"It was uncalled for," Fresh replied with an attitude.

"It was. I realize that. I knew deep down that you didn't want Channa again. I just... I let my ego get the best of me."

"Now, what if I did that, Drake? If I let my ego get the best of me?"

125

I frowned. I didn't know where he was going with this. "Come again?"

"You heard me, nicca. What if I let my ego get the best of me that day when you walked in with my bitch and told me that she was no longer my bitch because she was now your bitch?"

"That's not how it happened, Fresh."

"No, but that's how it felt, Drake. You keep fuckin' forgetting that I'm your right hand man because I want to be. I'm not one of these little niccas that you recruit. I hold just as much weight in The Cartel as your ass. I walked beside you because I want to."

"Yeah, man, I know, and I'm sorry."

"No, you're not, Drake. You're just down right now, so your eyes have been opened. If you weren't going through some shit, you wouldn't even be here."

I had plenty that I wanted to say, but I just sat there and listened to Fresh vent. Obviously, he had some shit he wanted to get off his chest."

"Do you know how many times Channa has asked me to fuck her after you two were already together?"

I shook my head in shock. This fucking bitch was so foul. I played myself by marrying her.

"She tried to fuck me the day of your bachelor party. Did you know that? That's why I been telling you since forever to leave that bitch alone. She's been foul."

"Why didn't you tell me?"

"Hell, I had been trying to. I didn't come out and say it because I didn't want you to accuse me of what you accused me of."

Before I could ask that burning question, Fresh answered it for me.

"I never touched her once she walked out the door with you. Never. Recently, Precious came home and found Channa butt ass naked in our bed. Channa thought it was me coming home, instead of Precious. That's why Precious hates Channa. They are always going to have problems because of me. I did that by betraying Channa because I slept with her sister. Another

126

reason why I told you not to marry her. You were a rebound. That woman wanted me and she still does."

Fresh showed me all the texts from Channa. How she constantly begged him to take her back. How she was going to tell me that she was pregnant by Fresh if he didn't fuck her. She drove a wedge between me and my cousin and I allowed her to do so. I wasn't about to tell Fresh, but Channa was the reason why I thought he fucked her. She created that doubt by implying that Fresh still wanted her.

It was my turn to sigh. When the waitress approached us, I order two shots of Cîroc. I had been sipping on it since Quay's party a few months back.

"I'm glad you finally told me," I said, feeling like the biggest fool alive. "I was stupid. I should have listened. I didn't. Trust me, I paid for it dearly. That woman has ruined my damn life over the last ten years. I can't blame that on nobody but my damn self. I was selfish and did a fuck nicca move. I'm truly sorry. I just want us to get back to where we used to be."

As soon as the waitress sat the shots down, I took them both to the head. I wasn't even a drinker, but these last few weeks had me drinking and popping pain pills back to back, just to ease my mental and physical anguish.

"How can I make this right?"

Fresh shrugged.

Damn, I hurt him deeper than what I thought.

"Just let me know. Whatever it is, I'm willing to do…"

I got a call while I was pleading my cousinship to Fresh. I answered immediately, thinking that something was wrong with Dream.

"Is this Drake Diaz-Santana?"

My heart dropped at the formality. "Yes."

"This is Officer Mally. You need to come home immediately. Your house is on fire."

"WHAT THE FUCK!!!" I alarmed everyone in the place with my booming voice.

"We're trying to put it out and salvage what we can. You need to get here asap."

"I'm on my way," I said, jumping up from my seat.

"What's wrong?" Fresh asked, alarmed.

"My damn house is on fire."

"What?" Fresh asked in disbelief. "I'll be right there. Let me pay the tab."

I rushed out of Hooters on twenty. My face was so red that the air in the car couldn't cool it down. Shit got real when I pulled up on my block and saw a million fire trucks, police cars, and even an ambulance. I talked all that shit, but the first thing I thought was something bad happened to Channa. Fresh just pulled up behind me when I raced through the crowd.

"Let him through," the police officer said, referring to me.

I walked right up to Mega, who was talking to a fireman. "What happened?"

Mega shot me a look. I knew that meant to fall back from asking or saying too much. Some fuck shit went down.

"I'm Noah," one of the firemen said. "I was just telling your brother that someone set your house on fire. Your garage and your cars are destroyed.

I felt a lump form in my throat. I handpicked every last one of those cars. Then, I stared at our childhood home and blinked back tears. The home that we grew up in was destroyed.

"We're going to salvage everything that we can," Noah said. "I promise."

"Thank you," Mega said because I was in shock. Mega pulled me aside.

"It was Channa," he said, making my blood boil even more. "She drove pass me when I pulled onto the block. She was in that car that you just bought. I didn't think anything of it until I was about to turn into my driveway and noticed that your house was on fire."

Fresh raced over to us. "What the fuck happened?" He looked as distraught as I was. "Don't tell me them niccas we beefing with did a bitch move like this."

"No, it was Channa," Mega confirmed. "Not only did I see her driving off the block. My security cameras caught her loading up Drake's car around the time his house went up in smoke."

"I'm about to kill this bitch."

I had my gun in my hand before I knew it. I was on my way to find Channa's ratchet ass and put a bullet in her head. Fuck her and them kids. I was shooting that hoe on sight.

Fresh must've known I was about to set shit all the way off. He snatched the gun out of my hand and tucked it in his waist before anyone could see it. I was so outdone; I literally couldn't think straight. Fresh put his arm around my neck to keep me from leaving. He almost had me in a headlock.

"I'ma get Drake out of here. Can you handle this?" Fresh asked Mega.

"Yeah, I got it. I'll follow up with y'all after they put the fire out."

Fresh was walking backwards, pulling me away with him. "Give them my number as a person of contact. I don't want them contacting Drake."

Fresh pretty much drug me over to his car, forcing me to get in. Before I got in his car, I stood there in a daze as the firemen continued to spray water on my house.

"I can't believe this fuckin bitch has burned my shit up."

"Get in, Drake!" Fresh called out.

"I'm so outdone, man," I said, getting in to the car. I felt like I was about to have a nervous breakdown.

"Did you have anything of value in the house?"

"Not really," I said with disgust. "It's the principle about it."

"Let's hit the strip club. Ass and titties always makes my day better."

Chapter 22

Dream

I tried on at least ten outfits before I fell back on the bed crying. I was now six months pregnant and I couldn't fit none of the shit in my closet, once again. I felt like a whale. Lying back on the bed, I covered my face with my hands and balled.

"Stop crying," Drake said.

I felt his weight on the bed as he climbed towards me.

"What are you doing here?" I cried. "You're supposed to be at therapy."

"That shit could wait. I knew today was important to you." He scooted closer to me, putting his hand on my stomach. "You want to stunt on these hoes on your first day back, right?"

I took my hands off of my eyes and laughed. "What are you even saying? Where did you learn to talk like that?" I laughed some more.

"From you." Drake laughed too. "All them damn conversations about those chicks at your job."

"Baby," I said, jumping up from the bed. I wasn't even crying anymore when I saw the maternity skirt suit and kitten heels. "You did this for me?"

"Listen," he said, pounding his fist into his hand. "If you ain't right, I'm not right. Whatever I gotta do, I'm going to do it, feel me, ma?"

"I love it," I squealed.

Drake kissed me and I felt like I was on top of the world. I never expected him to show up here with my clothes for my first day back.

"Fuck these haters, boo," he said, repeating one of Mercy's favorite lines.

I cracked up. "Fuck 'em," I cosigned, throwing my hands in the air dramatically.

"Fuck 'em then, shit."

I laughed so hard. Drake was imitating Mercy so well. I was too tickled.

He continued to imitate her, "I got your bitch. Drake, you better get this hoe before I stomp a hole in her ass. Tell her ass she's messing with the wrong one. The next time she disrespects me, I'm going to put a hot slug in her ass."

"When did she say that?" I wondered, cracking up.

Drake cracked up too. "When you were in a coma. I took Mercy out to lunch. We were on our way to see you, and Channa rolled up. Mercy went off."

I smiled, taking off my pajama bottoms. "That's my bestie. She got my back, for real, for real."

"I'm trying to have your back, for real, for real," Drake said while coming up behind me, squeezing my big breasts. "I love these big ass titties."

"Don't get used to them because I'm not keeping them after the baby is born."

"Well, let me enjoy them now," he said, spinning me around. My breast was in his mouth before I knew it.

Drake picked me up and put me on the dresser, spreading my legs. "Lean back, baby, so I can work this tongue."

I moaned when I felt him licking between my legs frantically. "Slow down," I squealed. "You're about to make me cum."

"That's the object," he said, sucking and licking on my clit simultaneously.

"Aaaah! That shit feels gooood," I said, gripping Drake's head when I felt his tongue inside of me. He was licking from my ass to my clit.

"Cum on my tongue, ma," he begged.

I couldn't fight my orgasm any longer. "Oooh! Ooooh! Ooooh! Draaaake!"

"Release them juices, ma, so I can lick this pussy clean."

That's exactly what I did as soon as the words left his mouth. I held onto my thighs as I came. Drake's tongue felt so fucking good that I couldn't even speak. I bit my lip and released my sweet juices. Drake licked my pussy like he was starving.

"That shit was so good, all over my face."

He stood to his feet and pulled his pants and boxers down. His dick was inside of me within seconds. He ripped my night shirt off of me and started sucking my breasts.

"Damn, I love sucking your big titties," he exclaimed while thrusting inside of me harder.

Drake just entered me and I felt like I was about to cum again.

"You love this dick, ma?"

"Yes, baby," I stated as my legs started to shake. The tremble started at my toes. I screamed as loud as I could. The orgasm was so sweet that it took its muthafuckin time going through out my body before it rested in my pussy. "Drrrraaaaakkkke!" I finally cried out, squirting cum all over the place.

"Flip that ass over," Drake said, yanking me off the dresser. I was still weak, so I almost lost my balance. He caught me and leaned me over the dresser, sliding his big dick inside of me.

"Oh, shit, Drake."

"You better take this dick," he stated.

I showed him how much I planned on taking his dick by throwing my ass back. I might have been pregnant, big as a house, but I was throwing the hell out of my pussy.

"Damn, Dream, you tryna make a nicca tap out?"

"Yes," I said smiling.

He grabbed my breasts again, kneading my nipples between his fingers. I felt like I was going to lose my mind. My orgasm was building once again. Drake had me so fucking sprung off his dick. I moaned loudly as I anticipated the feeling that was about to attack my pussy.

"Yeah, baby, take this dick like only you can."

"Drrrraaaaakkkke! Your dick feels so damn good."

"Your pussy feels so damn good, ma. I need you to cum, so I can bust a nut."

My orgasm ripped through my body like a hail of bullets. I was bucking against Drake so hard that I thought I was going to hurt the baby.

"Don't stop fucking this pussy, baby," I moaned while cumming.

Drake gripped my arms, pulling them behind my back as I lost my damn mind cumming. He continued to dick me down as I screamed for dear life.

"Give me that dick. Fuck me with that big diiiiiiiiiick," I exclaimed as I creamed.

"Now, let me get mine before you be late for work."

I surprised Drake when I moved away from him and kneeled, taking his erection into my mouth. I didn't care that I was tasting my own juices. I just wanted Drake to cum harder than he'd ever came. I was an expert at sucking his dick now. I knew exactly how he liked it. Slowly, I sucked on his dick, licking it with pleasure. Then, I spit on it a few times and licked it off.

"You so nasty," Drake said, looking me in the eye.

"Nasty for you, baby. Can't nobody suck this dick like me."

"You my little freak?"

"I'll be anything you want me to be," I said truthfully. I was far from being the Dream before the coma. Since waking up, I was a fearless bitch. Ride or die was becoming natural every day.

I swallowed Drake's dick whole, showing him that I meant business. I loved sucking his dick now that I was a pro. Grabbing his ass, I forced his dick even further down my throat until it was practically touching my esophagus. I tried to stick my finger in his ass, and he hit me in my head.

"Quit all that fuck shit, Dream. You play too damn much with that fruity shit."

I smiled with his dick in my mouth, but I never quit sucking. I gripped his hips instead, continuing to suck. I knew I was sucking Drake right because his eyes were closed and he looked in a zone. He was about to cum. Instead of sucking his cum down my throat like I usually did, I pulled his dick out of my mouth and jerked his seed all over my face. I had never done that, but knowing that these bitches were after my man caused me to step my game up.

Channa was my biggest rivalry. She was married to my man and pregnant by him. If I wasn't carrying his baby, I felt like I would always be in her shadow. Then, there was Arizona and Arabia. I know Drake sent them away. He told me he did. That didn't change the fact that, at one time he had deep feelings for Arizona, and he was quickly falling for her sister. I had to beat out all these hoes who wanted my man. He was mine, and I intended to fuck him, suck him, and kill for him if I had to just to keep him.

Drake took his dick out of my hand and stepped out of his clothes. "Take a shower with me."

I was hot and sticky, so I followed behind him to the shower. We had another quickie in the shower. I guess we both couldn't get enough of each other. This time, I bent over in the shower while Drake rammed me from behind until he came.

Afterwards, we got out of the shower and dressed. I put on the new skirt suit that Drake bought me. I looked stunning when I looked in the mirror. Once I fixed my hair and applied my make-up, I was ready for my first day. Drake held the door open to the white Mercedes. This car must've been new because I'd never seen it before. As we drove downtown, he constantly rubbed my stomach and kissed my hand. When we pulled up, he tongued me down.

"I love you, ma."

I stared into Drake's sincere eyes and replied back, "I love you too."

We kissed a few minutes more before I reminded him that I was having lunch with Mercy, and she was giving me a ride home.

"Aren't you glowing this morning," Mercy exclaimed, looking me up and down. "Looks like someone had something more than breakfast."

All I could do was smile. Drake's loving had me feeling radiant.

"Must be nice," Mercy said, acting like she was jealous.

I smirked at her and we both cracked up laughing.

"You could be getting some good dick too, if you would give Mega a chance."

"Okay, that is my clue to exit."

"Good D will change your life. It'll clear up your skin."

"Girl, get on with all that. I had one period pimple, and the shit is gone now. I'm flawless again, bitch. Getcho life."

I cracked up as Mercy did a runway walk down the hall. I shook my head at her crazy ass and opened my office door. I was in shock when I saw all of the roses adorning my office. Immediately, I thought of Drake. He'd outdone himself this time. I was just about to call Drake when my manger stepped into my office.

"Oh, you're here," he said, shocked to see me. "I was just about to…" he stopped speaking and smiled. He hugged me and then stared at my stomach. "We'll talk about that later. Welcome back. I'm glad you're okay. Now, follow me."

He practically pulled my arm out of socket as he led me to the conference room filled with everyone on our floor. Well, everyone except for Mercy. I didn't know where she was at. I could really use her assistance right now. I stared at the time and realized that she was probably somewhere hunting down a fresh pot of coffee.

"What's all this?" I asked because the conference room was filled with flowers too.

I opened my mouth to speak again, but I was silenced when I saw Spencer standing before me. This nicca had been missing for weeks and, now, he wanted to pop up at my job.

"What is this?" I whispered when I got in his personal space.

"I'm giving you what you always wanted."

He smiled and I could see bullshit in my future. He pulled out his phone and went live. After grabbing my hand, he got down on one knee and pulled out a ring box.

With the camera all in my face, he said, "Dream, I should have done this a long time ago. I knew from the moment you walked into the wrong class that we were meant to be."

Everyone sighed. I heard ooohs and aaaaahs.

"Dream Holloway, will you marry me?"

"Don't do this," I mumbled.

He knew how much marriage meant to me. Why would he make a mockery out of it? I wanted to say no so badly. I looked at my supervisor's face and all of my co-worker's faces. They looked so hopeful. At one point in my life, I wished for this day. It figured Spencer would do this shit after I'd moved on with Drake.

"What did you say?" Spencer said loudly.

"You heard me," I mumbled again. "Don't do this."

"She said yes everybody," Spencer told everyone.

He slipped the ring on my finger and stood to his feet. Everyone cheered loudly and screamed.

How could he do this? I wondered, with tears in my eyes. Everyone was congratulating me and I hadn't even said yes. I wanted to pick up one of the chairs and throw it at his ass. Just as everyone was celebrating, Mercy walked in.

"What's going on?" Mercy looked around as she sauntered in with a cup of coffee.

"Dream just got engaged," one of our co-workers announced with excitement.

Mercy rushed over to me, smiling. She looked at the ring and hugged me. The smile wiped off her face when she looked to my left and saw Spencer.

"What the hell is he doing here?"

I was so hurt that all I could do was cry.

"Please tell me that you didn't play Drake for this sorry ass nicca."

"Meet me in my office," I told Mercy. "I'll be there in a few minutes."

"Bitch, you better. Drake is going to murder your pregnant ass." Mercy sauntered off.

"Okay, the celebration is over people," my manager stated. "Congratulations to Dream and Spencer, but time is money and money is time."

Everyone groaned as they filed out of the conference room. Before long, it was just me and Spencer.

"I was thinking we can have a small wedding-"

SLAP!

I smacked fire from his ass. "You know I didn't say yes."

"Yes, you did," he lied again. "I heard you."

"You didn't hear shit," I snapped.

I was so angry that I had to leave or I was going to end up having a miscarriage, whooping his muthafucking ass.

"Don't follow me either."

"I got to get back to work, but I'll see you later wifey."

My blood boiled while I made my way to my office. People wanted to congratulate me more and make small talk about my fake ass engagement, but I played all of them to the left. Before another person could ask me anymore questions, I scurried inside of my office and closed the door.

"This day is crazy already, and it's still in the am."

"True, but it's about to get even crazier," Mercy stated.

"Why you say that?" I asked, slightly out of breath.

Mercy held up her phone and I watched the video of the engagement replay before my eyes.

"This shit is everywhere. You better hope that Drake doesn't see it."

"Awww, fuck!" I yelled.

I tried to call Drake. There was no answer.

"Damn!" I screamed, tossing my phone on the floor.

"Calm down. You're going to upset the baby. How about we do that offsite visit together? Then, we can go get lunch. The fresh air will do you some good, and we can talk without all these nosy heffas lurking."

Listening to Mercy speak reminded me of Drake imitating her earlier.

I giggled. "I think that's a good idea because I might kill Spencer if he comes back."

"What do you think Destiny is going to say when she finds out?"

I picked my phone up off the floor. "Who cares. I just wish he proposed to her and not me."

Mercy laughed loudly. "That'll never happen."

Chapter 23

Drake

"Your therapist is bad as fuck," Quay whispered in my ear.

Out of all the niccas I had to ask to come with me to my last therapy session, I had to ask this horny ass nicca. Quay always had sex on his mind. Money is always number one. Sex shortly follows.

"Which one?" I asked, entertaining his lustful thoughts. I had two therapists. I assumed he wasn't talking about the white one who took care of my arm.

"You know which one. The one with the small waist and fat ass."

I snickered at this nicca here. "You're talking about Kay Kay," I answered while pushing myself to do these leg lifts on this machine.

"Kay Kay," he said seductively. "She looks like she needs some dick."

"If you don't get your ass back," I laughed. "It feels like you're whispering sweet nothings in my damn ear. I ain't Kay Kay, nicca."

"I'm saying, set that up tho, Drake."

"Nicca, chill. You always act like you're pressed for chicks when you got a million. If she's just a piece of ass to you, you need to act like it. You're the only muthafucka I know that acts like a damn virgin seeking his first lay."

Quay grinned. "I can't help it if I think with my dick."

"Obviously, I can't help the shit either."

We both laughed loudly, which got Kay Kay's attention.

"Are you over here getting in trouble?" she asked, approaching us.

I see why Quay had a thing for her. She was bad. Her workout attire was banging. If I wasn't so focused on my leg, my dick would be hard too. Since dedicating myself to Dream and Dream only, I had been doing good by keeping my dick in my pants. I planned on keeping it that way. I'd admit, working out with Kay Kay had been a little tough. She'd been professional in every way, but I was still a man. Quay was right. She did have a fat ass. I could look, as long as I didn't touch.

Quay spoke up." It was me. I think I hurt myself trying to use this machine. I think I might need therapy too. Ouch," he faked, holding his leg.

Kay Kay giggled. "Boy, you're stupid. You haven't used one piece of equipment since you been here."

"Are you doubting me, ma?" Quay inquired, looking at Kay Kay like a piece of meat.

She looked over her shoulder and smiled at him before she stooped down, tending to my leg. "I'll address your doubt after I do my job."

Quay licked his lips. "I'll enjoy the view while you do your thing, ma."

I locked eyes with my cousin and he smiled. This wild ass nicca here. Quay fell back, while Kay Kay and I spent another hour together working on my leg. She massaged my leg, I worked out some more, and then she helped me stretch. I couldn't lie, the shit felt good. It felt like I had my leg back.

"You're good as new," Kay Kay said, helping me up and hugging me.

"I feel like my old self again," I exclaimed.

"Good. I'm glad to hear. That means I did my job."

"Drake, you ready to do this!" my other therapist called out.

"Yeah, I'm ready, Shelby," I said, about to walk away. I had to double back and holler at Quay. "Nicca, don't fuck her up in here while I'm having therapy."

"But, what if she want it, tho?" he asked with that cheesy grin he always gave when he was up to something. "I gotta give her what she wants."

"You better wait. Do that shit when I don't have therapy. I'm trying to get a clean bill of health and bust out this bitch."

"Cock-blocking ass."

"You fuckin' heard me," I gritted. "Do that shit on your own time."

Quay grinned. "For you, I'ma chill. But, just so you know, I'ma bang your therapist." He thrusted his pelvis for added emphasis.

"Your ass will be last on my list of people to call next time."

"Whatever, you called me cause you know I make therapy fun."

I flipped Quay the bird and walked over to Shelby, and Quay sat on one of the leg machines talking to Kay Kay. I just knew that Quay would go against me and take Kay Kay to the back, but he didn't. He kept it PG, talking to her for the next two hours. Honestly, I didn't think he had it in him.

"We're done," Shelby announced.

I jogged in place, happy as hell that I had my arm and my leg back. I couldn't wait to get back to business, back to breaking niccas down. I was sure they were stepping on my name because I'd been hurt and gone too long. It was time to show my face and put in some work, so that muthafuckas understood that Drake couldn't be broken.

After I showered and changed, I told Quay I was ready to go. He hugged Kay Kay, and I hugged her and Shelby too. I told them both no offense, but I didn't care if I ever saw them again. They laughed at me and told me take care.

"I saw the goo goo eyes Kay gave you as we left. You better not had fucked her."

"Take your panties out of your ass, nicca. I didn't fuck her. I did finger her and suck on her titties until she came."

"Gawd, your ass is nasty."

"I learned it from your nasty ass. You were fuckin' in middle school."

I cracked up. "I might be a little nasty."

"Hell yeah, you got two women pregnant at the same damn time. Bruh, that's nasty."

I laughed even harder. "You got a point. I love pussy. What can I say."

"I do too. Don't hate the player, hate the game, nicca."

We were jonin' going back and forth, cracking on each other like we did when we were kids, when Quay got serious all of a sudden. I was driving, but I could tell he was watching some kind of video.

"Bruh, you not about to believe the fuck shit I'm about to show you. Pull over."

I did as he said and pulled over, looking at his phone. Sure enough, I didn't believe it. My mouth hung open as I watched this punk ass nicca Spencer surface. He'd been missing for a hot ass minute. I see he showed up bearing gifts. I had a gift for his ass, my fuckin' gun.

"I'm going straight to her job," I said, darting into traffic like speed racer.

I pulled up and double parked. "Stay here, Quay."

"I got you," he replied, sliding into the driver's seat when I got out.

I walked into IHealth like a tornado. The receptionist must've known I was on a war path because she didn't even stop me. Lucky for her she didn't because I might have knocked her the fuck out. I went to Dream's office and she wasn't there. I looked a little more until I bumped into one of her co-workers, who said she was off site. I got the address from her and left out of there on a mission.

"Drive to this address," I told Quay, jumping into the passenger's seat.

"You got it. Is this where Dream is?"

"Yeah, her and Mercy are off site. I'm about to pop up on her ass."

"Bruh, you think that whole thing was real? It's the internet, so shit ain't always believable."

"That shit really happened. I'm positive."

"What you gonna do when you do see her?"

"Snatch her ass up. Ain't no way I'm going to sit back and let her marry that lame nicca. She belongs to me."

Quay snickered. "You say it like she don't have a choice."

"She don't. She's mine. That pussy is mine. The baby is mine. She better act like she understands that shit or we about to have a problem."

As soon as we pulled up, Mercy and Dream were walking to Mercy's car. I was about to hop out when Quay suggested that we follow them instead, so that's what we did. We trailed them to a small restaurant. They parked and got out, so did we.

"Don't act no fool in here, Drake," Quay said when he saw me grab my gun.

"I'm not going to act a fool, unless Dream gives me a reason to."

She was key-keying and slapping the table, having a good damn time with Mercy while that nicca's ring was on her finger.

"So, when the fuck where you going to tell me about this shit?" I asked Dream, startling her.

"Drake, you scared me," she said, grabbing her chest.

"I should be scaring your ass. You out here doing scary shit. Now, answer my damn question," I exclaimed, sliding into the booth next to her. I sat my gun on my lap, just in case she thought I was playing. "Choose your words carefully, if you don't want to be carried out of here in a body bag."

Dream was already crying, looking guilty, and pissing me off.

"It's not what you think," Mercy said, trying to defend Dream.

"You stay out of it," I snapped at Mercy. "This don't concern you. It's between me and Dream. Fall the fuck back."

Mercy sighed.

I continued. "She's wearing the proof on her finger," I said, grabbing Dream's hand." So, it's exactly what I think. You on bullshit, ma," I said, addressing Dream again.

"Drake, you're overreacting," Mercy defended.

Quay shut Mercy down. "Stay in your place, ma. This ain't got nothing to do with you. He already told you to keep your nose on your face, feel me?"

Mercy eyed Quay hard before she rolled her eyes, keeping quiet.

I directed my attention back to Dream. "Fuck is you on? I had to see this shit on social media? You couldn't tell me yourself. If you wanted to be with that nicca, all you had to do was say so. I would have stepped the fuck off. You and him could live happily ever after," I chuckled out of anger. "I got hoes still trying to get at me, but I choose you. Let me know, so I can do me."

"Wait, what hoes?"

"Don't changed the fuckin' subject. This ain't about me. It's about your ass getting engaged for the world to see. That shit went viral."

"Drake, it ain't even like that," she cried. "I didn't say yes. I was questioning him why, when he slipped the ring on my finger. He lied on me. You gotta believe me."

"I don't believe shit. That ain't what it look like to me, ma, but it's cool. You can have that nicca. Fuck you and fuck his bitch ass. Y'all deserve each other. This shit just came full circle. I should have never fucked with your ass in the first place."

I got up from the booth and Dream scooted out too. "C'mon, Quay," I demanded.

Quay grilled Mercy and Dream before he slid out, standing by my side. We were walking out when Dream ran up to me, trying to stop me from leaving.

"Drake, don't do this. I want to be with you. I'm giving Spencer back his ring."

"I can't fucking tell," I said, knocking her arm off my shoulder. "Don't fuckin' touch me, ma. Go touch that nicca, your fuckin' fiancé."

"He's not my fiancé," Dream bawled. "I swear, it's not how it looks."

"Fuck what you talking about. That ring on your finger from that nicca is all I need to know."

"But, what about our plan?" Dream had the nerve to ask me.

"Fuck you and that bullshit ass plan," I barked, walking out of the restaurant followed by Quay.

"You think she's telling the truth?" Quay asked me as we approached the car.

"Fuck her." I was so pissed; I couldn't think of nothing else to say. I wanted to shoot up the restaurant, just to let off some steam.

"I mean, that Spencer nicca is gunning for you. He could be on that bullshit, for real."

"True, I'ma fuck around and kill that nicca. He's trying me. He has no idea that I will body his goofy ass."

"Let me look at this video again," Quay said, pulling out his phone. "Shit ain't right."

Chapter 24

Drake

"Take me home," I cried in Mercy's arms. "He doesn't love me no more. Take me home."

"Shhhhh!" Mercy quietly patted my back as my head rested against her bosom.

I managed to make it back to our booth before I collapsed in her arms.

"Drake left me," I whined.

Mercy smoothed my hair out of my face. "He didn't leave you, Dream. He's just hurt by your actions. Why did you take the ring from Spencer in the first place?"

"I don't know. It all just happened so fast." I picked up a tissue and blew my nose. "And it was my first day back, people were looking at my stomach, and I just felt weird from the moment I walked in. I didn't want to cause any drama."

"You know what you need to do, right?"

"No, what?" I asked because I truly didn't know. My brain felt cloudy, like it was on overload. Just thinking about being without Drake had me depressed.

"You gotta give that fuckin' ring back and prove to Drake that he's your king. Do that shit live like Spencer did you if you have to. Whatever it takes to get your man back."

I sniffled. "I'ma do what I gotta do."

"Shit yeah. Don't lose your man over that stupid nicca. I'll bet any amount of money he was doing that more for Drake than you. Spencer ain't stupid. He knows about Drake, I'm sure. He wanted to push him out the way so that he could have you all to himself. Don't let that nicca win. You better than that. Besides, the nasty fucker is with Destiny, and we both know she's been ran through."

Her last statement made me laugh.

"Is everything okay?" the waiter asked.

Mercy gave a half-hearted smile. "Pregnancy woes."

"Can I get you ladies anything else?"

"No, just the check please," she told the waiter.

He tore the paper off of his pad and placed it down on the table faced down.

I tried to reach for the bill, but Mercy lightly slapped my hand. "Girl, I got it. You just pull yourself together."

I dabbed at my eyes and fixed my make-up while Mercy paid the tab. When she came back, I was ready to confront Spencer and give him his ring back. As soon as we got into the car, I was about to text Spencer when my mother called me crying. She said get over there asap.

"What did she say?" Mercy asked frantically, as she hit the expressway headed to Chatham.

"She didn't say," I said through tears, once again. "She just said it was bad and that I needed to come right away."

Mercy drove fast and crazy like she always drove. We were at my mother's house in no time. My father answered the door and he was all shook up too.

"What's going on?" I asked, looking from him to her.

"Baby, we didn't want to alarm you, but we…" My mother started crying hysterically, unable to finish her sentence.

My father stepped up, clearing his throat. He had tears in his eyes that he refused to let fall. "We didn't want to alarm you while you were in the hospital, but we filed a missing person's report on your sister a long time ago."

"Wait, you mean everything you told me in the hospital about Bey was a lie?" I asked in confusion.

"No, your mother had an argument with Bey, but that was months ago. What she lied about was the fact that we filed a missing person's report, and there was a detective assigned to her case."

I sat down, totally flabbergasted. "So, what does all this mean?"

My father choked back tears. "We got some bad news, honey. Bey is dead."

"NOOOOOOOOOOOOOOOOOOOOO! SHE CAN'T BE!" I yelled, falling out of the chair onto my knees.

Mercy rushed to my side to help me, but I didn't even want to be helped. I wiped my tears. My parents were both crying too.

"How?" I asked angrily. "How do you know that she's dead? Tell me, dammit. How?"

"Her body was delivered to my office in a box," a man that I never saw before said. He must've saw the confused look on my face and decided to introduce himself. "I'm Detective Morley."

I was so hurt by the news that I didn't even see the detective standing off to the side.

"Dream, I understand if you have any questions. I'll be glad to answer them."

I was at a loss of words. Every time I opened my mouth, a fresh stream of tears coated my cheeks. I could tell my parents felt the same way because they were hugging each other, crying as well. Thank goodness Mercy was there. Just like she always did, she spoke up in our defense.

"So, you said they delivered her in a box. Can you clarify that?" She was texting as she spoke, as well as holding on to me to make sure that I didn't fall. I noticed that she'd been texting since we walked in.

"Well, we've been in constant contact with her captors and well... things didn't go as planned," Detective Morley stated.

"What do you mean things didn't go as planned? Mercy asked angrily. "Is that code for your department fucked up? That your department didn't do its job? That someone dropped the ball and now my best friend's sister is dead? Say something?"

Dream & Drake 3: A Cartel Love Story

Detective Morley sighed loudly. "You're right. All of the above."

While Detective Morley and Mercy were going back and forth, there was a knock at the door. Mercy told the detective to pause while she answered the door. He looked a little uneasy, but he didn't stop her from going. That's when Mega walked in, followed by Drake.

"What's going on?" Drake asked clueless. Immediately, he rushed by my side on the floor. "Ma, are you okay?"

I fell into his arms, sobbing. "No, Drake, I'm not."

My parents were so distraught that they were still hugging each other and crying.

"Tell them what you told us," Mercy demanded.

Detective Morley ran the story down to Drake and Mega, telling them that he was in his office when he got a special delivery. He didn't think anything of it until he noticed that it was leaking blood. That's when he opened it and saw cut up body parts. When they ran the blood, it was a match to Bey.

Mega started laughing and that threw us all off. Everyone in the room stared at him as he laughed hysterically.

"I'm going to kill this punk," my daddy said, lunging at Mega. Mercy and my mother held him back.

"Daddy, it's not what you think," I said, defending Mega.

"That's the oldest trick in the book," Mega said nonchalantly, totally ignoring my father's tirade.

"I don't follow," the detective said with a perplexed look on his face.

"Did you test the body?" Mega asked confidently.

Detective Morley stared at him confused. "It was her blood."

"Yes," Mega stated with authority. "It was her blood, but was that her body in the box? Was that her remains that the blood was on?"

The detective stared at all of us. "You know, I don't know."

Mega smiled. "Double check. I'll bet any amount of money that it's her blood, but the body of another person."

Princess Diamond

Detective Morley stepped outside to place a call. He was about to insist that the body be tested to see who the remains belonged too immediately.

I stood to my feet, charging at Mega. "You said my sister wasn't dead. You told me to trust you and you would get back to me, and this is what I get hit with."

I balled up my fist and continue to hit Mega in frustration. He let me hit him a few times before he grabbed my wrists. Drake held me from behind, easing me away from Mega so that I wouldn't be able to keep hitting him. I took a seat on the sofa, crying my eyes out even more.

"You need to stop all that crying," Drake demanded. "If my son comes here retarded because you're acting a damn fool, I'm going to beat your ass."

I wiped my teary eyes with the back of my sleeves. "You better not put your hands on me."

"Then, stop all that crying and shit," Drake whispered in my ear.

"What do you care? You were about to leave me," I spat.

"I'm not leaving shit. You about to give that nicca back his ring before I break your finger trying to get it off."

"And what about my sister? She's dead and we're sitting around here doing nothing."

Mega spoke up this time. "I told you, your sister isn't dead." He kneeled before me. "Do you trust me?"

I stared into his gray eyes. He was so close that he was making me nervous. I could see the killer hidden behind his eyes, and it scared me.

"Do you fuckin' trust me?" he asked again. This time, he sounded more vicious.

"Yes," I said nervously.

He whispered, "Your sister is alive. This fuck off detective don't know shit. I wouldn't lie to you, ma."

I still wasn't convinced. "Do you trust him?" I asked Mercy.

She nodded. "He's crazy as fuck, but I trust him. I don't think he would lie about Bey being alive and she isn't. I felt like he knew more about what was going on from the moment he took her phone."

"I do," Mega said. "Let me handle this my way. Trust me when I tell you, Bey is coming home safely."

"Are you sure?" my mother asked in a soft voice. "Can you promise me that?"

"I promise you that I will risk my life saving her," Mega said positively.

"So, you know where my daughter is?" my father inquired.

"No," Mega said.

Everyone sighed in agony.

"Let me explain," Mega acknowledged. "I almost had her, but they keep moving locations. I believe that the body that the detective has belongs to another missing girl and not Bey. We won't be sure until the lab checks it out. I'm almost certain that I'm correct."

"Listen," my father said in a stern voice. "Whatever you have to do to bring my baby back home safely, I'm with it. I don't care if the shit is illegal. Do you need money?" he asked, reaching into his pocket. "A ransom or anything like that? I'll pay you for my baby girl's safety." My father's voice cracked and we were all in tears again. Well, everyone except for Mega and Drake.

"That's not necessary, sir," Mega said truthfully. "Bey and Dream are like family. It will be my pleasure to find her. I have a whole team looking for her..."

We all hushed when Detective Morley came back into the room with his phone in his hand. "They're going to test the body again."

"As they should," Mercy said with an attitude. "Half ass stats being presented to us."

"Well, I better go. They'll have the findings within a few hours. I want to be at the lab when they find out. I'll follow up with you, who can I call?" Detective Morley asked.

"Me," my father said.

"Okay, I'll follow up with you in a few hours."

As Detective Morley was leaving, Mega asked him if he could talk to him as they walked out. The detective said okay and they spoke quietly walking towards the door.

My father stared at Drake. "I guess I owe you for looking out for my baby girl."

Drake waved him off. "You don't owe me nothing but your blessing."

"My blessing?" he asked. My blessing for what?"

"To marry your daughter. When my divorce is final, I want to make things official with Dream."

"You have my blessing," my father said. I could tell that as much as he used to despise Drake, his approval was sincere.

I never saw it coming, but Drake got down on one knee before me. He pulled out a gold ring box, opening it with the biggest ring that I'd ever seen.

"Dream, I haven't been perfect. I've made a lot of mistakes but, if you do me the honor of being my wife, I promise to protect you, provide for you, and profess my love to you always. I want to marry you, not just because you're pregnant, but because you complete me. Will you marry me?"

I jumped into his arms, knocking him to the floor and kissing him all over his face. "Yes! Yes! Yes!"

I held out my hand. Drake snatched off Spencer's ring and he placed his ring on my finger.

"I love you, ma. I'm sorry for earlier. I didn't mean it."

"I'm sorry for putting you in that position. I love you too."

We laid on the floor kissing for what felt like forever until my father cleared his throat. "I said you had my blessing, but I won't allow my house to be disrespected."

Drake stopped kissing me. "I'm sorry, sir. It won't happen again," he said, helping me up off the floor.

"Yes it will," my mother said with a large grin. "You two love each other. It'll happen over and over again, won't it, Donald?"

My father lovingly kissed my mother. "If they're anything like us, watch out now."

I was just happy to see my parents smiling after they were just crying a few minutes ago. The fact that my father was giving Drake a chance made me smile. I loved him and I planned on marrying him as soon as possible.

Mega walked back inside. "We gotta go, Drake. The detective said we can be there for the results."

Drake kissed me and then let me go. "I'll be back, ma. Keep it tight while I'm gone."

"What about Spencer's ring?" I questioned.

"I'll give it back to him. You just stay away from that nicca. Don't go back to that house unless someone is with you. I'll come back here to get you; you're staying with me."

"Okay," I agreed.

"You two make sure you find my baby," my father said once again to Mega and Drake.

"We got you," Mega assured him before they left.

Once they were gone, I spoke to my parents candidly. We knew there was a possibility that Bey could be dead, but we much rather believe that Mega had everything under control. None of our hearts could handle her death right now. Call us naïve, but we choose to believe in her life and not her death. Deep down inside, I think we were all scared.

Mercy decided to stay the night with me. We slept in my old room together, like we did when we were kids.

"You think your father really gonna accept Drake?"

I toyed with my ring. "Does he have a choice?"

"Shit, not really. That nicca pretty much claimed your ass. What you gonna tell Spencer?"

"I don't know. Honestly, I don't even want to think about it."

"Well, I'm going to be with you every step of the way. And I better be your maid of honor; I don't care if Bey's ass do come back. I better be number one," Mercy pouted. "I'm just saying."

"How about I choose both of you?"

Mercy grinned, showing all of her teeth. "I can live with that," she said hugging me, squeezing me and the baby tight.

"You're too close," I said, trying to push her away, but she was hanging on tight.

Mercy kissed me on the cheek and rolled over, putting her butt on me. "Goodnight, Mrs. Drake Diaz-Santana."

I wanted to booty bump her out the bed, but I decided to get her back the same way she got me. "Goodnight to you too, Mrs. Mega Diaz-Santana."

Mercy whipped her head around. "You tried it."

*****

Of course, I woke up first. Actually, I barely slept because the baby laid on my bladder all night. All I did was piss. Getting in and out of bed finally woke Mercy up. My parents were gone. I was not sure where they went. Probably to my father's house. Don't even ask me why they lived in two separate houses. It'd been like this since Bey was in high school. What I didn't understand was they lived separate, but slept together at night, alternating houses.

"Why your parents couldn't cook for us before they left?"

"I know, right," I said, putting on a too small shirt and pants. "I need to swing by the house and get some clothes."

"What if Spencer is there?" Mercy asked.

"He's not. I found out that he'd been working his days off to get extra money."

"Probably for the wedding that he's not about to have," she laughed.

"Probably so," I laughed too.

"Okay, we'll swing by your place and get your things. Maybe pack a few items just in case, and then go to my place to freshen up before we get some breakfast."

"Well, we better get moving then because I'm already hungry."

"Your big butt stays hungry."

"That's not nice, Mercy."

"It's true," she stated while slipping on her clothes.

We walked out of the house looking like the walk of shame. Not one of us, but both of us had on the same clothes from yesterday, looking thotish.

"Bitch, you got me out here looking like I been fucking all night, and you know I'm getting no kinda dick."

I sighed. "And I'm used to my morning wood."

"That's nasty." Mercy turned up her lip as she pulled up in front of my house. "We're in and out, right?"

"Right," I said, getting my huge self out of the car.

Mercy followed behind me. As I opened the door, she got my mail out of the mailbox and sifted through my mail, being the nosy ass that she was. Meanwhile, I went upstairs to pack some of my things.

"I'm glad I'm staying with Drake."

Mercy flopped on my bed. "That's a great idea because I think Spencer's a basket case. Dump that zero and stay with the hero."

"Listen, I felt bad because I shouldn't have accepted it. At some point, I loved him. It was not my intention to lead him on."

"Somebody sent you a flash drive," Mercy said, holding it up for me to see.

"Pop it in the computer," I said while packing.

Mercy sat at my computer, powered it up, and then inserted the flash. While I was packing, I realized that she was quiet. I was almost done stuffing my suitcase when I turned around. Mercy was completely frozen.

"What's wrong?" I asked Mercy, stopping what I was doing and walking over to the desktop. What I saw next shocked the shit out of me. "Wait, play it from the beginning."

It was a video of me in the hospital. I was lying there in a coma and Spencer walked into the room. I looked so angelic lying there. No tubes or nothing. He kissed my lips and sighed.

"I can't," Mercy said, breaking my stare.

"I need to see this," I exclaimed. "It says a lot."

"I can't believe he was so nasty to do that to you."

I braced myself as Mercy got up and I sat down, trading places with her in front of the computer. I continued watching.

Princess Diamond

Spencer raised my gown, touching me down below. I cringed when he climbed into the hospital bed, holding my legs open.

Tears rolled down my face as I watched Spencer violate me. He was beyond sick. I couldn't believe that I loved this man at one point. As if that wasn't bad enough, he had the nerve to talk to me as if I was awake, asking me if it felt good to me. I was about to stop watching when he asked me if I was ready to have his baby. All I could do was hold my stomach and cry. The baby that I was carrying right now could be Spencer's, and this was how he or she was conceived.

I jumped up from the computer, covering my eyes with my hands. "Cut it off!" I screamed. I couldn't watch anymore as Spencer reached his peak.

"What do you want to do, take this to the police?"

"No, I'm about to call Drake."

Chapter 25

Spencer

"I ought to bust your shit wide open," Destiny screamed the moment I walked in from work. She had been beating me in the head nonstop.

Grant it, I knew this would be her reaction. That's why I hit up the bar before I came to her house. I figured she saw social media. Who knew that my little video proposal to Dream would go viral? I sure in the fuck didn't know. If I knew it would have gotten that much attention, I wouldn't have posted the shit.

My reason behind doing it was to tell our friends and family that we were an item and to get rid of her little boo thang that kept hanging around. He probably thought I was out of the picture because I was down for a few weeks. The video was supposed to put a stop to all that bullshit. What I didn't factor in was Destiny's reaction.

To be honest, I was just trying to win Dream over. I hadn't thought twice about Destiny or what she might think. That was, until she blew my shit up to the point where I had to cut my damn phone off. It got so bad that she showed up at my job and I had to tell security stop her. Her name was now put on the list of people who were no longer welcomed in the building. She showed the blackest part of her ass. When I say she went off, she went off. She broke some shit and everything.

I tried to run away from Destiny into the kitchen, but she was still hot on my ass, beating me in my back because she was too short to reach my head.

"You muthfucka. I trusted you. After being with me for weeks, this is what I have to deal with."

Punch! Punch! Punch! Punch!

"I cook for your ungrateful ass. I clean for your ungrateful ass. I go out of my way for your ungrateful ass."

Punch! Punch! Punch! Punch!

"Am I not good enough for your ass, huh, Spencer?"

Punch! Punch! Punch! Punch!

"Chill, Destiny!" I hollered, trying to push her away. I tried to block her punches. It wasn't working. In the mist of our struggle, she ended up socking me in the eye. Nothing major. It only hurt a little. When she got like this, it was hard to calm her down, so I did my best to remain calm.

"You don't think none of this shit affects me, muthafucka? That bitch been in a coma for months, but I been by your side. That fuckin' ring belonged to me. I'm the one that's been holding you down. She don't even fucking want your ass. I went to see her; did you know that?"

"You did what?" I asked angrily. I was trying to remain calm, but she done fucked up now.

"I went to see Dream and she don't want you."

"You're such a hater. Why'd you go see Dream?"

"Because I wanted her to know about us. Your ass been laid up here, it's about time that she knows the truth. You're fucking me every night. I'm sick of keeping our relationship a secret."

I started pacing the floor. This shit was all bad. That might be why Dream was so hesitant about taking my ring. I wasn't delusional. I knew that she was hesitant about marrying me. I just wanted to get us back on track, now that we had a baby on the way.

"Why the fuck would your stupid ass go over there? What the fuck did you say to her?"

Dream & Drake 3: A Cartel Love Story

"You think Dream is thinking about your stupid ass? She's not. She got a fine ass nicca who loves her. He got money, unlike your broke ass."

"Shut up, Destiny. That shit ain't true."

"It is true. My uncle always complains about that nicca. How much he don't like him, but he's won Dream's heart. How she's fell for that nicca and it's like he has a spell over her. The same nicca that saved her from the accident the night she was hit. The same nicca that took her to Puerto Rico. Have you ever taken her to Puerto Rico? Fuck no. Your broke ass can't afford to do shit. You're lucky I'm still rocking with your broke ass. Oh, and he's about to buy her a house. That's what he told my aunt. You don't have a chance nicca. I'm the closest thing you'll ever get to Dream. She don't want your ass."

Punch! Punch! Punch! Punch!

"You heard me, muthafucka, she don't want your ass!"

My hand was around Destiny's throat before I knew it. I was choking the life out of her and I didn't even care. I feel like she was the reason why Dream hadn't answered my numerous calls. I must've had texted and called her at least forty times today. Not one time did she respond. After proposing to her, I felt like we were making strides to our new beginning, but Destiny fucked that all up.

While I was choking Destiny, she reached behind her and grabbed the knife from the counter. I guess she was preparing dinner before I came in. She tried to slice me with the knife, but I knocked it out of her hand and kept on choking her. She kneed me in the balls and I doubled over. What a cheap ass shot. Women always used that shit against men. I groaned for a moment, while she gasped for air. By the time she reached for the knife, I had recovered and I was right on her tail.

She scooted across the kitchen tile, grabbed the knife, and swung at me. Luckily, she missed. She swung again and, this time, she sliced my arm. It wasn't deep, but the shit hurt like a muthafucka. I'd always had a very low tolerance for pain so, when she cut me, I just blacked out. I grabbed her wrist and the knife fell out of her hand. I picked the knife up with one hand and grabbed her throat again with my other hand.

"I hope Dream marries that other nicca and not you," Destiny said, adding insult to injury.

She had no idea how close I was to the edge when she said that rude ass comment. Thoughts of that nicca fucking Dream went through my mind and I completely lost my fucking mind, stabbing Destiny in the chest.

I dropped the knife, cradling her in my arms. "I'm sorry. I'm so sorry."

"I'm sorry too," she cried. "I just wanted you to choose me."

"Sssssh," I hushed her. "Don't talk."

Blood was already spilling out of her mouth as she spoke.

"I'm going to call an ambulance."

"No, I want you to take me to the hospital," she said, coughing up blood.

"Destiny, you need immediate attention. I can't take you to the hospital. I'm going to call 911 so they can tend to your wounds right away."

"I'm pregnant," she said, shocking the fuck out of me.

"You are?" I really felt like shit for losing my damn temper now.

"Yes. That's why I was so angry. I hoped that when I told you, you would propose to me."

"It's not too late," I told her. I didn't know if I really believed that, but I didn't want her to die either. I just wanted her to hold on. "Hold on, Destiny."

I laid her down gently on the floor, as I fumbled with my slacks to get my phone. I dialed and then hung up.

Destiny's eyes were still open, but there was no life behind them.

"NOOOOOOOOOOOOOOOOOO!" I screamed out.

I was so angry with myself that I started tearing the whole kitchen up. When that didn't bring me satisfaction, I picked up the bat that she kept by the fridge and began doing damage in the dining room and living room. Finally, I collapsed in the living room, crying my eyes out. Not because I was about to go to jail, but because I really regretted stabbing Destiny.

I sat on the floor holding her lifeless body, until reality set in that she was gone and never coming back. Instinctively, I carried her downstairs to the basement, where I left her for dead. I cried for a few minutes because I was going to miss her crazy ass. She was definitely off her rocker, but she didn't deserve death.

Next, I cleaned up all the blood. The stains on in the kitchen, down the basement steps, anywhere else that I thought it might be. Last but not least, I stripped out of my clothes, putting them inside of a garbage bag. Once I showered, I drove far away and dumped my clothes in a dumpster.

It was time to get out of dodge. With Destiny being dead and in the basement, it was only a short amount of time before everything pointed back to me. I packed all of my things, and went to a hotel.

I laid in the bed trying to get comfortable, but I couldn't. Every time I closed my eyes, I saw her choking on her own blood. The events kept replaying in my mind. I wondered, if I walked away, would there be a different outcome right now. I got up and took one of the sleeping pills that my doctor prescribed. Rarely did I take them.

As soon as I got back in the bed, my phone vibrated.

Worrisome ass nurse: I'm sick of asking you for my two-fifty.

Me: I don't give a fuck. I'm not paying your ass.

Worrisome ass nurse: Does that include me telling Dream what you did to her?

Me: Do what the fuck you gotta do. I'm not paying you shit.

I powered my phone off because I didn't want to hear shit else she had to say. She was bluffing. There was no way she was going to tell Dream shit. Telling on me meant she had to tell on herself too because she turned a blind eye while I did what I had to do. I guess the bitch didn't realize I would figure that much out.

Chapter 26

Drake

I was at the trap with Mega and Axel. Just like Mega said, the blood belonged to Bey, but the body didn't. It belonged to a Tonya Carol who had been missing around the same time that Bey had gone missing. What Mega didn't tell Dream or her parents was that Mega had been tracking these niccas because he thought they had something to do with Playez getting shot. The only thing was, each time he got close to them, it's like someone tipped them off and they disappeared. We were starting to think that there was another snake in our camp. Of course, Yolo was a suspect, but he hadn't been in the loop within months. So, it had to be someone else.

"Anyone new I should know about?" I asked, sitting down at my desk. I was in my office. It wasn't that nice. Just a sound proof spot for us to talk while we were here.

Axel mugged me. It wasn't nothing new. He always wore a frown. This nicca was street for real. "Now that you mentioned it, I got my eye on two niccas that don't seem right."

"Who?" I questioned, while Mega listened carefully.

"Zino and Gremlin."

"Gremlin is one of my best workers. He's been down with us for years."

"I don't give a fuck," Axel said with malice. "All the more reason for us to check this nicca out even more."

Dream & Drake 3: A Cartel Love Story

I put my hand up to stop Axel from popping off. "Say no more. You've been here more than me. If you feel like we need to check this nicca out, then that's what we're going to do."

I glanced at Mega and he already knew what time it was.

"I'm on it. So, I've been putting together bits and pieces. I truly think Bey's kidnapping, Breeze and Playez getting shot, and your car accident are all linked together somehow. Now, I know we took out the people who had captured Breeze, but I'm starting to think that maybe we didn't get everyone. Maybe someone was missing that day or something. There's more to this story. It has to be. I couldn't get on top of things when I was in New York but, now that I'm here, I can see that I've missed a few details."

"I was thinking the same thing," Axel agreed. "You needed a fresh set of eyes on this shit. Sometimes, when you see things every day, you tend to overlook minor details that stand out."

I couldn't argue with my brothers. They were right. "Listen, I know I can be stern. I know I rule with an iron fist too. I also know that I come down on y'all. However, I trust your decision. If you think this Gremlin nicca needs to be looked into, I'm on board. I just want to be in the loop though. Just because I'm not getting my hands dirty don't mean that I'm not involved. I'm still in charge."

Mega nodded. "Cool. We'll let you know what we find."

"What about Dekon and his brothers? How are they working out?"

"Just fine," Mega said. "I keep my eye on them. So far, they haven't done anything out of order."

I was glad to hear that. I hated to go back on my word and kill all four of them. I didn't want to, but I would kill them in a second if need be.

I was playing around with the settings on my phone when Dream called. "Hey, baby, how are your parents doing?"

I heard Dream crying on the other end.

"What's wrong, ma? What happened?"

"Spencer," she cried. "He... he... he," she cried some more.

163

"Check this out," Mega said, downloading a video. "Mercy just sent this to me."

Axel, Mega, and I watched as Spencer violated Dream. Well, we didn't get that far. I stopped the video before it got to that point. The moment he climbed on top of her, I already imagined the rest.

"I saw all I needed to see." The video was still playing and I ended up seeing this punk, bitch nicca violate her anyway. "Cut this bullshit off and delete it from the laptop," I demanded. "Dream, baby, I'm on my way. Hold tight."

She sobbed uncontrollably on the phone before she answered, "Okay."

After Dream was off my line, I turned to Mega. "Find that muthafucka and take him to the warehouse. He just gave me the perfect reason to wet his ass up."

"Done," Mega said, loading up both his guns.

"I'm going to go and check on Dream and I'll meet you there in a bit."

Mega and I walked out together. He went to find Spencer's sicko ass. I went to comfort my baby.

"Where she at?" I asked Mercy when I walked into her house.

"She's upstairs," Mercy said solemnly, pointing in the direction of the steps.

I jogged upstairs two at a time to get to Dream. She was curled up in the bed in a fetal position, crying. I kicked off my shoes and curled up behind her.

"I know, baby, I know."

"Did you see what he did to me, Drake?"

"I saw it, baby." I sighed because this shit was really under my fucking skin. "Well, I saw as much of it as I could see." "Are you hurt?" I asked her. "I mean, are you hurt, like down there."

"I don't think so," she exclaimed, clenching her legs tight when I touched her hip. "I was asleep when it happened so, if he did hurt me, I wouldn't know now."

She started crying even harder.

"Dream, tell me what's on your mind?"

Dream & Drake 3: A Cartel Love Story

"The note said it happened more than once. I'm afraid, Drake. Our baby might be Spencer's baby. I might have conceived while I was in a coma."

"I mean, is that shit even possible?" I was trying not to get upset, but this whole revelation had me stressed the fuck out. I think I sighed like seven times before she answered me.

"Yes, as sick as it sounds, it is definitely possible. I'm so hurt because I was hoping that maybe I got pregnant before I went in the coma. Now, I'm thinking maybe it was nasty ass Spencer who impregnated me."

"Okay, okay, okay… first off, we not about to say the word impregnate. I can't handle it." Just the thought of what Spencer did had me about ready to throw up everywhere. "Gawd, I can't take this fuckin' shit. I swear, I'm so damn angry."

"I am too," Dream said, consoling me. I was supposed to be consoling her. We were both sitting on the side of the bed; she was rubbing my back.

"You don't understand, ma; it's my job to protect you. I was at the muthafucka almost every day, and I didn't even know this shit was going down."

"You didn't know, Drake. I don't fault you."

"This shit breaks my heart. You're my fiancée. If I can't protect you while you're asleep, how the hell can I protect you while you're awake?"

We sat in silence for a moment. I didn't know what she was thinking, but all I saw was blood. Spencer's bloody body on the warehouse floor.

"I gotta go," I said, standing up.

"What you about to do?" Dream asked, knowing good and well I was about to put this work in.

"Handle this nicca. What the fuck you think I'm about to do?"

"Don't kill him, Drake."

Her request caught me off guard. "Whose fuckin' side are you on? This nicca just did some foul shit to you and you defending him? Fuck outta here. This nicca deserves to die. What, you still love him?" I asked, staring her ass down.

165

She just stared back at me with tears in her eyes, but she didn't say nothing. Her silence told it all. I could have spit fire.

"Regardless of how you feel about me, Dream, I'm still going to go and handle this nicca. On everything, after this, you and me ain't never gotta see each other again."

"I didn't say that, Drake," Dream sobbed loudly. "You're putting words into my mouth."

She reached out for me and I backed away from her. "It's what you didn't say. You still feeling this nicca." The shit pissed me off so bad that I just turned and walked away.

Mercy was at the bottom of the steps when I came down. "You out?" she asked, sizing me up. I'd been around Mercy enough for her to know when I was on ten.

"Yeah, I'm out this bitch."

Dream made her way downstairs too. "Drake, let's talk about this."

"Get ya girl," I said to Mercy. "She's going to need your support, now that we're done."

"Drake!" Dream called out as I rushed to my car. "Drake! Don't leave me, Drake! Please, Drake, I need you. I'm sorry. Please. I'm on your side."

A part of me wanted to turn around and run back to her. I couldn't. After all that we've been through, it hurt me that she was more worried about this nicca than she was about me. I was the one in this shit with her. I was the one she called. It was me who might be taking care of this pussy nicca's baby. Man, this shit was too fuckin' much.

I had to push Dream out of my mind. It was time to put this work in. Before heading to the warehouse, I went home and changed into my goon attire, all-black everything. Thirty minutes later, I was walking into the warehouse where Spencer was already hanging up by his arms. From the looks of things, Bull and Icepick had already done a number on him. His face was swollen badly, and he had black and blue bruises all over his body.

"I'll take over from here," I told everyone.

Dream & Drake 3: A Cartel Love Story

Mega, Bull, and Icepick went to the other room. I grabbed the remote and pressed play. The screen came down and the speakers piped up. It replayed the video of what Spencer did to Dream. The shit was nasty as fuck, but I had a point to prove. I was willing to stomach the shit until the end, when it finished. I cut it off and faced Spencer's pathetic looking ass.

"So, what was the point?" I asked calmly.

"I wanted to get my girl pregnant," he spat.

After I punched him in the face and knocked his two front teeth out, I asked his punk as the same question. "I'll repeat, what was the point, muthafucka?"

"I wanted to get her pregnant," he whined, spitting out his teeth.

"So, raping her while she was in a coma was your solution to that shit?" I said, connecting the belt I had in my hand with his flesh.

"Listen, man, she was my girl before she was yours."

I stared at his ass like he was crazy. Pretty much nothing he said was going to fly. I was just picking with him before he was killed.

"So, you felt like her body belonged to you? That you could take what is rightfully hers without her consent?"

"This shit was between me and my girl."

"Can I get the oil, please?" I called out.

Immediately, oil gushed down all over Spencer. I was sure he was shocked, but I wasn't. I wanted this muthafucka nice and slick for what I had planned. As soon as the last drop of oil fell, I lit his bitch ass up with that belt. I mean, I took out all the frustration I had of the accident, my brother's being shot, and what he did to Dream. Plus, I didn't like his muthafucking ass. I beat on this nicca so bad that the belt broke.

"Send them in," I huffed.

The door opened and a bunch of hungry niccas came strolling in. I stopped counting when the line was out the door. Spencer's eyes nearly popped out of his head. Although they were swollen shut, he managed to look surprised.

Princess Diamond

I walked up to Spencer and tapped him on his bloody face. "Guess what, nicca? These men are here to visit you."

Spencer strained his neck to look at the long line of men. "Why?"

I cracked up because this lame nicca was really clueless. "You see, I told them what you did to Dream, and they wanted to have a few words with you regarding the matter."

The chains that were holding Spencer up lowered him to the ground. Spencer hit the floor as the chains went back up into the ceiling. Wasting no time, the first guy undid his pants, put on a condom, and dived onto Spencer, ripping his ass in two.

The ear-piercing howl that he let out told me that I made the right decision. Dude was ruthless, fucking Spencer like the bitch that he was.

"Make sure he's alive when you finish," I announced as I walked out of the room, joining Mega.

"This was a good idea," Mega said, eating popcorn.

Periodically, he would look at what was going on, just to make sure shit was going according to plan. Icepick and Bull were guarding the exits, just in case shit went left.

"Torture is always a good thing."

"What, nicca?"

Mega laughed. "What I'm trying to say is, you could have just put a bullet in his head. I think revenge is better. Maybe it's just me."

I laughed too. "Naw, you know normally I do just pop these niccas and keep it moving, but he hurt my baby. I couldn't let him get away with that shit."

"From what I heard, she ain't your baby no more."

"Damn, Mercy got a big ass mouth. She's still my baby. I'm just not speaking to her at the moment."

Mega and I waited around until all the men finished busting Spencer's booty hole wide open. Once they were finished, we both entered the room to the bloody mess. Just like I asked, Spencer was still alive, barely, but as long as he had air still in his lungs, I was good.

"I'm sorry," Spencer slurred. They fucked the wind out of this nicca.

"I stooped down next to him. "I didn't hear you. What did you say?"

"I'm sorry. Tell Dream, I'm sorry. I thought I was doing right."

I snarled. "Save the bullshit lame ass, wack ass, pussy acting, no heart nicca. Stop fucking begging me like I like dick." I had to squint my eyes at this super fuck nicca. "Let's do this shit," I said, totally fed up with this muthafucka for real.

Mega and I both pulled out machine guns, ready to wet this nicca up just like I imagined it. This was more my style.

"Don't kill me," Spencer begged.

We opened fire on his ass. His body twitched as we sprayed the shit out of him. Even after he was dead, we didn't stop shooting until our guns were out of rounds. Then, adding insult to injury, we both spit on his ass.

"Puto!"

Chapter 27

Channa

I was not sure how, but I managed to avoid Drake at all costs. He put a bounty out on my head, his own fucking wife. I said wife and not ex-wife because we weren't legally divorced yet. This nicca had me dodging everyone. I hadn't gotten my nails done, hair done, or nothing. He had me walking around Chicago looking like a bum. I even switched doctors and I was going by an alias, just to make sure Drake didn't show up to my next appointment.

It was amazing what a little pussy could make niccas do. Since I didn't have any money, I was fucking left and right, trading my coochie for services. I realized that, partially, it was my fault why I was in the predicament I was in, but I blamed Drake too. He took everything away from me. The divorce was cold as fuck. He had no remorse, leaving me pregnant with his babies. Never mind my feelings. Fuck me. As long as that bitch Dream was good, right? Fucking bastard.

Action, my new boo, just gave me a few thousand to go shopping with. I'd been playing wifey to him ever since he picked me up from the lawyer's office. That's right; this good pussy I got had him taking real good care of me too. A part of me wished that I met him first, instead of Drake. He knew my value and he appreciated me. From what he said, he was moving weight in the Bronx until his boy got popped and things got hot.

Dream & Drake 3: A Cartel Love Story

He knew he couldn't stay around the way, so he packed up his car and drove here. He claimed he was trying to get up with his boy, some nicca who never hit him back. Since their operation was shut down, he relocated here, hoping to reclaim his life as a rich dope boy.

He said it was harder than he thought because The Cartel ran shit in Chicago. I didn't tell him my affiliations with The Cartel, nor did I drop any names. The last thing I wanted was for Drake to know what I was doing. The drug trade was small. If I dropped names, it wouldn't take that long for Action to get connected to The Cartel without me, and that would fuck up my plan to get back on top.

I left the mall, struggling to carry all of the bags of maternity clothes and smell goods. Action was taking me out and I wanted to look cute. Even though we had to be careful, I was sure that Drake, nor members of The Cartel frequented this spot. It was far enough away from the city.

"I should have waited for him to go shopping," I said, tossing a few bags in the back seat and then the rest into the trunk. "This shit was heavy as fuck."

Pop! Pop! Pop! Pop! Pop! Pop!

Shots fired. I ducked down just in time. Breathing hard, I reached into my purse and pulled out my bitch, ready to fire back. I was about to jump up and open fire, when more bullets came my way. I was sure this shit looked straight out of a movie. At least that's what it felt like to me. I was out here like a sitting duck.

I tried to stand up again but had to fall back quickly, as bullets passed my head.

"Muthafuckin' Drake!" I screamed.

Crawling low to the ground, I made my way two cars over. Don't ask me how, cause I didn't have a fuckin' clue. With my big ass belly and swollen ankles, I must've had God on my side. My babies must have a purpose because I knew I was meant to be shot the fuck up, but I was spared.

I pulled on the door handle and, just by chance, it was open. I didn't know who this special fuck was that left the door unlocked in the city of Chicago where cars are stolen every five seconds, but I was grateful to their ass. I slid into the driver's seat and that's when I noticed that the keys were in the ignition. What kind of bullshit was this? Fuck it. I needed out and I was provided a way. I stayed low while backing the car out of the parking spot. When I realized that I was in a car that was behind the shooters, I pulled off at high speed, nearly hitting every car in my path. I laughed to myself as it dawned on me that I was in their getaway car.

"That's what the fuck they get," I laughed. "Sending amateurs to do a professional job."

I thought Drake would have sent someone like Mega. Come to think about it, I was glad he didn't send him. I would have been laid out on the pavement dead right about now. The more I pondered this whole situation, Drake wasn't trying to kill me; he was trying to scare me. That shit was a warning because if Drake wanted me dead, he could have had me killed. Deep down inside, I knew nothing could stop him from ending my life if he really wanted to.

"Hey, baby," Action said, looking up from the video game when I came in. "What did you get?"

Obviously, his whole tone changed when he saw my dirty knees, how dirty I was, and the frazzled look on my face.

"I got a lot of nice stuff," I said, plopping down on the couch next to him. "Too bad it's still in the car at the mall."

"Fuck you mean?" he pondered.

"My raggedy baby daddy tried to have me killed."

"You lying?" Action asked with doubt.

"Why would I lie about that? I know you haven't known me that long but, to your knowledge, have I ever lied to you?"

He shook his head from side to side. "Not that I know of."

"I'm telling you, these niccas were like the terminator or some shit. They had bullets, bullets, and more bullets. I was lucky to make it out of there without being shot."

"See, that's why I told you to wait for me, ma. Yo, I would have put those punk niccas down."

I almost said we both would have been shot the fuck up, but I bit my tongue. "No, I'm glad you weren't there. I barely got away."

"Yo, I'm not no scary dude, ma. I'm not sure about your ex, but I go hard. I ride for mines." Action stood up, getting extra hype. "There's no way I would have let them niccas shoot at you and I was around. Fuck!" he hollered, throwing the controller across the room, shattering it. "I'm telling you, we wouldn't have to put up with none of this shit if I had them bricks. What's up with that shit?"

I never saw Action this angry before. After being shot at and nearly losing my life, I was shaken up. Of course, I would never let him know that. "I'm on it," I replied.

I didn't tell Action that I never asked Yolo for the bricks. I had been flirting with him, buttering him up. "Let me text him and see what's up."

Me: What's up wit you?

Yolo: Snow, my pretty vanilla chocolate. I'm good. What's up with you?

Me: I got myself in a little jam. Drake hates my ass right now.

Yolo: What you do?

Me: I burned his house down.

Yolo: Lmao. That was you?

Me: Yes, lol but that's why I need your help. You still having problems with The Cartel.

Yolo: Nah, actually, I'm not. I been back at the trap for a couple weeks now. Shit's been sweet.

Me: Cool. You think you can get me a few bricks unnoticed.

Yolo: I got a few stashed at the crib. How many you need?

Me: I'll take whatever you can get me for now. More later.

Yolo: Aight. Meet me at the crib. I'm on my way home now. I got you. I'm good for three.

Me: How much you asking for them?

Princess Diamond

Yolo: As much as you've had my back, I wouldn't dare charge you. I remember how you looked out for me on several occasions. Consider it payback.

Me: Good looking out. But if you were going to sell them to me, how much would you be charging.

Yolo: Drake's shit is pretty pure. Probably 20 a key.

"What ya boy say?" Action asked, lighting up a blunt.

"He said 20 a key."

Action nodded, smoking on his blunt for a moment. "This ain't no stepped on shit, right?"

"Hell no. It's coming straight from Peru. It's as pure as you can get."

Action reached over and grabbed me by my jaw so fast that I couldn't even react. "Bitch, I'm not playing with you. I'm going to give you the 60k but, if you fuck me over, I swear I'm going to fuck your little world up. Don't cross me, ma."

"I'm not going to cross you," I lied. "You've been good to me. I just want to return the favor."

Action let my jaw go and walked out of the room. He came back and dropped a small bag filled with money by my feet.

"Don't fuck this up."

"I'm not," I said with an eye roll. "You act like I'm the enemy."

Action sat down, smoking on his blunt once again. "Yo, this shit ain't personal, ma. It's business. You should know that."

"I do. You can count on me."

He was getting way too hyped. I had to do something, so I did the only think I knew how to do. I sucked his dick until he passed out from pleasure. He was high, so I was sure he would be out for a while. I grabbed the bag of money, my suitcases that were secretly packed, and I hauled ass to Yolo's. Fuck Action's rebound ass.

Action was snoring like a baby when I walked out the door. I wasn't going to blow up my spot by leaving him a sappy note and shit. Real bitches didn't tell on themselves. I jumped into Action's new whip, a cocaine white Audi A8. I loved this car. I

174

knew he bought it for himself, but I swear it was made just for me.

I pulled up in front of Yolo's house at the same time that he did. As soon as I got out, he hugged me. I was a little apprehensive because it was broad daylight. I didn't know if he was still being watched or not.

"I'm good," he said, easing my nerves. "I wouldn't be out here like this if I had eyes still on me."

I sighed. "Ok, cool." I followed Yolo inside.

His eyes roamed over my body. "You look real good Snow."

I turned around in my high heels, so he could get a good look at me in my short maternity tank dress. I'd admit that other than a big stomach, I was still snatched. I was wearing the one cute outfit that I had left, since my other shit was left in Drake's car during the shootout.

I was getting hot under his gaze. "You looking at me like you want some of this."

"I do. If you got a minute."

I smiled and bent over, twerking while lifting my dress to show him that I didn't have on any panties. With the quickness, Yolo dropped his pants around his ankles, pulled his manhood through his boxers, and rammed into me from behind.

"It's so rough," I laughed, and then moaned.

He grabbed me by my neck. "Shut the fuck up and take this dick."

I loved it when he talked nasty to me like that. Action was the same way. He was rugged like Yolo. In many ways, they were a lot alike.

I threw it back on Yolo, circling my ass on him. I was standing up, riding his dick to perfection. A few seconds more, my eyes rolled into my head and I was creaming like crazy. Yolo skeeted shortly after.

"Damn, you always make me cum when you cum. That shit ain't fair."

I grinned, wiping the sweat from my face. "Good pussy will do that to you."

"Shit, this pregnant pussy is even better. I can't believe Drake is missing out on this."

"Fuck Drake," I spat. "We got beef."

Yolo sighed. "That's not a good look, shorty. Drake is the last person you want beef with. I should know."

"Yeah, well, I learned from the best. If he come for me, I'm coming for him and his bitch. Eye for an eye in this mutha-fucka."

"I hear you," Yolo exclaimed, putting the bricks into one of those large recycled shopping bags. "You be careful. I don't want to see nothing happen to you."

"I'm good. You just make sure you watch your back. Just because you're back in don't mean they trust you."

"I already know."

I went to pick up the bag and Yolo stopped me. "Let me carry it out for you. It's kinda heavy."

I wasn't going to disagree. It was heavy as fuck.

After Yolo put the bricks in the trunk, I gave him a hug and a kiss before pulling off. I wasn't sure where I was on my way to, but I damn sure wasn't going back to Action's house. He served his purpose. Thanks to him, I was about to be back on top. I had all of the customers that he just hustled up because I was eavesdropping on all of his conversations. Plus, I went through his contacts in his phone. Now, I got 60k and three bricks. Shit couldn't get no better than this. The power of pussy was a wonderful thing.

I was craving some steak tacos from around the way, so I stopped off and got those before I decided to drive to Wisconsin. I was chowing down as I drove, dropping taco juice everywhere.

Whoop-Whoop!

"You gotta fuckin' be kidding me? I know the damn police ain't behind me. Fuck! Keep calm, Channa. He don't know what's in the trunk."

"Hi officer," I said in a cheery voice when he walked up.

"Ma'am, were you aware that you were swerving?"

"I was trying to eat and drive. Pregnancy makes me greedy." I giggled and rubbed my stomach.

The officer looked at me with a straight face. "License and registration."

"Sure, officer," I said, reaching into my purse. I gave him my license. I looked in the glove compartment and didn't see the registration. "Um, this is my boyfriend's car. He just got it, so maybe he hasn't registered it yet."

The officer eyed me suspiciously. "I'll be right back."

I tried to keep calm as he sat in the car running my license. I knew my shit was clean but still. Finally, the officer came back to the car, handing me my license.

"Miss, I can't let you drive off in this car."

I thought everything was good by his demeanor. "Why not?"

"The tags are expired. Did you know you're driving around on expired New York plates?"

Action's stupid ass. "I'm sure there is a misunderstanding. I can go to the DMV and take care of it."

"I'm sure you could, but there is no way I can allow you to drive an out of state expired plate. I'm sorry, miss. I need you to get out of the car. Now, if you don't have a ride, I can give you a ride home."

Fuck!

I got out of the car with my purse and the handbag with the sixty-thousand that Action gave me. I stared at the trunk as the officer spoke to me.

"Listen, officer, I was on my way to Wisconsin. Maybe you can escort me to the DMV. I promise not to drive off until I have the plates registered."

"Ma'am, I can't do that either but, if you want me to get your luggage out of the car, I can help you with that.

I sighed. "No, that's okay."

"Yes, let me help. I feel bad. You look like you're about to pop. Let me carry everything for you. My wife is pregnant too and I wouldn't feel right if I didn't help you."

Shit, I would get the Good Samaritan cop. Fuck my damn luck.

Princess Diamond

"No, I got it," I said, going into the trunk carefully. I had the heavy ass bag of bricks in my hand, when the officer grabbed the bag and the damn drugs hit the fucking ground.

We both stared at each other.

I could have denied it, but I chose not to. I was busted red-handed. I turned around and put my hands behind my back because I knew what was coming next.

"Ma'am, you're under arrest."

I wasn't going down by myself. Fuck that. If I was going down, so was Drake and his bitch, Dream. I was fucked, so they were too. I'd be dammed if I did time by my damn self.

Chapter 28

Drake

I just got cleaned up from the shit that went down at the warehouse, when I got pulled over. I called Ross before the officer got out of the car and made his way over to me. I knew he was on some bullshit. Just as I suspected, more officers pulled up. I wasn't worried; that's why I had a lawyer on retainer for situations like this.

I was told to step out of the car and, immediately, I was wrestled to the ground and roughly handcuffed. Not once did I resist because I knew they didn't have shit on me. At least that's what I thought until I got to the interrogation room.

"Do you know a Channa Diaz-Santana?"

I chuckled. "What kind of fuck question is that? Of course I do," I said, eyeing this dude. 'But you already know that."

I just smiled. I still felt like they didn't have nothing at this point. Channa could complain that I was trying to kill her, but she didn't have no proof.

"Why am I here, detective?"

"Detective Grant."

"Why am I here Detective Grant?" I repeated.

"We just picked up your wife and guess what we found."

"Enlighten me." I leaned forward, crossing my arms.

"Three kilos of cocaine in the trunk of her boyfriend's car and sixty-thousand in cash. Anything you want to say about that?"

"No, but I bet you're going to tell me."

"Indeed, I am. Your wife said it was yours."

I laughed so hard that I bit my tongue. "That's bullshit. If that's all you have, I might as well walk right now."

"You wish it was that easy," Detective Grant spat. "I know you. I know your kind. I'm very aware of The Chicago Cartel and all of its dealings."

I laughed even harder. "I have no idea what you're talking about. Sounds like you watch too much tv, detective."

"No, son, I've been watching your family for years."

"Again, it sounds like hearsay. Nothing concrete. Can we get to the point?"

"This is the point, Drake."

"Oooooh, now you know my name. I see they taught you well at the academy. Bravo." I could tell that my comment got under his skin. "I hear you speaking, blowing a bunch of hot air. Time is money and money is time, Grant. Chop. Chop."

We stared each other down before he spoke again.

I smiled, making him even more irritated. "I think you're bullshitting right now because you don't have nothing on me."

"So, you don't know anything about the cocaine that your wife had when she was pulled over."

"Listen, let me spare you a few moments of guessing. You mean, my ex-wife. I haven't seen Channa since she walked out of our divorce hearing. She signed the papers. Any day now, we will be divorced."

"Yes but, as of right now, you're still married."

"Apples and oranges," I replied nonchalantly.

"You think you got this all figured out, don't you?"

I chuckled. "I never said that Detective Grant, you did? What is it you want? Because right now, it seems like you don't have shit. You're reaching, like I said, and you're hoping that I'll say something crazy. I hate to ruin your day, but I don't have nothing crazy to say. I'm legit."

"That's what you say, but your wife says otherwise."

"Um, ex-wife, and she's a bitter woman right now. Did she tell you that she burned down my house?"

Detective Grant shrugged. "No, I didn't hear anything about that."

I squinted my eyes with hostility. "Of course, you didn't. I'm sure you didn't see the police report or the statement from the fire chief because they had to call him to get his expertise on the gasoline fire."

"No, I'm afraid I didn't."

This nicca was playing games, but I had no problem joining in.

"How's your wife?" I asked him, catching this nicca totally off guard. "How is Rita and your three daughters: Keisha, Kendra, and Kelandra?"

He eyed me with the same squinted eyes that I just gave him. "Are you trying to be funny, you little punk?"

Now, it was time for us to reverse roles.

"You mad or nah?" I asked, tantalizing him. I was getting under his skin because it looked like steam was coming from under his collar.

"The next time you mention my family..."

I smirked. "The next time, you'll do what? Kendra's just my type, I'll fuck her, impregnate her with twins, and leave her ass to be a single mom. Think I won't?"

Detective Grant jumped across the table, and I quickly scooted my chair back, so I was out of his reach. He stretched his arm in my direction like a madman. Out of nowhere, the door sprung open, and a woman stepped in. I was assuming it was his partner.

"Grant! Let me speak to you in the hallway."

Detective Grant snapped out of his frenzy, grimaced at me, and then followed the woman out of the room. While they were in the hallway talking, I wondered where Ross was at. I called him over four hours ago, according to the wall clock. I hadn't even been arrested yet, when I called him.

Princess Diamond

I knew shit was about to get ugly when Detective Grant came back into the room with a stupid grin on his face.

"Listen, I'm going to give you one more time to come clean. We know everything, Drake. You might as well confess, so we can get you a good plea."

I sat there like I was contemplating what he actually said before I finally spoke up. "The only thing I'm confessing to is my big dick and even larger balls. That I cum a lot and that I love to fuck."

Detective Grant and the woman, who I assumed was his partner, both turned red, which was pretty hard considering their dark complexions. Their facial expressions were priceless. I couldn't help but to laugh hysterically.

Out of nowhere, Detective Grant sucker punched me. I jumped to my feet, preparing to defend myself with my feet if I had to because my hands were still cuffed behind my back.

I spit out blood. "You fucked now, Grant."

"And this is how you treat my client while you give his attorney the wrong information," Ross said, walking into the room followed by two more officers.

Both detectives stood there stuck on stupid, while Ross told their asses a thing or two.

"You have no grounds to hold my client. He's free to go," Ross demanded, while instructing the officers behind him to uncuff me.

"Not so fast," the lady detective said. "New evidence." She handed Ross a folder and smiled.

Ross looked it over, and I knew I was fucked when his wide smile turned into an angry stare. "What the fuck is this? And why am I just now seeing it?"

Detective Grant smiled at me cockily. "I guess your fast talking ass ain't know someone turned snitch on you. They gave up some pretty good information. Enough for us to hold your ass while we go before a judge. Oh wait, this is Friday. I guess you'll have to wait until Monday."

"Fuck you, Grant," I spat.

"No, Drake. It looks like you're the one that just been fucked."

"Don't say another word, Drake," Ross instructed. "I'm going to get to the bottom of this."

Grant smirked. "While you're at it, get to the bottom of Dream too."

I tensed up when he mentioned Dream. Sure enough, as I was being escorted out of the interrogation room, Dream was standing there.

"Drake!" she called out crying. "What's going on?"

"Nothing, baby. Ross is going to take care of everything. Just chill, ma."

Grant laughed because he knew that he had me when he brought Dream into the equation.

Detective Grant taunted Dream. "You and your little boyfriend are being booked on drug charges."

Dream's face told it all. "But, I don't understand. Drake, I'm scared!"

"Stop talking, Dream," Ross said. "I'm representing you and Drake. Unless I'm present, you don't say a word."

Dream broke down crying as they were pulling me away. I swear, seeing her pregnant in a police station crying made me go crazy. I tried to fuck up everything in sight before they finally drug me away. I didn't care that the last time I saw her we had an argument. She had my damn heart, and I would kill and steal for her. It didn't matter how much shit she said or did, or how much we argued or did each other wrong, I was going to always have love for Dream. That woman was my other half.

"Y'all muthafuckas about to pay for this shit!" I shouted. "You fuckin' hear me, putos!"

Chapter 29

Aquarius

I was at the bar. I needed a drink after spending all day working on a virus that shut down my online gaming site.

"What can I get you, sir?" the waitress asked.

"A Corona," I replied while looking at my phone. She was about to walk away when I grabbed her arm. "Keep them coming."

"You got it," she said before moving on to the next patron.

I needed a drink after I found out Drake got locked up. There was a snake among us. I ran everyone and I do mean everyone through clearance. The whole team got checked out, including family members. I knew my family wasn't grimy. Not saying we didn't have some shady people in our family, because we definitely did. My point was Drake's set up was smooth.

It was time to get shit popping my way and shut this nicca Yolo down once and for all. I knew Drake and Breeze thought I was paranoid, and maybe they were right to a certain extent. Being in jail did that to me, but I knew I was right about Yolo's ass. No, I didn't have the proof yet, but I would have it. All I had was a hunch, a gut feeling. My instincts were always on point. This nicca was a rat and I intended to flush his ass out. One thing I noticed about Yolo, he had an ego. I didn't know if it came from him being around Breeze too long or what. That was about to be his downfall. I was about to use that to my advantage.

Dream & Drake 3: A Cartel Love Story

I drank my Corona while waiting on Mega. I texted him earlier and told him to meet me here, so we could run my plan for Yolo by him.

"Hey sexy," a female said, standing behind me.

I swirled my bar stool around and came face to face with a very gorgeous woman. I definitely liked what I saw. She was hot. "Hello, beautiful."

"Why would a man like you be sitting at a bar all alone?"

"Waiting on a woman like you," I said and took another swig of my beer.

"Well, here I am. I have arrived. Now, what are you going to do now that I'm here?"

"Beat that pussy up," I replied with confidence.

I didn't know if my answer caught her by surprise or what, but she didn't seem as sure of herself as she did when she first walked up. Her little flirty game was cool and all, but I had to let her know where I stood.

"Listen," I started off. I was probably about to hurt her feelings, but I had to keep it real. "I'm only interested in smashing. If you not down with letting me fuck, we don't have anything more to discuss."

I expected her to walk away, slap me, or toss her drink in my face. What she did next totally shocked the hell out of me. She snatched the napkin off the counter and placed it in my lap. Removing her lip gloss from her purse, she traced the napkin with the gloss, right over my dick. I was thankful that I had on dark colored jeans for more than one reason, so the lip gloss that seeped through the napkin didn't show, and my dick imprint was hidden. After she finished, she took the napkin and boldly put her hand down my pants, placing the napkin in my underwear.

"I want to smash too," she whispered in my ear while copping a feel on my dick. It didn't take much to get me rock hard. She definitely had my dick straining against my boxers.

I picked up my phone and took her picture. "Cool. I'm glad we both understand each other." My voice was calm, but my hormones were raging.

"You just make sure you call me."

"I will."

She kissed my cheek and switched her way to the entrance. My eyes followed her ass as she made her way to the door. She held my undivided attention until she exited the bar and out of my sight. I reached inside of my pants and took the napkin out, plugging her number in my contacts. If she checked out, I was definitely going to call her. I looked forward to fucking her brains out.

My phone indicated breaking news with a live text link. I tried my best to keep up with the news. There was so much shit going down, I had to be aware and pass the information along. I clicked on the link and went straight to the website. I continued to sip on my second beer while I watched the news report that a house was blown up with people inside. So far, the body count was four males. They were trying to determine if it was a terrorist attack or a hate crime or if it was an accident. Police were everywhere and the street was blocked off.

I just so happen to look up and saw Mega walking through the door with his gun visible on his hip. I got bitches with no problem, but this nicca was a chick magnet. Every woman in the bar laid their eyes on him as he made his way over to me.

"Nicca, are you crazy, walking in here with your gun like that?"

Mega shrugged and took a seat next to me.

"You don't even care, do you?"

He smirked. "Not really. I got a license to carry this gun. It's for show anyway. I never use it. I just want people to see what I'm on before I get there. Buck up and get fucked up."

I snickered. This nicca was crazy for real.

"This is for you," the waitress said, holding a drink out for Mega. "Courtesy of that young lady over there," she exclaimed, pointing in the direction of another beautiful woman who waved at him.

"I'm good. I'm not drinking," Mega announced.

"Tell her thank you," I said.

The waitress sat the drink down next to Mega and walked off.

"Nicca, you see this crazy shit?" I asked him, showing him the news broadcast.

"Yeah, I see it," he replied nonchalantly.

"This shit is crazy. Four people are dead."

"Six people," Mega corrected.

"What did you say?" I asked, looking up from my phone.

"I said six people are dead," he repeated. "They haven't found the other two bodies yet."

"How do you…" my voice trailed off. When I made eye contact with Mega, that's when I realized that he was the one behind this incident.

"Aww fuck," I exclaimed, turning my phone off. "I should have known."

Mega smirked. "So, what's up with this plan? I'm still on the clock, if you get my drift."

I just shook my head. Mega never ceased to amaze me.

"We can talk about it later if you want. I didn't know you were at work."

"I mean, I am, but I have a few minutes to spare."

I was just about to speak when his phone vibrated. He pulled his phone out of his pocket and started texting.

"Oh, I saw your little jump off outside. She's hot. Definitely slide up in that."

"How did you see her?" I asked. I could have sworn that she left way before he got here. "You know what, don't answer that question. Once again, I don't even want to know."

Mega chuckled. "It's best you don't."

I chuckled too. "All work and no play ain't healthy. Relieve a little stress, you feel me?"

"Oh, I definitely feel you. I'm working on it," he said, still texting.

"Who is that?" I asked while leaning forward, staring at his screen. I should have known it was Mercy. "Nicca, your ass is obsessed. That girl don't want your ass. You need to leave her the fuck alone before she gets a restraining order on your ass."

"She's not about to do that," he said with his eyes glued to his phone.

"Why not? You harass her enough. I know I damn sure would if I was her."

"Nah, bruh, I'm breaking her down."

"How do you figure that?" I had to hear his answer. She looked like she was pushing him even further away if you asked me. It'd been months since they first met and she hadn't shown the slightest bit of interest his way.

"Because she's texting me back now."

"But, what is she saying tho? Cause all I saw was her telling you not to contact her anymore."

"Exactly."

I was confused as hell for real now. "Exactly what?"

"When I first started texting her, she would ignore me. I wouldn't get a response back at all. Nothing but crickets. Now, she responds to me immediately. She won't admit it, but she looks forward to my texts and calls. True enough, she tells me not to text her or call her anymore, but she doesn't hesitate to reply. I think she likes the chase. I know I do. I love to conquer, and I plan on conquering her soon. I'm just letting the pussy marinate."

"You on some pimp type shit. I hope she's worth it."

"She will be," he said, smiling at the text that he just got.

Mercy was beautiful, but she didn't seem worth all the time Mega was putting into her. I would have dropped her ass a long time ago.

"Anyway, I'll get back to her," Mega said, putting his phone away. "Tell me what's up?"

"There's a rat in our camp," I blurted out.

Mega's smile quickly turned into a frown. "Who?"

"Yolo," I said in disgust. "I told Breeze and Drake months ago. I know they were following papi's orders, but papi ain't here," I said, referring to my uncle who was their father. "This nicca is the only one I could think of who would be right under our nose and have full access to knock us all off."

"You should have told me this a long time ago. I never did like the nicca," Mega stated, enraged.

"Well, everyone thinks I'm just being paranoid because I never liked his ass. I figured you would feel the same way too. How was I supposed to know?"

"Nah, I hate the nicca too. I don't understand why papi took him in. He should have killed him right along with his parents. That's the code."

"Wait, what?" I nearly spit out my drink. "Papi killed Yolo's parents."

Mega answered by nodding his head.

"This all makes sense now. You think he knows?"

"He might," Mega replied.

"Damn, I wish I had talked to you a long time ago." I sighed. "This shit is even more fucked up than what I thought it was. Yolo definitely has a motive. If he knew papi killed his parents, then that would be the reason why he was so hell bent on getting back at us. It would also mean that you and I are in danger too."

"That nicca will have to be slick as fuck to catch me."

"I'm sure Breeze, Playez, and Drake said the same thing."

Mega nodded. "You have a good point."

"So, we stopped watching him and let him come back to work."

"Hold up, stop right there. What? Where's he at now?" Mega asked confused.

"Drake put him in time out months ago. We had someone following him, and we got nothing. That's why I said let him think everything's good, even though it's not. He'll let his guard down again because that's just the type of nicca he is. However, this time, I'm going to put Unique on him. I know she can get the job done. I'll just have to take one for the team."

"You about to smash?"

"If I have to," I answered. "I'm making up some shit as I go along. Fake her out until she gets down with the program."

"Just wave a few dollars in her face. She'll turn snitch on anybody. I never understood what Breeze saw in her. He needs to learn how to pick better women and stop thinking with his dick all the damn time."

"I agree but, for now, she is exactly what we need. She's sexy. I might as well enjoy myself."

"You should just let me kill Yolo and be done with this shit," Mega stated like it was a normal thing to shoot someone.

"Well, I would, but I don't want papi to call us in violation. Now, I know why he's protecting this little nicca. I'm assuming he feels guilty about Yolo's parents. Fuck all that. He's putting our lives in danger. I know for a fact that, if Yolo was anyone else, papi would have had him taken care of a long time ago."

"Yeah, I'm sure he does feel guilty. Yolo's father was a close friend of his. I think his murder was an accident. Papi doesn't talk about that story too often. From what I gather, they just hit a lick and papi was cleaning his gun and it went off, killing Yolo's father by mistake. His mother retaliated, shooting back at papi, and he put her down too. Yolo was in the bed sleep, so Papi took him with him. Their grandmother took the other two boys."

"What other two boys? And why am I just now hearing about this shit?"

"Yolo has two younger brothers that look just like him. They are twins. Papi had me keeping tabs on them for years. They on some street shit but, from what I can tell, they have no idea about any of this. They're small time hustlers, just trying to maintain. They're not a threat but, if they ever become one, I'll be hot on their asses."

I sighed. I got an eerie feeling about all this. "Does Yolo know?" I asked with concern. This could be bad news for us, if Yolo was aware that he had siblings. Being an outcast among us would definitely cause him to seek out his family.

"I don't think so," Mega stated. "To be honest, I don't think he knows about anything I just told you. I just think that he feels isolated because we're all family and very close. He's alienated himself because ain't nobody did anything to him. He's had a very good life, despite the circumstances. Everything papi did for us, he did for him. Yolo was treated like his own."

I laughed. "But you just said you hated the nicca."

"I do, but I never treated him badly. I just don't fuck with him like that. Never have. Never will."

I shook my head. "We better hurry up and get some dirt on this nicca before all of our asses be dead."

"Like I said, he better come hard if he wants to catch me." Mega looked at his phone. "I gotta go. Hit me up later and tell me how everything went with Unique."

"Will do."

I finished off his drink and paid my tab. I needed that drink after the information that I just learned. Carefully, I made my way to my bulletproof car. I had to handle this Yolo shit first.

I headed home before I went to see Unique. I had to get my shit right and look the part. Right now, I had on some basic shit that wouldn't impress her the least bit. She was the typical thot bitch who got turned on by materialistic shit, so I had to turn into the type of nicca that she would be attracted to.

Pulling into my four-car garage, I parked my work car and walked inside. I felt the emptiness of my house. I would be glad when this beef shit was done, so I could get back to what I love to do—fuck. Eventually, I wanted to settle down. That's the one thing Drake had right. Dicking down different pussy every night got old.

Having a steady piece of ass was priceless right now. The thing with that was these bitches ain't loyal. They not checking for a nicca for real. Either they want my money, my body, or both. It was hard to find a real chick who wanted my heart. Until I felt like I found that woman, I was going to continue to fuck around. Ghetto dick would be all I had to offer.

Once I showered and dressed in a bunch of expensive labels from head to toe, I put on my gold chain, diamond stud earring with the matching diamond bracelet, and sprayed my fifteen-hundred-dollar cologne. Unique knew her shit. She could see and smell money a mile away. If Breeze didn't show her nothing else, he exposed her to a rich lifestyle. That's why I made sure I was wearing thousands and smelled like it too.

Before I left, I sat down on my bed and pulled the cash out that I took out the bank. I folded it in a knot and placed a rubber band around it. This shit was risky too. I was about to leave out the house looking like a drug dealer, something I rarely did. Unlike some of my family members, I liked looking normal, even though I was a millionaire. Blending in was always my goal. Flashy shit brought too much attention around the city. However, money talked and bullshit walked. That saying definitely held true in Unique's life.

I pulled up as Unique was waiting for the bus. Her car was down, thanks to me. I knew how to get her attention. I was sitting in my red, bulletproof, custom made Jaguar XF Sport. This car was sure to get her attention. Her eyes were checking me out before I could roll down the window.

Chapter 30

Unique

I sat on the bench at the bus stop with a serious attitude because I just got a brand new car. I went through hell and high water to get that ride, scheming my ass off. I fucked three different niccas just to make sure that I didn't end up on the bus, and I still found myself taking this route.

"Can you scoot over a little bit more?" some ratchet ass bitch asked.

"No, I can't," I clicked. She eyeballed me and I eyeballed her ass too. I wasn't moving shit. My feet hurt. I would fight her for this seat if I had to.

This Chicago heat wasn't no punk. It was beating down on my body like I was in an oven. My tits were sweating. My ass was wet. Water dripped from my midsection down between my legs. I was sweating so bad that my long hair was sticking to my neck. The season was fall, but it was still ninety degrees outside. The seasons were all fucked up.

I was just about to say fuck it and call a cab when this fresh ass Jag pulled up. I strained my neck to see who was inside, but it was tinted out. Regardless, I was determined to get this person's attention. I knew it was a nicca driving. This was just the come up that I needed. The window rolled down slightly. I couldn't see the man very well, just his calculating eyes. I could tell that he was fine.

"Get in the car!" he called out to me.

I hesitated for a moment. Who was this? Did he know me? Was it Yolo? Nah, he's been ignoring my calls for the last couple of months.

All of a sudden, the sky got dark and a cloud hovered over the city. Rain began to pour down, soaking my skimpy outfit and ruining my hair immediately.

"C'mon, Unique. You're wetting my shit up!" the guy yelled at me.

I didn't hesitate this time. I ran to the car, opened the door, and planted my ass in the leather seat. I closed the door and turned towards the driver. Imagine my surprise when I saw it was Quay.

"Why you look so stunned?"

"I just... I just thought you hated me."

"I know we haven't seen things eye to eye in the past. However, that doesn't mean I'm going to drive pass you on the bus stop either."

I pushed my wet hair out of my face, pulling it up into a ponytail. "I appreciate it," I said with gratitude.

Quay looked me over and smiled. His eyes were glued to my body. I looked down and noticed that my bra and thong were showing through my wet clothes. Damn. Something told me not to wear this shit, but I was trying to be cute. Now, I was sitting in Quay's car looking just like a stripper on wet t-shirt night. While I was in deep thought, Quay put a gun to my head, and I jumped.

"Don't kill me," I squirmed.

"Tell me what I want to know and I won't."

My voice trembled in fear. "What do you want to know?"

"Tell me about Yolo," he said with malice. "And choose your words carefully."

I was really scared now. I was sure that he was on to me. But, how tho? I sat in his car paralyzed, as I tried to come up with a lie.

Click.

Dream & Drake 3: A Cartel Love Story

Quay pulled the trigger and I felt my life flash before my eyes. I wasn't sure if the chamber was empty on purpose or if he was trying to play Russian roulette with my life. I would have pissed on myself if I hadn't peed before I walked to the bus stop.

"Omg!" I cried. "What do you want to know?"

"Everything," he said, shoving the gun against my temple.

I paused one second too long and Quay pulled the trigger again. Tears escaped my eyes because I just knew I was dead this time, for real.

"You gone stop fucking around and tell me what I want to know before I blow your damn brains out."

"Okay, Okay," I surrendered. "Don't shoot, please."

"Start talking then."

"Yolo asked me to set up Breeze."

He hit me in the head with the gun. "So, you were responsible for him getting shot?"

"No," I sobbed. "I wasn't helping him when Breeze got shot. I would never be a part of that."

"But, you'll set him up tho?"

"All he told me was to distract Breeze. I was in on it when he got out of jail, but Breeze didn't want me, so Yolo dropped me. Breeze picked Bey over me, so I was useless to Yolo. He stopped telling me things and cut me out of the plan completely. I haven't been a part of nothing in months, so I can't say shit else cause I don't know nothing else. I had no idea he was going to try and kill Breeze, or I wouldn't have agreed. He just said he wanted his spot in The Cartel, so I assumed Breeze would step down if Yolo shamed him enough."

Quay hit me in the head again and I cried even harder. "What kinda stupid thot shit you talking about? Yolo can't shame Breeze into stepping down. Things don't work that way. That's the stupidest shit I ever heard. You are as dumb as people say you are. So, that's all you know? I think you're lying."

He looked as if he was about to pull the trigger for a third time and send me straight to hell.

"I don't know nothing else. I swear," I mumbled with fright. My whole body was shaking.

Princess Diamond

"You better not know nothing else because the next time I pull this trigger on your ass, I won't miss."

"So, you knew all along. This wasn't some chance meeting at the bus stop."

"Damn right. I tracked your phone."

"Can I go now?" I asked nervously, reaching for the door handle. The doors were locked and I couldn't figure out how to get out quick enough.

Quay yanked me back so that I could face him. "You my bitch now."

"Why?" I asked, again in tears.

"I don't think you're in a position to ask questions."

I cried into my palms. "You're going to kill me."

"I'm not going to kill your stupid ass," he declared. "As long as you do as I say. How much was Yolo paying you?"

"Not much. He still owes me money. If I had that money, I would get my car fixed."

"Fuck that car. You're with me now. I'll make sure you get around."

"So, you're really not going to kill me?" I inquired again.

Quay had just taken off into traffic, but he quickly pulled over in the rain, putting the car in park again. "Look me in my face," he required.

I stared him in the eye, but then looked away. He gently touched my cheek, turning my face back to him.

"Do you find me attractive?"

I scanned the bulge in his pants and instantly got horny. A puddle developed between my legs, and it wasn't from the rain. I didn't know why I had a thing for men with power. The fear of dying, mixed with the thrill of being with a Cartel nicca, had me all the way turned on. Quay called a lot of shots. Just the thought of him ordering people around had my pussy aching.

"I always thought you were sexy. I just thought you hated me," I told him with my eyes on his crotch. He had a very large print.

"I don't want Yolo coming after you, so I'm going to make you my girl so you'll be safe, but that means you have to be down with me. No more of that fuck shit. Do as I say and ride with The Cartel. Can you do that?" Quay asked me, maneuvering back into traffic.

"I did it before."

"I mean, did you tho?" He gave me the side eye.

I smacked my lips. "What you mean?"

"You didn't hold Breeze down. What makes me think you'll be down for me?"

He had a good point. "I made a stupid mistake. I should have held Breeze down, but I didn't. I wasn't thinking straight," I huffed.

"Give me one good reason why you shouldn't die for that?"

I had to say something quick. Something that he wanted to hear. I said the first thing that came to my mind. "I'll set up Yolo for you."

Quay smirked. "Now we're talking. Are you sure you can do that without fucking up?"

"Yeah, I'm sure," I said, happy as hell that he wasn't threatening my life anymore. "What else you want me to do?" I practically begged.

I knew exactly what he wanted when his right hand pinched my thick nipples.

"Damn, your nipples hard. That shit stiff for me?" he asked.

"Yes," I said truthfully.

"That pussy leaking too?"

"Yes," I responded.

When he moved his hand from my breast to my thigh, I spread my legs so he could touch in between. I felt his fingers gently pull my thong aside, grazing my swollen lips. I parted my legs even more, as he touched my clit and drove with one hand until we made it to his house. I knew where he lived, but I'd never been inside. He pulled into his garage and ushered me out.

"Take that wet shit off."

"All of it?" I inquired.

"Yes. All of it. Your ass is practically out anyway."

Princess Diamond

"Okay," I answered, quickly stripping like he told me to. I was low key scared of him, but I was super turned on too. I hadn't been this horny in a very long time. I always thought Quay was hot. He had this presence about him that just said I'm that nicca and you better fuckin' know it, and I loved that shit. I left my wet clothes in a pile by his car inside the garage.

"C'mon in," he said, holding the door for me.

When I walked pass, he smacked my ass hard, leaving a sting that made my clit throb even more.

"You like that freaky shit, don't you?"

I just stared at him as he stepped out of his clothes. I didn't know why I didn't say something. I guess I was hypnotized by his body. Quay definitely had a nice body.

His stare was intense. "You look like the type who likes rough sex."

I really lost my voice when he stepped out of his boxers and released a big ol' horse dick.

I shrieked at the size of his manhood. Who knew he was packing all that in his jeans. I was about to speak when he grabbed me around my neck, turned me around, and threw me up against the wall. He tore a condom wrapper open with his teeth, and I felt him fumbling with it before he put it on his monster dick. The huge tip was spreading my vagina as he entered me with force.

"Please don't fuck me hard," I pleaded. "It hurts."

"Does it?" he asked while gripping my neck tighter, stopping me from speaking.

I stood up against the wall with tears sliding down my cheeks as he assaulted my pussy.

"Does it hurt?" he asked, as if he didn't know the answer.

"Yeeeeees," I cried out in pain. "Please go easy on me."

"But whores know how to take dick."

"I can't take it."

"So, you're not a whore?"

"I don't know what you want me to say."

"Answer the question."

He had me so confused that I didn't even know what he was asking. "What was the question?"

Quay stopped thrusting inside of me, laughing. "You're weak. How the hell can you set anyone up? You can't even take dick right."

"I can't take your dick!" I shouted. "You haven't allowed me to get used to the shit."

I slid off the wall, practically climbing on the counter, running from his dick. I guess my plea finally got to Quay because he stopped fucking me wildly with that horse dick. He lifted my tiny frame up in the air, kissing me passionately. I wrapped my legs around his waist, with his dick resting in between my legs. His throbbing erection slid back and forth between my legs. He could have easily slipped inside of me, but I guess he didn't want to. I was glad too because the light friction of rubbing against my hot vagina felt awesome. I held his face, kissing him with fever while he gripped my ass. The way he held me in the air had me on fire.

"Better?" he whispered in lust.

"Yeeess," I moaned.

"Yes, what?"

"Yes, daddy," I cooed.

"You ready for some dick now?"

My body tensed up a little when he asked me that question.

"I'm not going to hurt you this time."

"Okay, daddy."

Quay carried us to his kitchen table. His arm swept across the neatly plated table, knocking everything to the floor. Dishes crashed, but they didn't break. Silverware lined the floor as well. He scooted back on the table with me on top of him. My legs straddled him as we continued to kiss. Our tongues did all the talking. Quay was a great kisser, so I really enjoyed kissing him. The more we kissed, the hotter I got. I felt his hand reach under me, caressing between my legs. I was sure he was impressed when he felt my honey leaking down my thigh.

I felt the head of his dick at the opening of my wetness. He pushed the tip in and it stretched my walls again. This time, it felt good. I found myself slowly rocking on the tip as he sucked my tongue.

"Feel good?" he asked.

"Yes, daddy," I purred, taking in a few more inches.

He smacked me on my ass a few times. "Get it then."

I rocked slowly on his pole, until he was all the way inside of me. I thought he was going to rupture my insides, but I was drenched so he fit perfectly. He pushed slowly inside of me, as I savored the feel of his huge dick. It felt like it was in my throat, but I enjoyed every inch of it now. I began rubbing my clit and Quay moved my hand, rubbing it for me.

"Damn, Quay!" I screamed out.

My voice echoed off his kitchen walls. I arched my back, bouncing a little harder. I was about to cum, and it was going to be explosive. His big dick had my ass, pussy, and clit tingling all at the same time.

"You about to cum?" he asked.

"Oh gawd, yes!" I said with my eyes shut. I clenched my pussy muscles tight. "Shhhhhiiiiitt! I'm cumming.'"

I bounced on his manhood for a minute savoring the sweet, sweet orgasm. I squeezed my toes together as tremors radiated from within, and my juices gushed out.

"My turn," Quay said, picking me up and standing to his feet.

As amazing as his dick felt, I knew that I had to do something drastic to get his attention. I had to show some kind of loyalty. I knew he didn't fully trust me, but I wanted him to. I didn't want to run and look over my shoulder for the rest of my life because a member of The Cartel wanted to murder me. That's exactly what would happen if I crossed Quay. It still might happen if Breeze finds out when he wakes up that I tried to set him up.

Hopping off Quay's dick, I fell to my knees, staring his humongous tool in the face. I couldn't deep throat his dick, but I was going to damn sure try. I took the condom off that was coated with my thick, white cum and tossed it on the floor. Giving it my best effort, I took as many inches into my mouth as I could, sucking his dick for my safety.

"Daaaamm, girl. You trying to suck the skin off this mutha-fucka."

"I sure am, daddy," I said in between slurps.

Quay grabbed me by my hair, rocking his pelvis back and forth into my face. I had great gag muscles so, even as big as his dick was, I still didn't choke. I felt his body tense up and I knew he was ready to let his load go.

"Aaaaaaaahhhh. Fuuuuuuccccck!"

I felt his seed in my mouth. I was about to swallow when I decided to make it nasty. I pulled his dick out of my mouth and smeared his cum all over my lips and face.

"Damn, you made that shit look so fuckin' good."

I smiled, still sucking on his semi-hard dick. "I just want to please you, daddy."

Quay and I fucked and fucked and fucked until were both spent. Somehow, we managed to shower and get cleaned up before calling it a night.

I woke up in the middle of the night and found Quay's arm over my waist. He was snoring lightly but had a death grip on me.

"Where you going?" he asked groggily.

"Nowhere. I was just getting comfortable."

"Don't get up," he demanded. "I'm not playing with you."

"I'm not going anywhere."

He pulled me back into him and I snuggled back against his soft dick that was big, even when it was soft. I never thought that I would be with Quay. Never in a million years but, now that I experienced what he had to offer, I wanted in. I realized that he might only be using me, but I was sure that after I fucked and sucked him like only I could, he would be ready to wife a bitch up, move me in, and spend money on me. Yes, my pussy was just that good.

"Why you wake me up?" he wondered.

"I can put you back to sleep if you want me to," I said, tugging on his gigantic erection.

Princess Diamond

"You might as well," he said with an attitude, turning onto his back so that I could please him better.

I didn't pay him any mind while taking his dick into my mouth, preparing to suck him back to sleep.

"Shit, girl, your jaws are amazing."

So, I've been told, I thought, smiling inwardly.

Chapter 31

Aquarius

I woke up with Unique in my arms. Shit had been crazy. We been fucking for four days straight. I just couldn't get enough of her. Obviously, she couldn't get enough of me either. Once she got used to my dick, she fucked me all over the house, giving it to me like I never had it before.

She was definitely blessed, physically. I'd dated plenty hoes and none of the hoes I'd fucked around with were like Unique. Her pussy stayed wet and tight. I just knew it would be loose by the time we finished. Nah, her shit snapped right back. Then, I thought she would have a stank attitude. Not the case at all. She was so agreeable. I loved passive women. There couldn't be two bosses. I was in control and I make that point very clear. This was my fucking world. Either be a passenger or get the fuck out my ride.

My phone vibrated. It was a text. I didn't even want to roll over to get it. Reaching behind me, I got my phone and looked at the text. It was from Mega.

Mega: Where you been?
Me: In the house
Mega: For the last three days?
Me: Lol yeah
Mega: She got your ass, didn't she?
Me: Bruuuuh, you have no idea.

Mega: Nicca, focus. You about to let some pussy take you out.

Me: That'll never happen but, shit, I know why Breeze was sweet on her ass for so long. She got some of the best pussy ever.

Mega: I don't even want no pussy like that. It'll have me slip up and get murked.

Me: Hol up, you got a lot of damn nerve. You lost focus a long damn time ago with Mercy and you ain't even smelled the pussy. Get your ass on lol

Mega: LMAAAAAO! Stop trying to son me.

Me: Lmao. Nicca, talk to me after y'all fuck. Then, let me see where your head is at. You already sprung and all she did was stare at your ass.

Mega: Point well taken. But anyway... Yolo is here with me at the trap.

Me: Say no more. I'm back in action. After I hit this one more time...

Mega: *sigh* Bruh, damn!

Me: Calm down. You know I always come through. No slip ups ever.

Mega: You do, but your ass is worse than Drake and Breeze when it comes to being laid up. Work comes first, nicca.

Me: No pussy getting ass nicca. Don't judge me. Tryna stop my shine cuz you ain't fuckin. Hating ass.

Mega: CTFU

I locked my phone, put it back on the dresser, and smacked Unique on the ass. I must've put it on her because she was still knocked out. My hand roamed over her mounds. If they weren't so soft and jiggly, I would have sworn that they were implants. I already knew they weren't. Naturally, she had the body that other bitches were trying to get. That Barbie doll shape that was sexy as fuck.

I slapped her ass again and she stirred a little bit. I had something to wake her ass up, this morning wood. I flipped her onto her back, climbed on top of her, and slid my dick inside, grinding slowly.

"Damn, this pussy good."

"Mmmmmm."

"I bet your ass is up now."

Unique opened her eyes and smiled. "Good morning, daddy."

"You ready to take this dick?"

"Yes. Dick me down, daddy."

I sucked on her breasts while she worked her hips. I picked her up so she could bounce on it. Her moans turned into screams. She was cumming in no time. While she was still creaming, I laid her back on the bed, ready to release my load so we could cum together. I gripped her hair while biting her neck as my fluids leaked out.

"Shit, that was good as fuck," I panted on top of her.

The reality of what I just done kicked in. I jumped up and sat on the side of the bed with cum still oozing from my dick.

"What's wrong?" Unique asked.

I looked back at her, pissed the fuck off. She tried to comfort me and I pushed her away.

"What did I do?" she asked, crawling back up behind me.

I was so angry with myself for going in her raw. I wasn't worried about catching something. I was more worried about getting her pregnant. I never fucked without a condom, unless I wanted to. Usher's song played in my mind. That's what It's Made For.

Game rules, no cap no cut
But even Superman couldn't turn your love down, I
Slipped up, slipped in
Hey man what the hell you doin'?
Raw dog is a never
I know I know better
Heard her whisper
Don't worry, I'm safe
Didn't matter cause it's already too late
I was lost in the sauce, dead wrong

Princess Diamond

And I ain't stoppin' now
Parleein' in the bush again
Didn't think about what I was puttin' in it

Go on and hit it
That's what it's made for
She said, you got somethin on right?
That's what it's made for
Boo, are you trippin'
You know I got it
That's what it's made for

So I can do you like this, baby
So I can freak you like this, baby
Know you gon' felt it like this, baby
Girl, I forgot it
But we gon' still get down like this

I jumped up from the bed and Unique flinched. I guess she thought I was going to hit her. I sure as hell wanted to, but it wasn't her fault. It was all on me. Damn.

"Take a shower and get dressed," I said in a nasty tone.

I was ready to snatch her up when she didn't move. She just sat there looking at me crazy, like I didn't just ask her stupid ass to beat her feet.

"I said get the fuck up, shower, and put some damn clothes on."

Unique scurried out the bed, but she was still standing there looking stupid.

"What the fuck is wrong with you?" I swear, I was ready to put my hands on her. I was so damn close.

She gave me a simple look. "I-I don't have any clothes to wear. You told me to strip out of my wet clothes in the garage. I've been in the house with you since then."

"Why didn't you say that shit?"

I stepped towards her and she flinched. "Stop fuckin' flinching. I'm not going to hit you."

"Okay, but you're scaring me."

I grabbed her by the hand, nearly dragging her to the room across the hall. "Here," I said, pointing to the clothes in the closet. "This is my ex's shit. Find something to wear. You got ten minutes to be ready or we about to have a problem. And don't say shit about my ex or ask any questions because I'm not up for the damn discussion."

"Okay," she murmured.

I stormed back to my room and packed a shoulder bag full of gadgets that I would need for Yolo's house. After we got ourselves together, we went straight to his crib. I was about to break in, when Unique pulled out a key and opened the door. I looked at her ass sideways.

"What?" she asked clueless.

"Why the fuck didn't you tell me you had a key? I'ma bout to break in this man's shit when I could have just walked in."

"I'm sorry," she said, avoiding my gaze. "Here, you can have it." She placed the key in my palm.

"Man, I'm trying to trust your ass, but you keep showing me signs of being a snake ass bitch."

"Quay, I said I was on your side. I wouldn't be here risking my life if I wasn't."

"What the fuck are you risking? You need to be more scared of me than Yolo. That punk nicca ain't shit compared to me."

"I don't want you mad at me. I know you don't believe me, but I'm on your side. I'll do whatever you ask me to do."

"Aight. Stop running your mouth."

I needed to be able to think and she was talking too damn much. I walked around Yolo's house, trying to decide where I wanted to put the cameras and place the wires so that he wouldn't see them. Every room had two cameras and multiple wires. I wanted to hear this nicca breathing in his sleep. Nothing would get pass me. I called Mega.

"Can you see me?"

"Yeah," he said, looking into his phone.

"Aight. I got the apps on both of our phones, so someone is watching this nicca at all times. He's going to fuck up."

"Shit, you don't have to tell me," Mega exclaimed. "It'll be sooner than later."

"What about the recording? You hear that too?"

When Mega didn't reply to me, I assumed the audio wasn't as smooth as the cameras. I had Unique go into the other room and talk. Mega still didn't hear anything. After a few minor adjustments, everything was running smoothly. Mega hung up and I was packing up my stuff when Unique said something that made me think.

"You want this?" She was holding a phone.

"Yeah, let me get his phone," I told her. I was going to plant a chip in it too.

"This ain't his phone tho."

"So, what phone is this?" I asked her.

"His old phone. His new phone is on him."

I picked up my phone and dialed the number that I had for Yolo and, sure enough, the phone that was before me rang. This fuck nicca really thought he was slick holding two fuckin' phones. I couldn't wait until this nicca died. I was going to have the biggest smile on my face when he was gone for good.

I erased the call history, put the phone back, and told Unique to send Yolo a text.

"Keep it simple and say something you would normally say."

"Okay," Unique said, taking her phone out of her pocket.

I stood over her as she texted him, coaching her on what to say.

Unique: Hey. You keep avoiding my texts. I'm just trying to make sure you're good.

Yolo: I'm not fuckin with you no more.

Unique: You about to be fuckin' with me when you find out who I just got next to.

Yolo: Who?

Unique: Quay

Yolo: Oh word? How'd you do that?

Unique: How do you think? Just know that I'm his girl now. I've been with him for the last few days at his house. I just thought you would want to know that, but since you not fuckin with me no more...

Yolo: Wait. Hold on, girl. Sorry about that. You know you be on some shady shit sometimes, but I see you came through. You a bad bitch for pulling Quay's crazy ass. I didn't think you had it in you.

Unique: I know. He's about to take me shopping. I'm going to be staying at his house, so I won't be able to talk to you too much, but I'll keep you posted as best as I can.

Yolo: Yeah, do that.

I texted Mega about the two phones, and he said he would put the chip inside of the phone that's on him.

"Did I do good?" Unique asked me as she put her phone back in her purse. She was all smiles.

"You did great. Now, let's bounce."

I made sure everything was back the way it was before we came. Both of us had on gloves, but I wiped shit down anyway.

"Are you really going to take me shopping? Or was that just a lie that you told Yolo?"

I glanced at her. Damn, she would find the tightest, shortest shit that my ex had in the closet.

"We're going to swing by your crib so you can pack your things and come stay with me. Then, I might take you shopping."

She smiled. "Let me find out you like me."

"Maybe just a little bit."

She giggled, which made me laugh too.

I smirked. "Don't be trying to figure me out."

"I'm not. I'm just glad you're not mad at me anymore."

Little did she know, I was still low-key heated, but it wasn't her fault. It was mine. I got caught up.

"I know one thing, I'm getting a whole box of condoms and a Plan B before we go back to the crib."

Unique softly touched my hand. "Sounds good to me, zaddy."

Princess Diamond

Damn, a nicca could get used to being worshiped like this.

Chapter 32

Drake

Monday couldn't have come quick enough. I was so ready to get away from all these degenerate muthafuckas in jail. A weekend in a place like this was all I could handle. Overall, I kept my cool while I waited on my bail hearing. I spoke to Ross and he was pretty sure that he would be able to get me out on Monday.

Ross came to the jail early and prepped me for the bail hearing. He said Channa was in jail too and that she might be the one with diarrhea of the mouth. Channa better not be running her mouth. I had evidence to put her away for life. Not to mention, she burned my damn house down.

Just like Ross said, when I went before the judge, all of my charges were dropped. I was a free man. My victory was short-lived when Dream was escorted in. It had only been three days and she looked like she had been in jail a month. I couldn't wait until she was free. Imagine my surprise when her bail was denied. This so-called snitch stated that Dream was a queen pin. Somehow, this muthafucka managed to give evidence that convinced the judge that Dream was the real threat not me. So, the judge revoked her bail and back to the slammer she went.

Ross knew I was about to act a damn fool and land my ass back in jail. This time, for choking out the judge. Before I could open my mouth, some huge nicca yanked me out the courtroom.

I was fighting his ass tooth and nail, but I couldn't get back in there to see Dream, no matter how hard I tried.

I was so muthafuckin' angry that I had popped a blood vessel in my eye.

"So, what now?" I asked Ross in anger, while sitting in his office.

"Drake, you've known me for a long time. Trust me. I'm going to get her out."

"But, when tho?"

"Don't I always come through?"

I sighed. I didn't want to answer. I was afraid I might say some stupid shit and fuck my relationship up with Ross.

"Look at me, Drake."

I stared his ass down.

"Have I ever let you down?"

I sighed again. This time, I thought about what he asked. "I trust you, man. This shit got me going crazy."

"I know it does, but I have another bail hearing set for tomorrow. I'm going to work hard to make sure that she gets bail. I can't lie to you; they have some strong evidence against her."

"Yeah, but the fucked up part is, Dream ain't even street. I'm that nicca."

"And it should be that much easier to prove that she isn't a queen pin versus you being a kingpin. This actually plays in your favor."

I lowered my head. I didn't see how this played in my favor when the woman I loved was locked up like some animal, and she's pregnant. "I don't care what you have to do to get her out. If that means I need to take a plea, then that's what I'll do," I said while raising my head, looking him in the eye.

Ross nodded and handed me a folder. "This should cheer you up a little."

I took the folder from his hand. I was not sure what's in here that would make me cheer up. As soon as I opened the folder, I immediately smiled. "My divorce is final?"

Ross nodded and smiled. "Not only is it final, but I'm working on that other thing you told me to do too."

Dream & Drake 3: A Cartel Love Story

"Depends on when Dream gets out of jail."

"Let's be positive."

"You're right."

"Why don't you go home and get some rest? We have court in the morning."

I took his advice. I went home, well, not to my house because it was still under construction. Channa didn't burn it to the ground like she thought. I did lose a lot but, after the insurance company came out and assessed the damage, they were confident that everything could be restored, good as new. That put my mind at ease, since it was our family home. For the moment, I was living between my apartment and Mega's house.

I stayed with Fresh for a little while, but that nicca got too many kids. Crying babies all night long just didn't do it for me. Yeah, that sounded ironic coming from me, knowing that I would have multiples in my house. However, it made a difference when it was my kids versus someone else's kids.

Fresh had his daughters super spoiled. They cried about damn near everything. As soon as their lips quivered and a tear looked like it was about to fall, Fresh was ready to fold and give in to their demands. This nicca was the reason why they were so rotten. Plus, I planned on having a nanny, unlike them. I was not about to be up all night watching no kids when I needed my damn sleep.

I didn't realize how tired I was until my head hit the pillow. I was out like a light. It was morning before I knew it. Time to face the judge. I got to Ross' office early with two cups of Starbucks.

"What are Dream's chances of getting bail today?"

"I'm not sure. I wasn't able to get her medical records. Let me look once more." Ross walked over to the fax machine and then came back.

"Nope, nothing."

"So, how is this going to work?"

Ross sighed. "I'm not sure."

I was a nervous wreck sitting in the court room. My heart dropped to my stomach when I saw Dream again. She looked

213

like she was having a real rough time. When she looked back at me, I blew her a kiss. She gave me a faint smile before turning back around. I watched the judge's face as Ross represented for Dream. The no-nonsense look that she gave told it all, and bad news followed.

"Bail denied," she exclaimed, banging her gavel down.

"Fuck you mean?" I barked. "Bitch, you done lost your damn mind. I ought to-"

"Order in the court!" She banged the gavel furiously. "Order in the court!"

My outburst caused an uproar that rippled through out the court like a domino effect.

"Mr. Diaz-Santana, do you want to go back to jail? Because I can make that happen, right now."

I was about to answer that question when Quay hit me in the back of the head. I turned around to look at him, which distracted me from fucking the judge up.

The judge continued, "As long as I'm residing over this case, you will not be allowed in my court room. Court adjourned." She banged the gavel, and I was escorted out, practically tossed out on my ass.

"Way to go, hero," Quay said, flopping down next to me. "Now, you can't even support your girl cause your ego got you tossed the fuck out."

"Damn, Quay. Don't you think I know that shit?"

"And on that note, I'm out. Call me if you need me." Quay threw up the peace sign and bounced.

I had been sitting outside the courtroom on a bench, waiting for what seemed like forever.

"What now?" I asked Ross as soon as he walked up.

"Another bail hearing tomorrow."

His phone chimed. He looked at it and smiled bright.

"Bingo. Her medical records are available."

I sighed. "Is this really going to work? I'm starting to think that this judge is just a bitch, and she hates me and Dream."

"It'll work," Ross assured me.

"I hope so. I don't think Dream can take too much more. I can't lie, I don't think I can either."

"She's coming home tomorrow. I promise. Do you still want me to set everything up for you two?"

"Yes."

Thinking about the surprise I had for Dream actually put a much needed smile on my face.

"Third time's a charm," Ross said, patting me on my back like he did his colleagues. "Tomorrow is the day," Ross sang, walking away.

I drove straight home, making the final arrangements to my surprise for Dream. At the rate things were going, I was never going to be able to surprise her. By the time I made the last phone call, I was pooped. I crawled into bed, dreading tomorrow's bail hearing.

I didn't get up early or go and get Starbucks like before. I was feeling a little bummed, trying to figure out why wasn't the evidence presented good enough. How did I get off and she didn't? Anyone with two eyes could see that Dream wasn't a street chick. There was no way she would be a queen pin.

I sat outside the courtroom tapping my foot. For the first time, my suit felt uncomfortable and I never tapped my foot so much in my life. Every negative thing ran through my head. What if Dream's bail gets denied again, then what? Would she get years in jail? What about the baby? My mind continued to race for hours as I rubbed my clammy hands. Finally, the court door opened, and Dream walked out. I rushed over to her, squeezing her so tight that I was sure I hurt the baby.

"Drake, I was so scared," Dream said, melting against me.

"I know, ma. You'll never have to experience that again for as long as I live."

I ushered Dream to the limousine waiting outside. My apartment wasn't that far away, but I rented us a nice hotel suite. I wanted her to relax and clear her mind. I was sure that was difficult, since she was eating for two.

"Can we stop and get something to eat?" Dream asked. "I'm starving."

"I'll have whatever you want delivered to the hotel."

Her stomach growled loudly and we both laughed.

"I got you, ma."

As soon as we got to the hotel, I ran Dream's bath water and bathed her. Her food was delivered at the same time. I watched her as she smashed a shit load of stuff, from hot wings to barbeque to crab cakes to caramel cake. When Dream was stuffed, I led her to the bathroom, stripping her out of her clothes and helping her in. She started crying as I washed her body.

"Drake, I'm sorry."

"About what, ma?"

"About how I tried to stop you from going after Spencer. I don't care what you do to him."

"He's a nonfactor now, ma."

Dream cried even harder. "You're right. It doesn't matter. I just want you to know that I choose you. You got my back and I didn't have yours. That's all I could think about while I was in jail. That you were going to leave me."

"Ma, it's okay, as long as you have my back from this point forward. And for the record, I'm never going to leave you. We just had a spat, like lovers do."

"I want to be your ride or die," she cried. "Whatever I have to do. Steal, kill, or go to jail. I'm with you all the way."

She had no idea how much those words meant to me. I'd been waiting for her to say that since forever. "Okay, that's so cliché, but I appreciate it, ma. I just need you to be in this with me, no matter what I do. I live a crazy life. I can't be with a woman who folds under pressure. If a nicca gotta be dealt with, I need to deal with them."

"I'm not going to fold. You see I held my own in jail. I didn't break down not one time. Although, I wanted to because I was hungry as hell."

I wiped the tears from her cheeks. "Yes, you did. You were gangsta in jail with this big ol' belly."

She giggled. "I didn't tell them pigs shit."

"That's why I love you, ma."

"I love you too, papi."

Dream & Drake 3: A Cartel Love Story

"Let me show you how much, ma."

Dream sat on the side of the luxurious bathtub as I feasted on her kitty. I licked from front to back before I slurped on her pearl. Once I stuck two fingers inside of Dream, she came instantly, squirting cum all over my face. I was just so glad she was free and I planned on showing her how much. I continued to suck on her clit until she came again.

We took it to the bedroom, doing a sixty-nine. She sat on my face, and I continued to eat her from behind pleasuring her into bliss once more. Needless to say, Dream was worn out by the time I slid into her hot and juicy pussy. She laid there unable to move and just moaned as I stroked us both into harmony.

Just as I was about to cum, Dream jumped up from the bed full of life and took my dick into her mouth. She sucked on my tool hungrily, as I emptied my fluid into her mouth. I thought she was done, until she shoved me down on the bed and began sucking on my semi-hard dick. Once it was hard again, Dream mounted me and rode us both into ecstasy.

Chapter 33

Yolo

I might have been back in good graces with The Cartel, but shit was still all bad. Working under Mega had me on pins and needles. This nicca was more unpredictable than Breeze. Being in his presence, I had to watch my back, my front, and my side. He never said he was gunning for me but, deep down inside, I had a feeling that he was. That's why I decided to strike him before he got to me. I was setting things into motion asap.

I decided to pay Nemo a visit. He was an old friend of The Cartel. Someone who hated Mega and Quay just as much as I did. Mega was contracted to kill him, but somehow, he escaped death. I was sure that Mega didn't know that he was still alive. In fact, I was positive that if Mega knew, Nemo wouldn't still be breathing right now. Nemo had been hiding and laying low. I wasn't sure how he stayed out of the sight of The Cartel when they ran Chicago. If I hadn't accidently bumped into him, I wouldn't have believed he was still alive either. I just hoped I was as fortunate to escape death like he did. Something told me that I wouldn't be so lucky. Either way, in my absence, my plan to kill would still be in full effect, whether it's now or later.

Having a nicca like Nemo in my back pocket sure helped. It was only a matter of time before the bricks that I gave Channa got traced back to me. Had I known her ass was going to get arrested, I wouldn't have given her the shit. I wouldn't have even known she got popped until she called my phone from jail.

I pulled up to the spot that Nemo picked. The moment I got out of the car, there was a gun in my face.

"Is it this serious?" Nemo had been around The Cartel too long.

"You damn right," dude with the gun said.

I moved to the side with my hands in the air. Nemo's goons searched the car. They took the bag of cash out of the back seat and ushered me to the Yukon that was parked behind me. I sat in the back with dude holding a gun on me, while two other dudes sat in the front. Three more dudes were standing guard by my car. I guess Nemo thought I was about to set him up. The guy in the passenger's seat turned around and I realized it was Nemo.

"Is it all here?" Nemo asked while looking over the bands.

I scrunched up my face. "Of course it is. The five-hundred thousand like we agreed on."

He looked the money over in the bag once more. "It better be."

"When will it be done?" I inquired. I wanted them niccas dead asap.

"Soon," he stated. "Let me put a plan into action. I'm going after Mega first. Quay can wait."

Now, it was my turn to have an attitude. "Wait, what does that even mean?"

"It means, you need my help nicca. I don't need yours. I guess you fuckin' forgot I know them, so let me handle shit my way."

"Whatever. Don't take too damn long. I don't want them to get to me before I can get to them."

Nemo chuckled hearty. "That shit might happen anyway."

One of Nemo's goons signaled for me to get out of the car. As soon as I got out, his goons got back in, and they sped off. I just hoped that I didn't fuck myself by asking this nicca to help me. I wasn't sure if I could trust his ass either. He seemed shady as fuck too. As I pulled away from the secret location, I got a text stating there was an emergency meeting and to get to the trap asap. Then, Zino was on my line.

"Nicca, I'm telling you, they on to us," Zino whined, sounding just like a damn female.

"Calm your scary ass down," I spat.

"Why the fuck did you give that bitch those keys? The shit points back to me, damn." This nicca was really tripping.

"If anything, it points back to me," I corrected his scary ass.

"Well, Gremlin said he wasn't coming. I shouldn't show up either. I ain't tryna die."

"Listen, scary muthafucka, you're really going to fuck yourself if you don't show up. Missing a meeting makes you look very suspicious in their eyes, especially since you're already at the damn trap. What would be your reason for leaving? Think some damn time."

"I don't know. I don't know. I don't know," Zino stuttered. "I ain't tryna die man. Naw, man, not me. Uh-uh."

"Just be cool, shit. I'm on my way. And whatever you do, keep your fuckin' mouth shut. Act like you're good, even if you're not."

"Aight."

Zino hung up and I dialed Gremlin. No answer. I left this dumb ass nicca message. "Aye, we have a meeting. It's mandatory. You need to be there, feel me? See you there."

I hoped he got the message. The last thing that I needed was him to up and disappear.

"Good Afternoon, everyone," Mega said, walking into the trap in The Heights followed by his crazy brother, Axel.

Some spoke. Others gave a head nod.

Axel took a seat on the desk in front of us, mean mugging us all. I could tell he was shitty. "I called this emergency meeting because shit ain't right, and I plan to get to the bottom of it," he said with authority.

Oh, gawd. What the fuck now? If it ain't one brother, it's another one. All of these niccas were crazy as fuck. I sat there with my lips sealed tight. I didn't want them pointing no fingers at me. I hadn't been in much contact with my old crew because all of them niccas were dead. However, I'd been in constant contact with my new crew Zino and Gremlin. Zino just so happened to be sitting right by me. If I knew this nicca was going to be doing a finger-pointing session, I would have sat far away.

Axel sat before us looking angry and heartless. "There is a snake among us."

The room was tense as fuck.

I looked to my right and Zino was sweating bullets. This nicca here looked like he was scared shitless. I just hope he didn't do anything stupid. Axel continued to look at each one of us, like he could see into our soul. If I didn't smoke weed before this, I was sure I would afterwards. This whole experience was intimidating, to say the least.

"This meeting is long overdue. Some of you I know, others I don't. That's not the point; the point is you need to take a good look at me and remember my face. I'm not Breeze or Drake. I'm Axel and I don't give a fuck about your problems, your family, or you. The only thing I give a fuck about is this product hitting the fuckin' streets on time and turning that into a profit. If you can't do your job and make this money, you're a dead man walking. Now, I've said a lot. Is there anyone who wants out? You're free to leave."

Zino jumped up like a lightning bolt.

"Man, if you don't sit your ass down," I said through gritted teeth. I couldn't stand a scary ass nicca.

"Naw, man, I'm out."

I watched as he looked frantically around the room in fear and then bolted for the door.

Pop! Pop!

Two clean shots to the dome. Zino and another dude were running towards the door. They were both shot in the back of the head by Mega. Their bodies dropped before either one of them could register what had happened. The looks on their faces proved my point.

Axel chuckled. "I guess we know who the snakes are. Does anyone else want to leave?"

We all sat there in fear of our lives. Nobody said shit. Everyone looked as if they were holding their breath. I know I was. If they were on to Zino, it was only a matter of time before they figured me out.

"Just know that if you're full of shit, your ass will be fertilizer." Axel pointed to the two dead bodies on the floor. "Get the fuck out of my face. Meeting's over."

I wanted to run like Zino did, but I didn't want to get shot too. Running would make me look guilty. The last thing I wanted to do was look guilty. I just got back on good terms.

"Yolo, let me holler at you!" Axel called out as soon as I was about to leave. Everyone continued to file out as I turned around, walking back.

"Yeah, what's up?" I asked with my game face on.

"Take a ride with me."

"Hold up," Mega stated, patting me down. He took both guns that I had on me and handed it to one of the workers in the trap. "Now, you can leave."

I followed Axel and Mega to the SUV.

"Get in," Axel demanded.

Shit wasn't right. I could feel it. "Where the fuck are we going?" I exclaimed, stopping mid-stride.

"Are you a soldier or are you a pussy?" Axel stated with his gun drawn. "I'm not going to ask your punk ass again. Get the fuck in the car or have your brains blown out."

I got in the car like I was told, dreading what the next step was. Axel got behind the wheel. Mega occupied the passenger's seat. We pulled off, and I noticed that another car pulled off with us. The suspense of where we were going was killing me. I didn't know if I was the issue or if it was someone else. Axel or Mega could have killed me right there on the spot, but they didn't, which really had me thinking. What the fuck was really up.

"Zino was your boy, correct?" Axel asked.

I nearly shit my pants when he asked me about Zino's dead ass. I quickly thought about how I should answer. I could lie and say no but, then again, Axel might already know that we were cool. Fuck it. I decided to tell the truth. "Yeah, and?"

"And I hope you don't feel some type of way or no shit. The nicca was a thief. He got exactly what the fuck he deserved."

I just stared at him in the rearview mirror, trying to fill this conversation out.

"Did you know about what he did?"

"C'mon, man. You know I didn't have no idea. If I knew, I would have told you. Come at me better than that."

That's a lie. I knew Zino took the keys. I was the one who told him to do it. I was hustling bricks on the side to get my money up. I couldn't take over shit if I didn't have no bread. However, when Channa called and said that she needed them, I had no problem handing them over to her. She'd always looked out for me. It was only right.

"Well, it's your job to know. Personally, I think that should have been you lying face down on the floor breathless."

I nodded my head to let him know I understood. I would have opened my mouth, but I didn't want to put my foot in it.

Axel gave me a wicked grin. "It's not too late."

I sighed and stared out of the tinted window.

Was this the end of me? Was I really about to go out foul like Zino did?

Chapter 34

Beyonne

I laid face down on the mattress all cried out. I cried so many tears that I couldn't cry anymore. I was never going to get out of here. I stopped fighting my attackers and allowed them to do whatever it was that they wanted to do to me. I no longer tried to escape, nor did I give them any lip. There was no more slick talk left in me.

The thought of being rescued seemed impossible. Everyone had forgotten about me. I was at the point to just give up completely. Dying seemed like my only way out. I was tired of having a dick in my mouth. I was sick of getting my pussy ate. Whenever I did eat, the food was horrible. I'd lost so much weight that I was sure I looked anorexic. My weave was still in my head. Yes, my weave from months ago. It was hanging on the ends of my hair, down my back. All my nails popped off. My skin was ashy. I couldn't see as well because my contacts popped out a long time ago. Basically, I was fucked. That's what I was trying to say. Life as I used to know it no longer existed. I even stopped praying. Nobody was going to find me. I was just going to die like this.

For a while, there was another girl here, Tonya. She kept me company. I was not sure what happened to her. Knowing these insane bastards, they probably killed her.

Dream & Drake 3: A Cartel Love Story

Rutta appeared before me. "Get up. Today is your lucky day."

"How so?" I wondered.

"You're about to get all this girlie shit."

I didn't know what that meant, but I got up anyway, following him out of the basement and upstairs to the bathroom. I expected him to fondle me or force his penis down my throat, but all he did was stare. I was used to him watching me shower, so none of that bothered me anymore. The shower felt good because I hadn't gotten one in over a week.

Once I was clean, Rutta led me out of the bathroom into one of the bedrooms, where two women were waiting for me. I saw hair and nail items laid out, so I assumed that I was getting my hair and nails done.

"What's up with all this? Are you letting me go?"

"Something like that," Rutta laughed.

I wasn't sure what he meant by that, but I was happy as hell to be getting this type of treatment. I was sure there was a motive behind me getting dolled up. However, at the moment, I refused to let my mind wander and just enjoyed the moment.

The girl who did my hair hooked me up. She gave me 28" Loose Wavy Virgin Peruvian hair. I'm talking about the premium shit. If nothing else, I knew my weave.

"Somebody spent a pretty penny on you, girl," the beautician said, handing me a mirror so I could look at my tresses.

For a moment, I was so caught up in how beautiful I looked that I forgot where I was.

"Now, let me work my magic on those hands and feet," the nail tech said.

"Yaaaaaas." That was all I could say when she finished. I held my hand up, admiring the French manicure design with rhinestone accents. For a minute, I thought I was around the way getting Ming to hook me up.

"Congratulations," the manicurist said.

"Thank you," I said with no clue why she was congratulating me. I guess she was loving the nail art as much as I was cause it was banging.

Princess Diamond

They packed their things up, about to leave. I contemplated leaving with them when a woman with a rack full of dresses sauntered in. I also saw Rutta standing by the door with an AK. Even if I wanted to escape, I would be dead before I made it to the front door. That's probably what happened to the other girl because she was saying all the time how she was planning to leave. I went to sleep one day and, when I woke, she was gone. I heard a gunshot shortly afterwards, and I never saw her again.

I stared at all of the beautiful gowns that resembled a wedding gown and I was really confused now.

"Pick one, honey," the foreign lady said. I could tell by her accent that she was from another country.

"What is all this for?"

"The sooner you learn not to ask questions, the better off you'll be."

She gave me a look that said it'll save your life and I immediately shut up. I was convinced that I was going to die in this dress. That's why they were getting me dolled up. I always said, when I died, I wanted to be buried in a wedding dress. Only a select few knew that secret. I supposed this was the day they were going to shoot me and send me back to my parents in style.

Sadly, I tried on dress after dress until I found the perfect one. A white strapless wedding dress with a sweetheart neckline, beaded waistband, chapel train, and vividly ruffled ball gown skirt.

"Is she ready?" Rutta asked from the other side of the door.

"One minute!" the stylist called out, placing a floral wreath halo veil on my head. "She's ready!" the stylist called out.

The door opened and she ushered the rack of dresses out into the hallway. Rutta stepped in with the gun pointed at me. I closed my eyes and held my breath, accepting my fate. Death.

"You look beautiful," a familiar voice said. "Just like I knew you would."

I opened my eyes and came face to face with my ex. "Reggie?"

"In the flesh, baby."

Dream & Drake 3: A Cartel Love Story

He was dressed in a black suit and shoes, with a white shirt, vest, tie, and pocket square. Under different circumstances, I would say that he looked nice.

"Don't tell me that you did all this?'

He shrugged.

That's when it all made sense. "So, you kidnapped me? Why?" I had a feeling it was him. I just didn't know why.

"Because I was with you for years and you never looked at me the way you looked at that Breeze nicca. You never offered me your virginity. You never told people about me, the way you told people about him."

"So, you had me kidnapped because you're jealous? I ought to beat your-" I started to charge towards him when Rutta pointed the gun right at me.

"I love you, Bey, but I won't hesitate to have you killed if you don't do as I say. Now, as you can see, I'm carrying out the plan that you ruined."

"What plan is that?"

"Marriage. We were supposed to get married. That's all we talked about until you dumped me for no reason."

"Nicca, I didn't talk about that all the time, you did."

"I knew that the only way I could have sex with you was to make you my wife, so we're sealing the deal. You get what you want, and I do too."

"What kind of sicko are you? Did you order Rutta to force his dick down my throat too?"

"Yes, but it was for your own good. I love head and I wanted you to be great at it. I didn't want you biting my dick and shit, fucking up the mood because you're inexperienced."

"You're crazy if you think I'm marrying you."

"Marry me or die. It's up to you. Either way, you're leaving here today. Either we're walking out as husband and wife or you'll be leaving in a garbage bag."

I said I was all cried out, but a fresh set of tears coated my vision. Pull it together Bey, I told myself. Maybe you can still escape. Reggie just proved that you're his weakness. Maybe you can catch him slipping. Play on his emotions, girl. You can do this. I blinked away my tears and regained my focus on plan B. Operation Get The Fuck Away From Crazy Ass Reggie.

I should have known better. Gremlin looked familiar, but I couldn't place his face until now. He was Reggie's brother that was in the military. I'd only seen him once or twice, so it never registered.

"If I marry you, do I get to pick where we honeymoon?"

Reggie grinned. I guess I was speaking his language now. "Yes. As long as it's out of the country. We can't stay in the United States. I have our passports and everything ready. As soon as we're married, we're on the next flight out of the country."

I swallowed hard to stop more tears from forming. The last thing I wanted to do was leave the country with this piece of shit. "I want to go to the Dominican Republic." I remember Breeze saying that his sister lived there. Maybe I could get a message to her if I was in the same country.

"Sounds perfect," Reggie agreed.

I smiled because I felt like I had a way out. Reggie reached his arm out to me and I walked out of the bedroom with my arm interlocked with his. As soon as we got to the top of the steps, wedding music started playing. I looked downstairs and realized that Reggie was serious as fuck. There was a preacher standing in the living room with wedding decorations.

"This is the best I could do," Reggie stated. "I promise, things will be better in the future. I have money. See that bag over there?"

My eyes landed on the black leather bag that had the money in it.

"I hustled all that up for you."

"I appreciate it, boo," I said with a smile, but I wanted to throw up in my mouth. Just the thought of me knowing that he did all this to me over the last five months made me want to murder him. I was taking all that rage and bottling it up until I was able to unleash it on his ass. Until then, I would do what I had to do to make this nicca believe what he needed to believe, so I could get the fuck away from him. This time when I escaped, I wouldn't get caught.

Reggie and I marched downstairs towards the preacher standing before him. The preacher looked behind us at Rutta, who was still holding the AK, and he cleared his throat.

"Let's get this started. A wedding is a celebration of the miracle of love. Beyonne and Reginald, today, in the presences of God, we celebrate this wonderful moment in your lives. Please join hands and look into each other's eyes."

Reggie and I faced each other. My hands were shaking so bad that I could barely hold his hand. None of this felt right. I wanted to bolt for the door and, if I got shot in the process, so be it.

The preacher continued. "Reginald, do you take this woman to live together in marriage, love, honor, sickness, and health, forsaking all others to be faithful to her as long as you both shall live?"

Reggie smiled bright and firmly said. "I do."

"Beyonne, do you take this man to live together in marriage, love, honor, sickness, and health forsaking all others to be faithful to her as long as you both shall live?"

"I...I...I..." I stuttered.

My eyes widened with surprise as he crept up behind Reggie, putting a gun to his head.

"You'll never fuckin' be me, goofy ass nicca."

Chapter 35

Drake

"Whaaaaat!" I yelled. I couldn't believe all the shit that Mega was telling me.

Apparently, Zino and Gremlin were both snakes. Zino caught a dome shot earlier because he tried to run, and Gremlin was at the warehouse with Yolo.

"So, Yolo gave Channa the keys she got busted with?"

"Yes," Mega replied confidently. "That's not all. I think Gremlin kidnapped Bey. If he didn't, he knows who did."

"Fuck! Don't do shit until I get there. I'm on my way."

"Oh, there's one more thing."

"What?" I asked, sounding aggravated.

"Hurry up. There's someone here that wants to see you."

"I'll be there in a minute."

His last statement threw me. Who wanted to see me? I hoped it wasn't some chick. The last think I needed was more drama for my love life.

My phone rang again as soon as I hung up with Mega. It was Ross.

"Bad news, Drake," Ross said with a sigh.

"How bad?"

"Twenty years to life bad. They're trying to throw the book at Dream."

"But why? None of that is going to stick."

"I don't think it will either, but there is a possibility that something will. Is that a risk that you're willing to take? Right now, the only options are, take this to trial or take a plea. The plea is for fifteen years."

"Fuck all that. None of that shit sounds good."

"You know what you gotta do then," Ross stated.

"I had a feeling it was going to come down to leaving the country."

"Look at the bright side. Your surprise for Dream is there too."

"True. Have you talked to Amante?"

"No, I haven't. Should I reach out to him?"

"Naw, I'll do it. Meanwhile, I'll be preparing for us to leave."

"You need to do it asap. The prosecutor has a real hard on for Dream. He's trying to get the court date pushed up."

"Fuck him. We'll be gone as soon as I handle some other business because that shit can't wait. It's mandatory."

"Okay, be safe, Drake."

"I will. I'll be in contact."

I hung up with Ross and started texting Amante. I gave him the short version of what was going on, in code of course. Then, I told him to reach out to Ross. Amante hit me right back. He told me that he found out about Channa a while ago and he's already on it. That's why I loved my cousin. He was a bona fide asshole, but he knew his shit. If anyone could figure something out, it was going to be him.

"What's wrong, baby?" Dream asked, stirring from her sleep. I guess my loud talking woke her up.

"Remember when you said you wanted to be my ride or die?"

"Yes, baby, I remember."

"Well, I need you to get dressed. Someone will be here to get you asap and take you back to your place so you can grab everything. Get what you want because you might not be able to get it later on."

"Okay, but what's going on, baby? Tell me. I can handle it."

"They trying to throw the book at you, ma. If we don't get out of the country, you might be doing time for some stupid shit. I refuse to let that happen."

Dream looked as if she was about to cry, but she didn't. She sat up in the bed and forced a smile. "I got you."

"Even if that means we might be on the run to another country?"

Dream looked me dead in the eye. "Yes. As long as we're together."

"That's my girl," I said, tonguing her down. I felt on her fat ass and quickly regretted it because it made my dick hard.

"You want some of this before you go?" Dream asked me seductively, opening her legs wide.

I wanted to play in her pussy so bad. "Nah, ma, shit is serious. I'll take a rain check tho."

Dream stared at me seductively. "Okay, papi. I'll keep it nice and wet while you're gone."

Shit, she was making it hard for a nicca. I thought about hitting it right quick. I pecked her lips and raced out the door before I changed my mind.

Shit was already going down when I walked into the warehouse. Yolo and Gremlin were hanging up by chains. Yolo looked untouched. Other than a sock being in his mouth, he was okay. Gremlin, on the other hand, he was bad off. Flashbacks of Spencer filled my head. He was looking just like him.

"So, what's the plan?" I asked Mega, who was standing to my right, along with Axel. Fresh and Quay stood to my left.

Mega whistled and the door behind us opened. I wasn't ready for who walked in. All I could do was stare in shock. Is this real? I had to blink a few times because I couldn't believe it. When he came closer, I knew that it was true, and I wasn't dreaming.

"Breeze!" I called out, sounding like Celie from the Color Purple.

Dream & Drake 3: A Cartel Love Story

I couldn't wait for him to make his way to me. I took off running to meet him halfway. Once I got there, I embraced him as tight as I could. I guess the impact was too much because we both fell to the ground, with me landing on top of him.

"Damn, nicca. You crushing my fuckin' balls and shit. I'm trying to use my dick later on."

"Breeze!" I yelled out again with tears in my eyes. I didn't care if I looked gay. I continued to hug and kiss my baby brother. I missed him dearly.

"Yeah, nicca, it's me. You act like I was going to die or something. You should know better than that."

I got up and helped Breeze up.

"How long?" I asked through tears.

"Almost two months."

"And nobody told me?"

Breeze wiped away a tear and cleared his throat. "Papi tried. Mega tried. I didn't want them to tell you. You were in the hospital recuperating anyway. I wanted to come back the same way I left you. Surprise."

I dabbed away my tears. "Are you good, tho? Is everything okay?"

"Not really, but I'm about to be good tonight. We finna put in this work, so I can find my boo."

I grinned and hugged him again. "It's about to go down now. Oh boy!"

"Oh boy!" Breeze repeated with a smirk. "About to put these niccas in the dirt."

Things still felt surreal. There was more that I wanted to ask him, but I could wait. He was here, we were back together, and shit was about to get super ugly. Breeze whistled and the door opened again. Icepick and Bull walked in with four Pit Bulls. I recognized two of the dogs as Amante's. They were ruthless as they came.

"Let's get this shit started," Mega said, spraying Gremlin with a watery dog food mixture. He didn't stop until Gremlin was coated from head to toe.

"Where is Bey?" Breeze asked.

Princess Diamond

Gremlin fucked himself when he tried to spit on Breeze.

"Fuck this shit." Breeze signaled to let the dogs loose.

Icepick let go two of the Pits and they lit into Gremlin like a piece of steak. One gnawed at his foot. The other at his hand. I mean, they were chewing on his ass like it was Thanksgiving. Gremlin's screams were piercing, as the Pits ate at his flesh.

Breeze whistled again and the dogs stopped feasting on Gremlin.

"Now, I'ma ask your bitch ass again. Tell me everything you know. Where the fuck is Bey?"

"Fuck Bey!" Gremlin spat.

Breeze chuckled. "Lower the chains."

As soon as the chains dropped, Breeze snapped his fingers and all four dogs attacked his ass. All of a sudden, he was trying to speak, but we couldn't understand shit he was saying because one of Amante's Pits was biting his face off.

Chapter 36

Breeze

"Fuck Gremlin's bitch ass. I never liked him no way!" I shouted before I turned to Yolo. "Lower this traitor ass nicca and take that shit out his mouth."

As soon as Yolo's feet hit the floor, he threw up. While he was puking up his guts, I kicked him as hard as I could in the ass. He nearly fell into the vomit.

"So, you thought you could kill me, nicca?" I laughed in this nicca's face. "And you were stupid enough to think that you would walk away. How fuckin' dumb could you be? Now, unlike him." I pointed to the pile of blood and bones behind me that used to be Gremlin. "I'm going to only ask you once. You better tell me what the fuck I want to hear off rip, or you're gonna end up like ya homeboy, ya dig?"

I just knew that Yolo was going to play hard like Gremlin, and we would be sweeping his remains into the gutter too. He shocked the fuck out of me when he sang like a bird.

"I'll admit to what I did and what I did only. I was jealous of you, Breeze, so I wanted to set you up to take over your position of The Cartel."

"Nicca, you still on that bullshit? You don't know how to let nothing go. You was getting money, good money. I guess it wasn't enough. You just had to be the fuckin' boss."

"You want me to keep it real, right? You want the truth, right?"

"Nicca, don't fuckin' talk to me like I'ma chicken. Just continue before my finger starts itching, and I accidently bust one off in ya chest."

Yolo continued, "That's all I wanted at first. That's why I had the stash house raided."

"I told y'all niccas!" Quay bellowed, stomping his foot for emphasis. "I fuckin' told y'all. This nicca been plotting on y'all asses for years, and y'all called me crazy. I was fuckin' right all along. I swear, y'all niccas need to listen to me more often. I said it was his ass. I said it. He would have been dealt with if it was left up to me."

"You were right, Quay," Drake said, patting his shoulder. "What do you want, a cookie, nicca?"

We all laughed.

"Nicca, don't try to cookie and cream me, nicca. He would have been gone if y'all niccas listened to me in the first place. Nobody would be shot. No money would be lost. All this chasing our tails when this nicca been laughing at y'all like a joke, cause he damn sure ain't been laughing at me. I ain't never liked his rat looking ass."

"You're right, Quay. We're sorry," Drake said dryly. "We should have listened to you."

"Continue," I told Yolo's punk ass.

"I was the one who told Davie's cousins what happened with him getting shot. That's why they went after you the way they did. At the time, I wasn't thinking right. I regret that decision, though. I hate that you got shot. I really do."

"Yolo, no the fuck you don't, bitch ass nicca. What about Bey? Tell me about her?"

"I didn't have her kidnapped, but I know who did."

"Do you know where she is right now?"

"I believe I do."

"You need to know for sure, nicca because if she's not there, that's your ass."

"I think Gremlin's brother has her."

Dream & Drake 3: A Cartel Love Story

I scrunched up my face. "Why the fuck would Gremlin's brother have her?"

"Gremlin's brother used to date her. He was at your birthday party. A dude named Reggie."

I sighed because I remembered that lame nicca. He was the fool she tried to make me jealous with. The one who took her home that night.

"She was in East Chicago, but they moved her," Yolo said.

Mega spoke up. "We raided EC. They're all dead and Bey wasn't in that house. We've looked everywhere else, so she has to be at this Reggie dude's house. I've already alerted my team to look there and Gremlin's house. I wouldn't be surprised, since they were brothers."

"Let's go then," I told everyone.

Yolo acted as if he was tagging along.

"Naw, nicca, not you. Your ass is history. You just played yourself being jealous."

Yolo looked at me shocked. I guess he didn't expect for me to respond the way that I did, but fuck it. I wouldn't be Breeze if I let this nicca walk up outta here. I snatched the sprayer from off the floor and hosed Yolo down with fresh dog food. Then, I whistled and all four Pit Bulls attacked Yolo. He didn't put up half the fight that Gremlin put up. I stood there and watched as they ate him alive. Once he was mangled beyond repair, I called the dogs off.

"I'm sorry," Yolo uttered with his jaw hanging off. Half of his face was gnawed off and his tongue was barely attached. I was surprised that he was still able to speak.

"I'm sorry too, muthafucka. I should have pulled the trigger sooner on your bitch ass."

I pulled out my gun and pointed it directly at his head.

Pop!

"Fuck outta here!"

*****

237

"Are you sure it's only four niccas inside?" I asked Mega.

Mega and Drake were sitting up front, and I sat in the back. In the car behind us was Axel, Fresh, Quay, and Icepick. Bull and a few other goons stayed behind at the warehouse, waiting for us to return.

"I'm positive," Mega confirmed. "They're about to go in now."

"Oh no, they aren't," I said. "Ain't nobody saving my bitch but me."

"What?" Drake inquired. "You sound crazy. We've been looking high and low for this girl, and you want her life to stay in jeopardy."

I sneered at Drake. "No, nicca, I didn't say I wanted her life to be in jeopardy. What I said is, they can't save my bitch."

"How the fuck do you sound, tho? Being in a coma really fucked you up."

"Nicca, you can suck my big balls. Either they allow me to save my girl, or I'm going to pop every last one of them niccas. Try me."

"Just secure everything until we get there," Mega told his team. "Are you happy now, Breeze?" Mega stared at me in the rearview mirror and I could tell that he wanted to shoot my ass. "This is all your fault, Drake."

"How you figure that?" Drake quizzed.

"Because you spoiled his ass rotten. Now, we can't get no kinda sense out of him. He thinks things are always supposed to go his way because of your ass."

Drake groaned.

"Don't talk about me like I'm not here. I'm the baby and I'm spoiled. Get over it. I bet y'all missed my ass."

Mega and Drake both sighed. I was getting on both of my brothers' nerves, and I loved it. I missed them a lot. I was giving them a hard time, but I loved them. I loved all of my brothers. I was just the closest to Drake.

I slapped the back of Drake's head and he turned around really fast, like he wanted to punch my lights out. I smiled and his frown softened.

Dream & Drake 3: A Cartel Love Story

"You didn't miss me?"

"Of course, I did," Drake said, turning back around. "But if you hit me in the back of my head again, we might be putting your ass down too."

I laughed hysterically because I loved pissing Drake off. I continued to pick with Drake until we pulled up to Gremlin's house, then it was game time. Everyone got out of the car with their guns locked and loaded. Mega's people were already inside. They had things under control, just like they said. Three of the four dudes were wrapped up in duct tape from head to toe.

"Where's the fourth dude?" I asked my uncle Cream. Mega worked for him. He was a couple of years older than Drake and raised by Gigi, so this nicca definitely had crazy in his blood. He learned from the best and it showed by the skills that he possessed.

Cream nodded his head towards the living room. I cocked my gun and made my way there, followed by Drake, Mega, and Quay. I couldn't believe my eyes. My damn woman was standing before the preacher in a wedding gown, about to marry this goofy ass nicca Reggie. Before I knew it, I had my gun to the back of his head.

"You'll never fuckin' be me, goofy ass nicca."

I could imagine the scary look on his face.

"Run that suit, nicca."

"What are you doing?" Drake asked, standing by me with a gun pointed at Reggie too. "This ain't what we planned."

"Change of plans, nicca."

Something happened to me when I walked in and saw Reggie about to marry my bitch. I had been dreaming of Bey for months. I knew I was falling for her before I was shot but, after being shot and missing part of my life due to being in a coma, I decided to live in the moment. Fuck what everyone else thought. I knew Bey was for me and I was about to prove it to the world. It was now or never.

"Do you love me?" I asked Bey sincerely, while Reggie stripped out of his suit. It was a really nice suit, by the way.

She was crying hysterically now. "Yes. Yes. I do."

"I never stopped thinking about you," I admitted.

"I never stopped thinking about you either," Bey admitted also.

I got down on one knee, even though, I didn't have an engagement ring. "Listen, I know we met on bad terms. I know that I never showed you how I felt before now, but I love you. I fell for you the moment I saw you. Will you marry me?"

Bey smiled and I already knew her answer. "Yes. I love you too."

"I know this shit is spare of the moment but, considering everything that just happened to you and me, I didn't think we would ever see each other again. I want to make sure that I never lose you again. Being my wife will make that official."

Bey smiled and nodded her head. Tears of joy continued to fall down her face.

"This nicca crazy as fuck," Quay mumbled.

"Call me crazy, then. You try almost dying and see how the fuck you react to shit. Fuck you and everyone else's opinion. If y'all niccas ain't with it, get the fuck on. I'm not asking for nobody's approval. This between me and mines. Either support the shit or step the fuck of," I snapped.

"I think it's romantic," Mega agreed. "Something I would definitely do." He patted me on the shoulder. "Go for it."

Drake shook his head. "C'mon man, can't you wait and do this shit right? Give her the proper wedding that she deserves."

"Fuck no," I stated. "I'm living in the moment. Neither one of us are promised tomorrow. We can do all that extra shit at a later date."

"But, what about the marriage certificate?" Drake argued.

"What about that shit? I'll get Ross to fix all that later. As of right now, when we walk out of this house, we will be husband and wife."

I gave Drake a very stern look, so he knew I wasn't playing no games.

"Okay," he conceded. "Let's get started."

I handed my gun to Drake and quickly undressed, putting on Reggie's suit. It fit me better than it fit him. I was sure I looked better in it too. The preacher seemed hesitant, but I guess standing in a room full of gunman would make you do what you needed to do. The preacher asked me my name, I told him, and he went through the whole wedding speech. He probably repeated the same shit he said when Reggie was standing in my place.

"Face each other," the preacher required.

Bey put her hand into mine and smiled.

"Do you, Breeze, take this woman to live together in marriage, love, honor, sickness, and health, forsaking all others to be faithful to her as long as you both shall live?"

"I do," I replied, kissing Bey's hand.

"Beyonne, do you take this man to live together in marriage, love, honor, sickness, and health forsaking all others to be faithful to him as long as you both shall live?"

"I do," she squealed.

"The rings please?" the preacher announced.

Mega handed us our rings that he got from Reggie.

"These rings are symbols of eternity, an unbroken circle of love. Today, you have chosen to exchange rings as a sign of love for each other. We ask that God bless these rings and this union. Breeze, as you place the ring on Beyonne's finger, repeat after me. May this ring forever be a symbol of my growing love for you."

I repeated what he said.

"With this ring, I thee wed."

I repeated what he said again and placed the ring on Bey's finger. It was a decent ring, but I planned on buying her a ring so big, she was going to have to use her other hand to carry it.

The preacher instructed Bey to do the same thing and she placed the ring on my finger. I was definitely going to upgrade my ring asap.

"Breeze and Beyonne, you have consented together in holy matrimony before God, pledged vows before to each other, and exchanged rings as a token of your love and commitment. In accordance with the law of the state of Illinois, with the authority of God's Word, I pronounce with great joy you as husband and wife. You may now seal your union with a kiss."

The moment our lips touched, I was sure I made the right decision. I held Bey in my arms, kissing her for what felt like an eternity. That's how long it felt like we'd been apart.

"She needs to go to a doctor," Mega stated as soon as our lips separated.

"I'll take my wife." I smiled bright at Bey and she returned the same smile.

"That's cool," Mega replied. "But, just in case, why don't you let Cream drive you."

"I'll go too," Axel volunteered.

"What about me?" the preacher asked with a shaky voice. "Am I free to leave?"

I almost busted up laughing. This nicca looked like he was about to shit his pants.

"You're free to go, as long as you don't remember anything but a wedding being performed," Quay said.

He snapped a picture of the preacher. He had his information within minutes, rattling off his address and names of his family members.

"You get my drift," Quay said wickedly.

The preacher man held up his bible. "Son, all I remember is marrying these two at whatever address you said I did. Other than that, I don't recall nothing."

"My type of preacher. I'll have a check in the mail for your services."

Quay nodded at the preacher and he scurried out of the house.

"Follow him," Mega told one of our cousins.

"I was already on it," my cuzzo said, leaving out right behind the preacher.

"We need to wrap this up," Mega said, duct taping Reggie's arms. His mouth, feet, and hands were already taped up.

They cleared out, while Cream and Axel escorted Bey and I to our family doctor. I trusted this man, so I knew that confidentiality wasn't an issue. Bey was scared, so she asked me to accompany her in the examination room. She said she didn't want to have any secrets. I listened as she told all the horrible things that happened to her. I would be a lie if I said hearing her experience didn't make me choke up a little. She was now my wife. When she hurt, I hurt. Luckily, she didn't contract anything and the doctor gave her a clean bill of health. He said he wanted her to get tested again next month, just to be sure. However, he was quite certain that she was disease free. He also suggested counseling. I advised Bey to go and I planned on being right by her side.

It had been a long day. Even though it was our honeymoon, I gave her a much needed break. I decided to pamper her. All the food that she asked for was delivered to my house. I gave her a massage and held her while she slept peacefully. She must've been tired because she slept until the next day. When she woke up, that ass was mine. I fed her again, bathed her, and now I was ready to fall off in some pussy.

"I want a do over," I said.

She rolled over in the bed facing me. "Like how?"

"I want to recreate the night that you were going to give the pussy up to me. Back then, we didn't know each other-"

"Shit, we barely know each other now."

"True, but we have a whole lifetime to make up for that. We're married now," I said, holding up my new diamond encrusted wedding band.

I had my stylist bring by two new rings for us. I trashed that cheap shit Reggie bought. Speaking of that punk, him and the other captors were drowned in acid. Mega stopped by to let me know that the job was completed last night. He also said to have our shit ready because we were headed back to the Dominican Republic tomorrow. That's why I wanted to bust Bey's cherry tonight.

Bey smiled and kissed me passionately. "Yes, we are. I couldn't be happier. There is no other man that I would rather spend my life with."

"I feel the same way, wifey. So, are we fucking or what?"

"We fucking," she said, kissing me again.

"Run them panties then."

Bey stripped out of her clothes, tossing them on the floor. I was already butt ass naked. I threw the sheet to the side and concentrated on her perky breasts, devouring them both at the same time. I was so hungry for her that I couldn't make up my mind if I wanted to put my tongue in her mouth or tongue her breasts, so I did both.

"Do you think I lost too much weight?"

"Nah," I said truthfully. "You look delicious, and your ass is still fat." I took in a handful of her rump. "I'm good. I can't wait to lick from your ass to your clit." I flicked my tongue, demonstrating how nasty I was about to attack her pearl.

Bey purred and I knew shit was about to go down then.

"Are you scared?" I asked her out of concern. "We can wait if you want to."

"No, baby, I want you to bust it wide open," she said, making my dick even harder.

"It's like that?" I said, stroking my erection.

"Hell yeah. I promised myself that if I ever escaped, if I ever saw you again, I was going to throw this pussy on you."

"That's my bitch."

I positioned my face between her legs, doing what felt natural. I licked her booty like groceries, and then sucked on her moist hole and, finally, licked on her clit. Bey bucked at my face, cumming instantly. I wasn't done with her. I rolled onto my back and made her straddled my face. Suffocated by her pussy, I asked her to ride my face until she busted off three times.

"You ready to feel this dick?"

"You know I am, zaddy."

"I'm not going to take it easy on you. You need to take this dick like a good wife should."

I knew Bey was scared, but she smiled anyway. "I'm ready," she said, lying on her back and spreading her legs wide.

I had every intentions of thrusting into her hard and fast, but I found myself massaging her clit again while we kissed. I entered the head of my dick slowly. Bey looked as if she was holding her breath, so I told her to breathe. I slid a few more inches in and tears escaped from the corners of her eyes.

"You want me to stop?"

"No, baby. Keep on going," she encouraged me.

I slid a few more inches in and she screamed.

I put my mouth on hers, kissing her. "I'm almost completely in."

"Hurry up," she cried.

I slid the rest of the way in and she bit my bottom lip as more tears fell. I grinded inside of her tight hole slowly. Bey continued to cry, until my strokes became pleasure.

"Is this my pussy?"

"Hell yeah!" she cried.

"Circle your hips so you can cum."

"How?" she asked me.

I slid in and out of her a little faster, rotating my hips. To my surprise, she did the same thing, mimicking me. Before long, we were both hungrily fucking each other. I was pounding her pussy out and she loved every minute of it.

"I think... I think... I think I'm cumming," Bey cried out, clawing at my back with pleasure. Her body twitched underneath me and I felt a warm fluid come gushing out of her vagina. I clenched my ass, my nut sac tightened, and I buried my face in her breasts, as I let go of months of semen inside of her.

"You know you're pregnant, right?"

"Boy, shut up and get off of me."

When my breathing returned to normal, I rolled off of her and saw that the whole bed was covered in blood.

"Awwwwww fuck! I need a shower, and you're cleaning this shit up."

Bey giggled. "You're the one that wanted to bust it wide open, remember, asshole?"

I kissed her lips. "And that pussy was good too, Mrs. Breeze Diaz-Santana."

"That dick was good too, Mr. Breeze Diaz-Santana."

I grabbed my wife's hand. "Join me in the shower. We'll get the maid to clean it up."

"But, I don't want her seeing my indiscretions."

"Fuck that. That's what she gets paid for. We can sleep in the guest room."

Bey kissed me and I led her to the bathroom. My dick was erect again, and I planned on fucking her in the shower.

Chapter 37

Drake

R&B sensation Urbane sang his heart out to All of Me by John Legend. A few feet away, I stood next to the preacher wearing an ivory tuxedo with ivory accessories accented in diamonds. This was my surprise to Dream. A destination wedding at Secrets Royal Beach Punta Cana in the Dominican Republic. After she went to jail over my bullshit, I knew I had to make her my wife.

Under the gazebo, Breeze and Mega stood as my best man and groomsman. Bey and Mercy were Dream's maid of honor and bridesmaid. Sitting before us was Dream's closest family members and mine as well, which included Playez and Promise. Playez was in a wheelchair since coming out of the coma. According to the doctors, after months of intensive therapy, he would be making a full recovery. Just like always, Promise stood proud by his side. I had no doubt that my brother would be just fine. He was a trooper. Nothing but death would stop him.

The flower girl and the ring bearer just walked down the ivory carpet, so I knew that Dream was coming up next. Urbane, aka Marcel, stopped singing and the wedding tune began. I stared at Dream's beauty as her father walked her down the aisle towards me. Although she was very pregnant with a gigantic belly, she was wearing the hell out of her cream spaghetti strap ballroom wedding gown. Once she made it to the outdoor altar, her father handed her over, giving me his blessing. Dream's hand trembled and I knew she was scared. Marriage was a big step. I had my reservations too, but I knew I wanted to spend the rest of my life with her.

I helped Dream up the stairs, and we both stood before the preacher as he talked about marriage, love, standing before God, and until death do us part. We joined hands and repeated after him, exchanging rings.

Next, we were led over to the sand and advised to use the two colors of pink and blue to symbolize our union. Following the blending of the two colors, a large portion of sand was placed into a decorative glass as a keepsake.

"Drake and Dream, may your love never fade. May you never take each other for granted. You have consented together in holy matrimony before God. You have pledged your vows, exchanged rings, and decided to take this journey together. I now pronounce you husband and wife. Congratulations, you may kiss the bride."

I lifted Dream's veil and leaned in to kiss her. I was about to go all in, but her eyes were pleading me not to. So, I gave her a soft sweet kiss that lingered just for a little bit. When we pulled apart, the preacher announced us as husband and wife.

"Ladies and gentleman, I would like to introduce you to Mr. and Mrs. Diaz-Santana!"

Everyone stood and cheered as we walked down the steps hand in hand. My mother had a broom waiting for us to jump over. I thought it was stupid but whatever. I didn't want to hear her mouth, so Dream and I held onto each other and jumped. Rice was thrown at us, as we made our way down the long walkway towards the photographer.

Our guests were excused to the reception area, but the wedding party was asked to remain behind for pictures. Naturally, that included both of our parents, bridal party, groomsmen, flower girl, and ring bearer. Dream and I were the only two dressed in all ivory with diamonds. Everyone else had on white and gold.

Dream & Drake 3: A Cartel Love Story

The heat was blazing. It felt like two hundred degrees, so we could only take so many pictures outside. The makeup artists were dapping at me and Dream constantly. As fast as they wiped sweat from our faces, it came right back. Therefore, the rest of the pictures were taken inside where it was nice and cool.

The entire reception was decorated with white and gold everything, including our wedding cake, wishing well, and the hired staff. People knew that if they didn't abide by my wedding colors, I wouldn't allow them to attend. It was a pet peeve of Dream's and I wanted her to be very happy on her special day.

Once the pictures were over, Dream and I went to our suite and changed. I had on a white suit with gold accessories, and she had on a beautiful gold evening gown with the same pearls from earlier. Everyone was seated and stood when Dream and I finally made our grand entrance as husband and wife.

After our announcement, we made our way to the dance floor for the first dance. Neither one of us was thrilled about this part because we weren't dancers. All eyes were on us and we both had two left feet, except when we slow danced. I was so glad when that part was over. The second dance was Dream dancing with her father and I danced with my mother.

Next, we were seated. Dream and I sat at a table in front of our guests with our wedding party by our side. The waiters and waitresses were starting to serve our food. You name it, we had it. From whatever seafood that you might have desired, to steak, to the finest cuisines. I made sure the food was superb.

"I want to propose a toast," Breeze said, clinking his glass to get everyone's attention. "Many of you know that Drake and I share a special bond. We argue and sometimes fight, but we couldn't be closer. Although, I give my big brother a hard time, I respect him and I appreciate his advice. Don't tell him tho." He winked and me and smirked. "I'm excited to gain a new sister. Dream couldn't be a better mate for Drake. When I think of the epitome of love, I think of these two. Cheers."

I held up my glass, tapping it against his. I took a sip and hugged my baby brother. "Thanks, man."

"It's well deserved. I mean it, man. If anyone deserves happiness, you definitely do." He smiled, and I thought I saw moisture in his eyes.

"You not about to get sappy on me, are you?" I joked.

Breeze wiped his eyes. "Naw, nicca, its allergies."

We both laughed.

Mega and my father stood up and gave toasts to our union too, followed by Bey, Mercy, and Dream's father. He openly said in front of everyone that he didn't think I was good enough for his daughter, but what father would just give his daughter away without having reservations. I was glad he cleaned it up because my family was looking at him sideways at first. He had no idea that he was seated among a room full of killers. Finally, her father said that he thinks Dream married the right man and he was glad she didn't listen to him. He genuinely hugged me. When he called me son, my family was at ease. Shortly after, the food was brought out, and everyone was quietly talking and eating.

Breeze tapped me on my arm and I turned to my right.

"I'm happy for you, big bruh."

"Thanks, Breeze. I'm just glad that you're okay. I was so worried about you."

"That's what I wanted to talk to you about. I'm not okay," he confessed.

"What do you mean?" I asked, worried all over again.

"I know I looked like a crazy person when I married Bey, but I just wanted to do some shit right for once. I fucked hoes, nah mean? I wanted something real. Just like you have. That talk that we had in the car after the police station. That shit replayed in my mind over and over. I let my immaturity fuck up what Bey and I had. Marrying her was the right choice."

"I think so too. I just wished that you could have given her a proper wedding."

"Yeah, I hear you, Drake, but me and Bey are good. She knows I'm a thug and I do thug shit. That nicca Reggie was trying to flex on me. I did what I had to do. Bey belongs to me.

Marrying her immediately felt like the right thing to do. That was the right time, the right moment."

"I feel you on all that, but it just seems like your rushing things. You have time."

"Not really, Drake. That's what I wanted to tell you. I wasn't trying to ruin your wedding day, but I still have a blood clot on my brain. The doctors want to do surgery, but I postponed it. They said I only have a fifty percent chance of living. Hearing that shit got me thinking about a wife and kids. I can't leave this world without having a little Breeze left behind. Bey is the perfect wife and mother."

I understood why Breeze did what he did. I felt so bad that I gave him a hard time. "Listen, man, I would have never given you a hard time if I knew all that was going on," I said, blinking back tears.

Breeze was holding back tears too. "Other than mami and papi, nobody else knows but you. They have me on blood thinners trying to make sure the clot doesn't get any larger. For right now, I'm good but, one day, I'm going to have to have that surgery. I'm putting it off as long as I can. When they tell me that I have to have it, I will."

I hugged Breeze again. "Damn, man. This shit got me so fucked up."

Breeze wiped his eyes and smiled. "Well, you better act like the thug that you are, nicca, because I'm ready to get all the way turnt. Shit, I'm pumped with pain killers and liquor. I'm feeling like I rule the fuckin' world. We about to party and bullshit the night away. Is you down or nah?"

I dried up my tears. "Hell yeah, I'm down. Let's get it in like we used to."

"That's what the fuck I'm talking about. This ain't a sad occasion. This is a happy occasion. I'm married. You're married. Let's celebrate."

Breeze called the waiter over. He poured us two shots of Tequila. Breeze raised his shot glass to mine.

"Out with the old pussy and in with the new."

"What?" I asked laughing. "What kinda toast is that?"

Breeze had to laugh himself. "Okay, what about this. To married life."

"That's more like it." I took a sip. "So, how do you feel about Quay and Unique."

Breeze shrugged. "I don't. Unique ain't my bitch. Quay told me what was up. We chatted about it. If it ain't Bey, I truly don't give a fuck. If Quay wants Unique for whatever, I'm cool with it all."

"How do you think Bey feels about all this? I know she doesn't like Unique."

Breeze made a sour face. "Bey ain't too fond of seeing Unique, but I told her to chill, so she's biting her tongue for me. It won't'be no issues tho. Bey will stay in her place and Unique will stay in hers."

"Good. Cause I got enough issues, shit."

"Hell, me too," Breeze said getting another refill on his drink.

Now that everyone was full and the formalities were out of the way, we hit the dance floor. I came from a family that loved to dance. It wouldn't be a black wedding if we didn't do all the different slides and line dances—Electric Slide, Cha-Cha Slide, The Wobble, Souja Boy, and the Cupid Shuffle. Then, the party really got started.

The liquor was flowing freely when the Milly Rock came on. Of course, Breeze and Bey stole the show. They were getting it in like auditions to a music video. You would have thought these two invented the Milly Rock. Right by them was Quay and Unique. The two couples looked as if they were trying to outdo each other. It was quite entertaining. Quay and Unique were giving Breeze and Bey a run for their money. Quay and Unique were out there looking like Usher and Ciara dancing. They were dancing so hard; I started to sweat just looking at them.

Things slowed down with R. Kelly's Step In The Name Of Love. That's when Dream and I showed out. If we couldn't do nothing else, we could step. Big belly and all, Dream moved around effortlessly as I twirled her around the dance floor.

Dream & Drake 3: A Cartel Love Story

When I walked off hot and sweaty, I got a call from my cousin, Amante. I knew he was working on a deal for Dream, so I answered immediately.

"What's up, cuzzo? You got good news for me?"

"First off, let me say congratulations. I wish I was there."

"Thanks. I wish you were here too. I could only imagine you and NeNe."

"No, you couldn't. I broke up with that bitch."

"Again?" I asked as if I was surprised. I should have known better. They broke up and got back together all the damn time.

"Yeah, she called herself taking Dom away from me. As soon as I get off the phone with you, I'm going to find her and beat her ass."

I knew better than to get in the middle of their lover's quarrels. I made that mistake before and ended up with bruised ribs. Never again. "Well, on that note, what news do you have for me?"

Amante sighed. "I tried Drake."

"You tried what? What does that mean?"

"It means that I could only get one of you off, Drake."

"Just give it to me straight."

"The prosecutor is a dick. He wants you bad. He was willing to let Dream walk-"

"What's the catch? I know one's coming."

"You already know. The catch is only if you turned yourself in."

"You're kidding me? He doesn't have nothing on me."

"He has a lot on you because Channa's bitch ass talked. She was arrested right before you were and ran her big ass mouth; she didn't throw you under the bus, she pinned it all on Dream, but the prosecutor isn't stupid. He knows that Dream isn't running an operation. He leveraged her to get to you."

I sighed stressed to the max. "This is so fucked up."

"It is, but I was able to negotiate on your behalf. I changed shit up and presented him with the truth. That Channa was the one accompanying you and not Dream. I made it look like she was the queen pin and you were working for her."

"Word?"

"You damn right.

"So, your time has been reduced to two years behind bars and three years' probation, in exchange for Dream's freedom."

I sighed again, loudly. "Damn, I'm going to miss the first two years of my child's life."

"Maybe so, but Channa got thirty years. Her kids will be married with their own kids by the time she sees them."

I couldn't help but laugh at that statement. If she wasn't so shady, we all could have been free, eating lovely. Nah, she just had to turn snitch.

"When do I have to turn myself in?"

"Once I tell them that you accepted the plea, you have to turn yourself in before the month is out."

I exhaled loudly again.

"That's the best I could do, Drake. Diarrhea mouth Channa fucked you up because I could have gotten you off if she didn't run scared. However, I'm still working on a few things."

"It's cool. I appreciate what you did. Two years ain't shit. I'll take the plea."

"I'll set everything up. Call me later, so I can discuss the final arrangements with you. Oh and by the way, Channa took the paternity test. The babies are yours."

"Did she say what we were having?"

"Nope. Her exact words were you can wait until they are born."

"Petty ass bitch," I spat.

"Exactly what I said too. Anyway, once again, congratulations to you and Dream."

I was a little bummed out when I hung up.

"There my husband is," Dream said, walking up to me and kissing my lips. "I love you."

I forced a smile. "I love you too, ma."

I had no idea how I was going to tell my wife that I was leaving her before the baby was born because I just took a two-year bid.

Chapter 38

Drake

Dream and I had been holed up together for the last week in our honeymoon suite at the resort celebrating. Other than occasional shopping and phone calls to our family and friends, we were busy doing nasty things. Being pregnant had turned Dream into the ultimate lil freak.

She told me that since I went out of my way to surprise her with the wedding of her dreams, she wanted to do the same for me. She gave me the best gift a woman could give a man— the gift of unlimited head. I mean, I woke up with my dick in her mouth, and she sucked me to sleep every night. I enjoyed watching her deep-throat my manhood every time I sat down. Off and on, she licked on my tool until I exploded in her mouth or busted on her face.

Call me crazy but, since Dream said I do, it was like she had this insatiable lust to give me head constantly. Almost as if she couldn't get enough of my joint being between her jaws. She was so obsessed with my erection that I was about to name her Super Head. Since the first time she bobbed on my stick, she'd become an expert head doctor, giving it to me exactly how I loved it.

I could be kinda picky sometimes. Dream noticed that immediately. Depending on the time of day, I liked my knob slobbed differently. I liked her to suck it slow in the morning. During the day, she could get it how she wanted to. At night, I wanted that nasty shit. Most times, I preferred to be standing, while she stayed on her knees giving that sloppy toppy.

We'd just finished another one of our all day fuck sessions, lying in each other's arms, basking in the nude.

"We're having dinner with my family tonight," I reminded her.

"Do we have to go? I want to stay here laid up with you," she fussed.

I had to admit having Dream all to myself for days had me spoiled rotten, so I understood why she didn't want to share me right now. We were still celebrating.

"Yes, sexy, we have to go. Besides, I have some important news to share."

She got excited. "News?" she repeated as her eyes lit up. "I can't wait to hear what you're about to say. I could only imagine how sweet this surprise would be. My last surprise was the house that you're having us built here next to your parents' estate."

I rolled out of bed, so I couldn't look Dream in the face. I highly doubted that she would be excited once I gave her the news.

"Just to think, that nice ass and big dick is all mine. I thank God every day for you. You're smart, loving, caring, and I know for sure you're going to be an awesome husband and father."

I kissed her on the lips and laid out my outfit.

"Can I pick out what you're wearing?" I asked.

"Sure. I don't have a problem with that."

I went into the closet and looked at the clothes that I just bought for her. Grabbing a long flowing dress that tied around her neck and the pair of heeled sandals that she loved on sight, I laid it across the bed next to my clothes.

"Wear your hair up in a bun." I handed her two jewelry boxes. "For you."

She shrieked with joy. "Another gift?"

"Of course, anything for you, ma."

I strolled to the bathroom to shower, while she opened the gold boxes. I was positive that she would be breathless when she saw the diamond necklace, matching diamond studs, and diamond hoops. Just like I thought, she was giddy like a kid on Christmas.

"Thanks, husband. You're the best," she said in a seductive manner.

I jerked the shower curtain back and stuck my soapy face out. "You can show me how much I mean to you later." I winked.

"I sure will, papi. I'ma suck your dick like Dracula."

"Oooooo weeee."

She giggled and stepped out of the steamy bathroom.

*****

"Dinner was lovely, Mrs. Diaz-Santana," Dream said to my mother. "I think I ate enough for three people."

My mother smiled and patted Dream's hand. "I have plenty leftover. I'm going to pack you and Drake plates to go."

Dream cheesed and I knew her greedy ass couldn't wait until she could go back for more.

"And you can call me Juliet," my mother told her. "We're family now. Mrs. Diaz-Santana is Sancho's mom, Meme." My mother laughed hearty. "Honey, I'm not that old. Besides, we all have the same last name now."

"Except for me," Mercy stated frankly.

My mother looked at Mercy and smirked. "You have a lot to learn, young lady."

Mercy gave my mother a confused stare. "Excuse me, Mrs. Juliet, but I don't understand what you mean."

Mega rubbed Mercy's back, lovingly. "Don't worry your pretty little head with the details. Our day is coming."

Mercy looked at Mega sideways. "How? We're not even a couple. You have to be my man in order for us to get married.

You're jumping the broom, when you need to be worried about basic shit."

The eye roll Mercy gave Mega made the whole table crack up.

"Bruh, you sure you want to be with her?" Breeze asked Mega. "She's kinda crazy. For real."

"I'm sure," Mega said with a smirk.

Breeze was eyeing Mercy like she was the plague. Meanwhile, Mega was eyeing Mercy like she just accepted his future proposal, and Mercy was completely ignoring Mega. The whole scenario was hilarious.

"I like her," my mother said truthfully. "She reminds me of myself when I first met your father. I hated his ass too."

My father laughed. "But look at you now," he answered in his hard Spanish accent. "Married with a lot of kids."

"Because you chased me until I gave in," my mother openly admitted. "I ran out of options."

We all laughed. My parents told their crazy stories all the time about how my father stalked my mother until she gave into him. He chased her for years before she finally gave him the time of day.

"So, you feel my pain," Mercy said to my mother.

"Yes, honey, I do. Mega is definitely his father's son. I can only imagine the hell he is giving you. He won't stop until he makes you his. Then, you'll be just like me. I didn't see my feet for years. Eight boys and three girls later."

"Eight?" I inquired. "Last time I checked, you only have seven sons."

"She meant, seven," my father said, trying to recover from that slip up.

I noticed how my parents eyed each other. It was obvious I was missing something, but I decided to drop it. They had a secret that they didn't want to let out. I had a long lost brother somewhere, or maybe I didn't. He might have passed away. That would make sense why my parents were being hush hush about it.

Dream & Drake 3: A Cartel Love Story

I looked around the room at all of my brothers and their girlfriends or wives. We hadn't been together as a family in months, so it felt good to see everyone. Despite our differences, we were very close.

"Anyway." I stood up, tapping my glass with a fork. "Can I have everyone's attention? As you all might know, well you might not know, I asked mami to cook this dinner, so we could all be here together as a family."

I stopped speaking and asked Mega to go and get Playez and Promise. They ate and disappeared. Once they returned to the dinner table, I continued. My sisters weren't in here. I decided to tell them later or let my mother tell them. They were going to take it hard, but Dream was going to take it harder, so she was my main focus. Mami and papi already knew, along with most of my brother.

"I just took a plea," I blurted out, lowering my eyes.

"For what? And why am I just hearing about this?" Breeze asked with a glare.

Dream was already sobbing and I hadn't even finished what I had to say. I sat down immediately, putting my arm around my wife as I continued.

"Channa got busted with some bricks and money that she got from Yolo. She turned snitch to get out of that jam. That led to me and Dream getting arrested. They let me go and dropped the charges, but they kept Dream. The prosecutor wanted to bring Dream up on queen pin charges because Channa tried to make it seem like I was working for her. They were about to throw the book at Dream and Channa would have walked. I had to do what I had to do."

Everyone at the table just stared at me in shock, except for Breeze. He always had a voice.

"Channa's ass needs to die. That'll take care of the problem."

"I can't. She's in federal custody."

"Well, she can die afterwards then," Breeze announced, already killing her off in his head.

259

Princess Diamond

"Will you let me finish? Amante worked with Ross and they got me a plea. I'm doing two years in jail and three years' probation, but Channa got thirty years."

A few people at the table gasped at the number of years Channa got.

"When do you turn yourself in, son?" my mother wanted to know.

"In two days."

"You're going away because of me," Dream cried. "It's all my fault."

She got up from the table and ran towards the nearest bedroom, which just so happened to be my parents. Bey got up to go after her, but I stopped her. I needed to talk to my wife alone. I walked into my parents' room, and Dream had thrown herself across their super king sized bed, crying her eyes out. I got into the bed and held her, resting my hands on her stomach.

"I'm sorry, Dream. I have to do this."

"But you're doing this because of me. They wanted me, not you."

"No, they always wanted me. They just couldn't get to me, so they used you as leverage. That's why it was so hard to get you out of jail. They were building a strong case against you."

"How can they build a case against me when I haven't done anything?"

I continued to rub her abdomen. "Well, because Channa provided them with all the information that would incriminate her and used it on you. She built the case against you that they could have built against her. It was her best bet to try and get off on the charges that they were pinning on her. What I'm trying to say is she threw you and me under the bus to save her own ass."

Dream rolled over, landing in my arms. "I can't live without you for two years. We just got married and I'm already a single mother."

"Yes, you can and you will. You'll have plenty of help. You'll always have your parents, Bey, and Mercy."

"But Bey is staying here in DR with Breeze."

"Maybe so, but Mercy will be by your side. I'm sure of that. My brothers will be by your side as well. Axel and Mega will protect you. Also, Fresh and Quay were great with kids. He can help you too. As an added stress reliever, I'm hiring you a nanny, two if need be. Whoever you like. Then, you have both of my grandmothers who will gladly step in. Between the two of them, they have raised over thirty kids. They're pros. You have plenty of help, babe."

Dream continued to sob in my arms. "None of that can replace you. What am I going to do without you by my side?"

"Be the first lady of my operation. Run shit like you would normally do, as if I were right by your side. I realize that you're devastated, ma, but now more than ever I need you to hold me down. Do you think you can do that?"

"For two years, Drake? Two years? How am I supposed to deliver this baby without you?"

I held her lovingly, as she continued weeping due to the bomb I dropped on her. I knew she was going to take it hard; that's why I had all of her things cleared out from the house with Spencer. I had all his things dropped back off at Destiny's, where it belonged. Imagine my surprise when I talked to her parents and they told me that Destiny was in the hospital fighting for her life. Apparently, she was attacked. I didn't know all the details. Dream's parents wanted to tell her about Destiny, but I shut that shit all the way down. It would be too much for her to bear. I feel sorry for Destiny, but fuck her and definitely fuck that puto, Spencer. My wife was my only concern.

Once she calmed down, I coached her out of my parents' room back to mine. My parents' estate was so big that all of the children still had their own room. As I ushered Dream pass my eldest sister, Jenny's room, I noticed that my parents were in there with them. They were all crying. I was sure that it had to do with me.

"Wait for me in my room," I advised Dream. "I want you butt booty ass naked too. I'ma give you some of this dick you love."

Dream smiled for the first time in hours. "Yes, papi."

Princess Diamond

I smacked her on the ass; she bent over and shook her ass in a way that I never seen before.

"No doubt, I'ma handled that, ma."

"Handle it then," she said, smacking her own ass again.

Dream drifted off to my room. I couldn't wait until I was inside of her again. However, I had to do damage control for my family. My father might have been the king, but I was the prince. Since I'd been born, I'd been the rock to all my brothers and sisters. When I walked into Jenny's room, all of my sisters were balling. I was sure my parents told them what was up. As soon as they saw me, all three of them rushed over to me.

"Drake, no," Jenny cried. "We need you."

I looked into my father's sad eyes, and I realized that he tried to comfort them.

I sat down on the bed with all three of them in my arms. My baby sister sat in my lap demanding all of my attention, while my other two sisters sat on both sides of me. I kissed all three of them on the forehead before I gently explained why I had to be gone for two years. By the time I finished giving my sisters the attention that they needed, they were all wiping their eyes.

"Can I talk to you?" my father said, stopping me before I could get back to Dream.

"Yeah, papi, what's up?"

"I know you have a lot going on, but I have to tell you the decision that I made about your replacement."

"That's a no brainer, Dream."

My father chuckled. "Mijo, this is a man's operation. She can't run things like you, but I know someone who can."

"Who?" I asked with doubt. "Because nobody can run things like me."

"Cream."

"Hell the fuck no!"

My father's eyes widened with shock. I was never disrespectful.

"Mega and Axel can handle things until Breeze comes back. We have a whole team in place. They been running shit."

Dream & Drake 3: A Cartel Love Story

My father squinted his eyes at me. He looked like he wanted to swing on me. I stood firm with my chest poked out because I wasn't backing down.

I hated Cream's ass for as long as I could remember. He was always tagging along with our family like the third wheel. Shit never made sense when it came to this dude. Then, he tried to boss me around. Never gonna happen. Cream was a bitch ass nicca. The end.

"Cream is going to take over your position. That's final."

"Final?" I repeated with an attitude.

"It's best," my father stressed.

"So, you've already made up your mind? I don't have a say, I guess."

"I've made my decision. Cream will be taking your spot."

"Well, I want Dream in there too. She can do it. You might not know her, but I do."

My father shrugged. "It doesn't matter to me if you want Dream a part of the operation or not. However, Cream will be running things while you're gone. I have spoken."

With that, my father told me goodnight and walked away. That's cool because I planned on putting Dream on game. My girl was about to show his ass that she had a bad bitch buried deep inside of her.

Dream was sleep when I entered the room. That didn't stop me from stripping down and getting in bed naked. I snuggled my body close to hers, spread her ass cheeks, and slid my dick right into her wetness.

"Shhhhiiiit." I sighed. Her pussy was dripping.

Dream stirred in her sleep.

"Exactly what I needed," I said, pounding her wetness.

She scooted even closer to me, throwing her ass back.

We were both in heat. Making love wasn't what neither of us needed. We just wanted to fuck. I pulled her hair. She sucked my fingers. I bit her shoulder. She smacked my face. I grabbed her neck, not too hard though. I didn't want to hurt my baby. Dream came and, then, when I was about to cum, she eased away from me and sucked me off, swallowing all of my seed.

263

Princess Diamond

"Sleep tight," I told her. "We have a long day ahead of us tomorrow."

I laughed because Dream was snoring before the words left my mouth.

Morning came before we both knew it. It felt like my head just hit the pillow when my mother was waking us up for breakfast. Like a family, we all sat and ate breakfast together. Things were quiet as we ate. Everyone seemed to be focused on eating. I didn't even let Dream's food settle before I snatched her away. Our first stop was the gun range. Dream was scared of shooting at first, that was until she got the hang of it. Then, she was popping off like a natural.

Next, I broke down my whole operation. I mean, everything from A to Z. Drugs, routes, who did what, and why. She got codes, money washing tips, numbers to important people, and, most importantly, access to my money. Well, I'm not that damn stupid. She only got access to half.

Our last day together was a bonding moment. Dream got a wealth of knowledge. Knowing that me and our unborn child depended on her and their fate for the next two years lit a fire inside of her to be that bad bitch that she always wanted to be. We ended the evening in church, where the pastor prayed for us. That night after making love for the last time as a free man, we both slept peacefully.

*****

The day I had to turn myself into federal custody felt like the absolute worst day, besides the day Dream got hit. I had nightmares of what this day would be like. So far, it was nothing like my dream. Everything seemed cool.

My family was there, minus my father and mother. Everyone stood outside the federal building, hugging me and saying their goodbyes. Despite how grief-stricken I was on the inside, I never let my true feelings show. I hugged everyone. My brothers, my sisters, cousins, aunts, uncles, and grandparents. Even Amante and Ross were there. I met with them right before my arrival. Finally, Dream was standing before me.

"I'm going to call you as much as possible," I said as she choked back tears. I hugged and kissed her stomach. "Make sure you bring my son to see me."

"I will," she said, allowing a few tears to fall. "This is for you."

I took the opened envelope from her hand and looked inside. There were two letters. I pulled the first one out and silently read it. It was the paternity results to the baby.

"My son is really my son?"

Dream nodded with tears. "Open the other one too."

I read the second paper with tears in my eyes too. "You're pregnant with twins."

Dream nodded her head frantically before kissing my lips.

"We're having twin boys everyone!" I shouted.

My family cheered. I was so elated that I raised Dreams shirt and kissed her stomach multiple times. Then, I looked to the sky and thanked God for my seeds. I was happy as fuck that I didn't have to raise that sick nicca's kids as my own.

I hugged Dream one last time, smelling her sweet scent.

"The news you just gave me will be my strength and motivation to do this bid."

"That's why I waited to tell you. I was going to tell you at the family dinner, but I figured you could use this good news at this very moment."

"I love you, ma."

"I love you more."

I held her hand while walking slowly towards the federal agents, who were waiting to apprehend me. They were personally escorting me in because they said I was a flight risk like my father. I kissed Dream once more and prepared to turn myself in. Right before I approached the agents, Cream stepped out of the shadows. I didn't even know he was amongst the crowd. I wanted to bust him in the face for trying to steal my spot while I was in a jam, but I decided to chill instead. He hugged me and the gesture seemed sincere, until he whispered in my ear.

"I'm going to take great care of your operation while you're gone and even better care of Dream. I know her pussy feels good. Tight and super wet. By the time you come home, your business and your bitch will both be mine. Drake mutha-fuckin' who, nicca?"

The rage that I had been containing blew the fuck up. I just snapped and popped the shit out of this nicca. I hit Cream twice in the jaw so fast that he never saw it coming. I was trying to break his shit, and it pissed me off that this nicca took them licks like my hits weren't shit. I knew for sure that I was busting his ass. Before I could crack his ass for a third time, the four agents on standby, apprehended me. I was coming at their asses like the Incredible Hulk. I took two of them down before they under-stood what was going down, restraining me.

Chaos erupted among my family as I was being forced to the ground, handcuffed, and tased. Some of my family members were going off and had to be restrained too. My last moment in the free world, I saw Cream comforting my wife as she cried on his shoulder. When I touched down again, I was going to show that nicca why I was boss. Cream's ass was going to be mine.

Chapter 39

Dream

After I told Drake I loved him, I turned my back because I just couldn't see my husband being cuffed again. I knew, when I woke up today, that it was going to be hard. Still, I truly had no idea how hard it would be. Maybe it was the pregnancy. I didn't know, but I was beyond emotional. I thought I could do this. I thought I was strong enough.

All that pep talk that he gave me went in one ear and right out the other. My feelings were so hurt. I thought I could be here while Drake turned himself in. I couldn't take it though. Tears were threatening to fall. My heart was breaking and I was so confused.

I heard the commotion and Drake's screams. In my heart, I knew he was putting up a fight because he didn't want to leave me and the babies. I was too afraid to look, so I kept my hands over my eyes. A few people bumped me as they came to and fro. I wanted to hold my stomach to protect my babies, but I didn't want to uncover my eyes. I was more afraid of what I might see, opposed to losing my children.

Just when I felt like all hope was lost, I felt a pair of strong arms wrap around me.

"I got you, ma," a familiar voice said, holding me in a loving embrace.

Princess Diamond

I opened my eyes and came face to face with my past. "Cream? What are you doing here?"

"I'm taking over for Drake, and I want you back, ma. Don't tell me that you don't want me too. I know your pussy is creaming for me right now."

His soft lips kissed my cheek and my neck, and my nipples hardened.

"I knew your body before you ever knew who the fuck Drake was. That pussy belongs to me, not him. It was supposed to be Cream and Dream. What happened to that?"

Damn. I realized that I just fucked up. My first love was kin to my husband. How could I be so stupid? This was about to be a long ass bid…

Author's Note

Thank you so much for supporting me. I appreciate each and every one of you. I hope you enjoyed the story so far. It's not over yet. I have so much more to say about these characters. Also, I have spin-offs as well.

In Dream and Drake 4, find out what happens while Drake is in jail. Cream takes over Drake's operation, but his main focus is making Dream his woman. Cream reminds her of Drake so much, and he's such a great help with the kids. He is her rock and support system in her time of need. Does Dream give into the temptation because she is lonely?

Mega finally conquers Mercy, but will it cost him his life. Mercy has a secret. This is the reason why she had been pushing him away. Will her love for him stop her from doing the unthinkable?

Quay is happy living his life single and free until he finds out his on-again-off-again girlfriend Yesi is a snitch. She has been giving information to the enemies. Will The Cartel spare her life when they find out? Or will they kill her in cold blood?

Made in the USA
Lexington, KY
09 March 2017